from Gods

MARY TING

dedication

Amanda Wright—Thank you for believing in my story. Your support was the reason From Gods was written. Most of all, thank you for being my friend.

To Mary's Angels—my street team—your eagerness to get my books out there is amazing. Your dedication, time, and friendship are much appreciated. I would be lost without you all. Extra times a million to Elliot McMahon and Janie Iturralde for all you do. Angel hugs!!!

For my Beta Readers: Jane Soohoo, Elliot McMahon, Janie Iturralde, Michele Luker, and Mindy Janicke. You are the best! I appreciate your honesty and your friendship. Love!!!

To Vanessa Stricker for running From Gods Fan page. I'm so honored! You Rock!

Ginormous thanks and hugs to my blog friends. I can't thank you enough for all your support and for loving From Gods. Thank you to all my old and new friends I've met through Facebook. Thank you for reading my books and for all your support. I am speechless and forever grateful!

PRAISE FOR:

"A fast paced adventure full of mystery, action, magic and romance! Readers won't be able to put this book down!" - **InD'tale Magazine**

"A story that is Electrifying with love. Get ready to be shocked!" - **Janie, Crossangels**

"From Gods takes mythology to a whole new level of imagination with its incredible plot and amazing characters. It's full of hotness that you never want to end!" - **Michele, Insane About Books**

"From Gods by the AMAZING AUTHOR Mary Ting is OMGods good!! If you even LIKE Greek Mythology, set aside some time because you will DEVOUR Mary Ting's Demi Gods and Vultures!!!" - **Mindy, Books Complete Me**

"This book is "electric" as it blends paranormal romance, mythology (which I love), action and suspense together for an amazing read. Mary Ting, you've done it again! This book exceeded

PROLOGUE

I REMEMBER IT clearly, as if it happened yesterday, the day my dad left and never came home. I was only eight years old, but when you feel like your whole world has been taken from you; you never forget.

"Mommy, where's Daddy? Why isn't he home?" I asked as we cuddled in bed.

"Skylar, I'm going to tell you something, and I want you to be a brave, big girl," she said nervously, lacing her fingers through my hair.

"Did something happen to Daddy?" I asked, feeling my heart pound faster.

"Daddy can't come home. He had to go away."

I knew what Mom meant, but I needed to be sure. Needing to go away meant he would come back home, eventually. "What do you mean? Will he be home for Christmas?"

"Sky—" Mom started to say, but she was unable to finish as I started to throw a tantrum. I didn't mean to, but something in the pit of my stomach suddenly alerted me that something was terribly wrong.

"Don't call me Sky." I jumped out of bed. I knew at that moment that my fears were true.

"Only Daddy calls me Sky." I looked out the window and recalled how he had told me that I was beautiful, like the sky. It was the reason why they named me Skylar. He had given me that name.

I started to calm down after seeing the beauty of the night, taking in a deep breath. "Is he...dead?" My fists were tight as I prepared for the news.

"No, honey. Daddy isn't dead. It's just that he's never coming back. I don't have a reason to give you."

Never coming back. Though I understood those words clearly, I refused to believe it. "No. He has to come back. I need Daddy. He's supposed to tuck me into bed and read me bedtime stories." I hugged my arms tightly to my chest, trying not to break apart. I thought my body was going to shut down to stop the emotions that I couldn't handle.

"Sky," my mom called softly, standing in front of me.

"No. Don't call me Sky. It reminds me of Daddy." Tears welled up in my eyes. "Why can't he come home? I don't understand. Doesn't he love us anymore?" As my lips trembled, tears poured down my face. Mom's words had shattered my heart into a thousand pieces. It was the first time I ever felt like that. I sobbed as if my dad had actually died.

"Of course he loves you," Mom reassured me, stroking my hair. I could see tears glistening in her eyes.

"He doesn't," I sobbed. "Daddy doesn't love me anymore." The sobbing became uncontrollable and I gasped for air. My throat felt dry and my eyes hurt, but I didn't care.

Mom embraced me, trying to give me comfort, but nothing could have eased the pain at that point. I wanted my dad to be home. I wanted the security and the daily routine. I wanted everything to be how it was. From that day, no one called me "Sky" and eventually, it felt as if my dad was dead to me.

ONE

SKYLAR'S EYES QUICKLY swept the lanes, looking for a police car. Driving down the highway at night, at seventy-five miles per hour, made it difficult to spot one, but she didn't want to get caught texting. When the coast was clear, she reached her hand into her purse to pull out her cell phone, becoming frustrated when she couldn't find it. She frantically felt around every inch of her purse. *Why can't I find my phone? Oh my God! I hope I didn't forget it.* After grabbing every object her fingers touched, she finally pulled out the phone. With a sigh of relief, her muscles relaxed.

She knew texting while driving was illegal in her state, but since no cops were around, she wanted to text her cousin to let her know she was almost there. Holding the wheel with her forearm and placing her phone right in front of her, her eyes shifted back and forth from the road to the keys, typing a few letters at a time.

Skylar and her cousin were best friends, and every year in late August, she visited her for a few weeks. This was the first time she had driven to her aunt's house by herself. They lived in a very small town, and it took about an hour and a half to get there from Skylar's home.

Almost there. Can't wait to C U.

After she pressed send, she shoved the phone back inside her purse. Hearing her favorite song on the radio, she cranked up the volume a bit and sang along. Shortly after, she heard a high-pitched sound. Unsure where the noise was coming from, she turned the volume down. Shocked, she felt the dreadful sound rush to every nerve in her body, awakening her, terrifying her, making her heart thump so fast she thought her chest would split open.

Surely I'm over reacting. After all, there are loads of cars speeding. But when she heard the horn signaling for her to get off the freeway, she looked in the rearview mirror and saw the reds and blues flashing and twirling—for her. In that instant, she felt her blood pressure shoot up. *How in the world? Where did that come from? I was so careful. Darn it.*

Exiting the freeway, she drove into the first place that looked safe...a gas station. The only person pumping gas replaced the nozzle, got into his car, and drove off, leaving her alone in the lot with the cop. She wished she could follow the other car and drive away, but instead she parked away from the gas pumps.

No other stores were adjacent to the station; in fact, it was pretty much a stand-alone building in complete darkness. Who knew what could be lurking? *What did I expect? I'm in east nowhere USA!* Inside the station's mini market, the light was on, indicating it was open, but from what she could see, there was nobody there besides the cashier. At least that made her feel safe—somewhat.

Glancing at the side view mirror, she realized that the officer was obviously taking his or her time getting out of the vehicle, since she saw no one approaching. Turning off the ignition, Skylar waited anxiously, biting her lip, thinking of ways to convince the cop not to give her a ticket. Tapping her foot and picking at her nails, it was like waiting for a courtroom verdict.

Being around cops was intimidating enough, but being pulled over by one was even worse. People got tickets all the time, but this being Skylar's first, made it difficult to bear. How would she explain this to her mom?

As she apprehensively waited for the officer, she wondered what she had done to get pulled over. It was almost impossible for him to know she had been texting. Her mind reeled with unpleasant thoughts. What if he was a bad cop? What if he planted drugs in her car and made it seem like they were hers? More "what ifs" circulated through her head—watching the news and bad movies had definitely invaded her mindset.

Tap! Tap! Tap!

Skylar jumped, startled by the sound. "Sorry, officer," she whimpered, starting the engine just to roll down the window and then quickly shutting it off again. The flashlight shone brightly, hindering her view, but she got a breath of the hot, sticky air that clung to her skin. Having the air conditioner on in her car, she had forgotten how hot it was out. Even at night, the weather was intolerable.

Hoping not to offend him or her, she moved a little to the left and got a clear view of his gorgeous, young face. With instant combustion, her heart fluttered a mile a minute and her stomach churned nervously. She felt her face grow hot as she flushed and her body temperature shot up, either from the sight of him or the searing weather—perhaps the combination of both. Whatever it was, he was the gravity pulling her in. She was wrapped in his invisible force, taking in all of his hotness, and she was almost sure he was looking back at her with the same intensity. *Breathe...breathe...exhale.*

She had heard of love at first sight, but this was more like lust at first sight. *What is wrong with me? Stop staring!* Sheepishly, she unglued her eyes from his beautiful greenish blue ones; she couldn't tell exactly what color they were. Trying not to stare, she saw a pearl drop of sweat trickle down from his hairline. She didn't want to look into his eyes again, for fear she may get lost in them and not be able to look away.

Shifting her view, she focused on his uniform; it fit perfectly to the curve of his muscles. His clean-shaven face brought out his high cheekbones, and every part of him looked flawless, from his hair to his broad shoulders, and all the way down as far as she could see. She had seen good-looking cops, mostly on television, but for goodness sake...sizzle!

"Could I see your driver's license?" he said flatly in a low, masculine voice.

Pause

Even the tone of his voice made her heart race. *Get a grip! Do you have a girl friend?*

"Your driver's license?"

Pause.

"Your license?"

"Oh, I'm sorry, but this is my first time being pulled over. Did I do something wrong?" She blushed, focusing on his nametag— Officer Doug.

"I need to see your driver's license."

She reached into her purse, pulled out her wallet, and then her license. "Here. It's really not a good picture."

The officer's lips formed a thin line. "We don't judge." He winked.

OMG! He winked at me. Skylar felt her cheeks flush again, and she wondered if he noticed.

"Skylar Rome?"

"Yes, that's me." She pointed to her license.

After staring for some time, he handed it back to her. "You're new to this town, aren't you?"

"Yes. No. Well, yes. I mean...." *Oh my gosh, I can't even talk.*

"Can't make up your mind?" The officer chuckled, obviously amused by her nervousness.

Skylar giggled. "I visit my cousin here every summer. I was on my way there. Did I do something wrong, officer?"

Skylar wanted to know what she had done to get pulled over so she would not do it again, though she wouldn't mind being pulled over by him again.

The officer didn't answer her, even though she'd now asked twice. He seemed flustered, looking intently into the empty darkness around the gas station, as if he could see something there.

"Ms. Rome, can you open your trunk?"

"Oh, sure. I only have my bags in there." She did as he requested and popped the trunk from the inside. "Should I come out?"

"No," he said, a little too sternly. "Stay there and don't move."

His tone startled her at first, but she didn't think much of it. After a few seconds, he came back. "Skylar."

"Yes?" She looked into his eyes and blinked, mystified. She could've sworn his irises pulsated and turned the color of silver.

"Just be careful," he warned, and walked away.

Skylar exhaled a deep breath she didn't realize she was holding. With a sigh of relief, she placed her driver's license back inside her wallet. When she cranked the engine, she looked to the left to make sure it was safe to make a U-turn, but she jumped again when she saw the officer standing beside her car where he had stood before. *Did he change his mind and decide to give me a ticket?*

"Don't text while you're driving. It's dangerous. It's also against the law if you didn't know," he scolded.

"Oh, okay. I'll remember next time." She smiled. "Thank you." *How did he know?*

With a nod, he turned away and headed back to his car.

Skylar looked in her rearview mirror, but he was already gone. *That really happened, right?*

She took out her phone and read a text from her cousin. *Can't wait!*

Skylar texted back. *I got pulled over by a gorgeous cop. He let me go. Explain when I get there.*

Ecstatic that she didn't get a ticket, she pushed the pedal and drove out of the gas station.

KAYLA LIVED IN a two-story house. All the houses on that block were cookie-cutter homes, built practically touching each other. It was difficult to tell which one was Kayla's, especially since there were hardly any streetlights, so Skylar looked for not just her address, but also the white mailbox that glowed in the dark.

The first thing Skylar did when she arrived at her cousin's house was run to ring the doorbell. Kayla swung the front door open and pulled her cousin in for a tight squeeze. "I'm so glad you're here."

Kayla wore a gray tank top and cotton shorts. Her brunette hair brushed Skylar's face, and she noticed that it was longer than it had been on the last visit, now passing her shoulder blades. "You grew your hair?" Skylar said, pulling her back. "I love it."

"Me too," Kayla giggled, flipping her hair. "Your hair got longer, too. Great minds think alike." Kayla giggled again. "Enough about our hair. So...what happened? A hot looking guy pulled you over?" Her eyes were beaming with curiosity.

Skylar nodded with a shy smile. "Hottest guy ever."

"Did he give you a ticket?"

Skylar swiped her hand across her forehead. "Nope. Thank God, or Mom would kill me."

"You got lucky. He probably thought you were cute and let you go."

"What?" Skylar blushed, thinking how cool that would have been if those thoughts had run through his mind, but what did it matter anyway? What were the odds of seeing him again? She figured the chances were slim to none.

"It's not a big deal. I got my first ticket about a month ago. You have to go to traffic school to get it off your record. You can even do it online. So did you ask him to cuff you?" Kayla snorted.

"I wish I'd thought of that. I was too busy trying to get my mouth to work. I was staring at him like an idiot." She shook her head, thinking how silly she'd acted. "Let me get my bags."

"Do you need help?"

"Nope." Skylar ran out, clicked the remote to unlock the doors, and came back in with two duffle bags and her purse.

"That's it? Just two bags?" Kayla exclaimed.

"I'm only staying for three weeks, not a year. I'm not like you," Skylar teased. "So where's your mom?"

"She's still at work. We keep the diner open until midnight during the summer, don't you remember?"

"Yes, of course, but for a split second I had forgotten."

"I bet I know why," she smirked. "So, did you get his name? Maybe I'll run into him next time and I'll tell him my cousin has a crush on him."

"You wouldn't dare." Skylar slapped Kayla playfully and ran upstairs with her bags in her hand, and Kayla at her heels. As Skylar settled into the guest room, the girls sat on the bed and discussed their summer plans.

TWO

THE SUN'S RAYS seeped through the window, warming Skylar's face. From the intensity of the heat, she knew it was going to be another scorching day. Squinting against the brightness, she let out an irritated moan. *Grrr...is it morning already?* She wasn't ready to start the day.

The moon had been full and brilliant last night, capturing her eyes. She'd left the curtains halfway open, wanting to escape in the beauty as she lay in bed. Unfortunately, she had forgotten to close them before she fell asleep. Moving a bit to the right to dodge the light helped, but then she smelled eggs and bacon, which made her stomach rumble with hunger. Instead of taking her time getting out of bed, she sprang right up.

Quickly, she washed and changed into shorts. She realized the curtains were still open as she pulled a T-shirt from the drawer, and was startled to see the shadow of a man behind the curtains of the house next door. She rushed to close hers, not wanting to give anyone else a peep show—especially when she was only wearing her bra and shorts.

That's odd, she thought. Skylar recalled Mrs. Song, who was a widow, occupying the house next door. What was a man doing there? She brushed it off, thinking it could have been her son or a friend. After she looked presentable, she went downstairs to the kitchen.

"Good morning, Auntie Kelly," Skylar greeted, giving her a warm sideways hug and a kiss as she inhaled the aroma of the food. Scrambled eggs—Skylar could hardly wait to take the first bite. Kelly stopped stirring the eggs and turned to wrap her arms around her niece.

Skylar's aunt was also wearing shorts and a T-shirt. She looked like she just got out of bed, especially since she wasn't wearing any makeup, but despite that, she looked great. Just like Skylar's mom, Gina, Kelly was naturally beautiful, and had flawless skin. With her hair dyed lighter, she looked young for her age.

"Good to see you," Kelly replied cheerfully, releasing her hold and placing her hands on Skylar's cheeks. "You are getting more beautiful every time I see you."

Skylar felt her cheeks turn warm. Shyly, she looked away. She was never good at taking compliments. "Thank you."

Kelly released her face, smiling. "How's your mom?"

"She's good, I think." Skylar hesitated, though she didn't know why her answer was uncertain. Perhaps it was the fact that her mom was in love, something she wasn't used to. It had been just the two of them for the longest time, until she met the second love of her life. Mom was happy, and Skylar was happy for her, but was she really in love, or was she lonely? What did Skylar know of real love anyway?

"Her fiancé is treating her well?" Kelly continued to ask.

"Yes, from what I can tell. I mean, he's nice. I like him...I think," Skylar mumbled, shrugging her shoulders then turning to Kayla, who was already sitting at the table, still wearing her pajamas.

Skylar plopped down next to her. Kayla looked irritable, and was obviously not paying attention to their conversation.

"So, Auntie Kelly, how about you? Dating anyone?" Skylar asked. "Mom doesn't share that part of your life."

"There is a good reason why she doesn't. Nothing serious. If I'm lucky enough to meet someone and fall in love again, I'll be sure to let you know." She winked.

Skylar could tell her aunt felt uncomfortable discussing that topic, so she stopped asking further questions and turned her attention to her grumpy cousin. "You're up early this morning. You didn't wake me up."

"Didn't want to bother you so soon," Kayla grumbled and rolled her eyes.

Skylar knew Kayla's eye rolling wasn't meant for her, and she wondered what was up. She opened her mouth to speak, but closed it when Kelly approached and placed Skylar's plate and a glass of orange juice in front of her. "Thank you, Auntie."

"It's my pleasure to feed my favorite niece."

"I'm your only niece."

"Is that so?" Kelly laughed, smirking. "Then I'm happy to feed my only niece."

Ready to devour her breakfast, Skylar kept one eye on Kayla and the other on the view beyond the windows. The dining room was her favorite spot in the house. The long windows provided a clear view of the front yard. Beaming in from between the branches of the trees, the sun's rays gave the illusion of heaven's light.

"How was the drive here?" Kelly asked, nipping at the bacon she had just taken out of the pan.

Kayla almost spit out the juice she had just drank, and coughed several times to get her breath back. Skylar shook her head, silently asking Kayla not to say anything. "It was fine. Nothing happened," Skylar reassured.

Kelly arched her brows in confusion, looking suspiciously from Skylar to Kayla. She parted her lips to speak, but then closed them and shook her head with a grin.

"What's wrong?" Skylar finally asked when Kelly turned to wash the dishes, giving her the chance to talk to Kayla. She could hardly get her words out. Her mouth was too full of eggs.

"I have to work at the diner today."

"Okay, so we'll change our plans. No big deal."

"Then I have to work tomorrow, and the next day, and the day after...you get the point?" Kayla sighed heavily. "We are short on waitresses. Mom says she can't afford to hire another one right now, and it takes time to go through the interview process. So I'll have to fill in the shifts."

"Sorry, Skylar," Kelly said, seeming to have eavesdropped on their conversation. "I know you had plans, but that doesn't mean you can't work around them. This can happen when you own a diner. When you go to college, make sure to pick a good career."

Skylar took her last bite of eggs. "Maybe I can help at the diner?"

Kelly and Kayla both flashed their eyes happily at Skylar. "Yes. We can work together, and then I won't be so bored," Kayla uttered, emphasizing the word "bored."

"You'll be too busy to be bored." Kelly's eyes steeled at her daughter. "But that is a great idea. I could use the extra help. Let me ask your mom if it's okay. I don't want my sister getting mad at me for making her baby girl work during her last summer before she goes off to college."

"I'm sure it'll be fine, Auntie Kelly. Mom wanted me to look for a job so I could start learning about finances. Besides, I should start paying for my own gas, but you don't have to pay me. I would only work for the experience, and this way I'll get to be with Kayla."

"Nonsense, Of course, I'll pay you. It won't be much, but it should help pay for your gas. Did you hear that, Kayla? Skylar thinks she should pay for her own gas...hint, hint."

"But I practically work for free. It's against the law to pay me so little," Kayla pouted.

"I'm your mother. I can do or say anything, within reason. Now hurry up and eat, 'cause both of you are due at the diner in one hour," Kelly said, scrubbing the counter near the stove. After the grease marks disappeared underneath the sponge, Kelly excused herself from the room.

"What a way to spend a Saturday," Kayla whined.

"It'll be fine. At least we can be together. You'll have to teach me. I won't know what I'm doing." Skylar got up, cleared their empty plates, and set them in the sink. After she washed them, she turned to see Kayla still in the same position, her eyes staring blindly at the refrigerator, elbow on the table, and her right fist propping up her head.

"Hey...it'll be okay," Skylar cheered. She hated seeing Kayla upset.

"I know. It's just that we had our summer all planned out. We're supposed to go to the beach and get tan."

"We can go out at night, and don't forget, there are the weekends. Too much sun isn't good for you anyway. Besides, you already know going to the beach is not my first choice for fun. I only go for you."

"That's where the cute guys spend their summer, and you are grossly too positive," Kayla teased. "Gross, gross, gross. But that is just another reason why I love you."

"You know I'm not like that all the time, right?"

"Girl, I've seen your dark side and all that self-defense stuff from the classes your mom made you take. I bet you can do some major damage," Kayla giggled, pulling Skylar in for a hug, leading her out of the dining room. "Maybe the hot cop will be there. They do eat, you know?"

"I hope not. I don't think I can breathe around him," Skylar exaggerated.

"Hmmm...maybe I can cuff the two of you together."

"Then I'll definitely faint."

THREE

KELLY'S DINER WAS always a fun place to be. It was small compared to most restaurants, but it was cozy and just big enough to accommodate the local customers. Inside, the tile floor was always squeaky clean. Toward the back were the restrooms and the kitchen, but the coolest part of the diner was the large opening where the chef could be seen cooking.

It was shortly after the breakfast rush, and the aroma from the food still lingered. The diner was empty and quiet except for the soft music that filled the air with a welcoming ambiance.

Being that this would be Skylar's first job, she was overflowing with excitement and nervousness. Though her stomach constricted with anxiety, she could hardly wait. She would be making her own money, and that alone thrilled her tremendously.

"Hello, Jack. Hello, Mona," Kayla greeted. "This is my cousin, Skylar. You remember her, don't ya?"

"Hey, Kayla," Jack said from the kitchen, holding up a spatula. "I may be old, but I have a good memory, especially when pretty girls are involved. Of course, I remember. Welcome back, Skylar."

"Hey, Jack," Skylar replied, blushing.

"Hello, Skylar," Mona welcomed her warmly. She wore all pink and a white apron. Mona had lost some weight from what Skylar could remember, and had dyed her hair a lighter shade of blonde. But what she remembered most was Mona's love of perfume. She smelled like honey mixed with wild flowers.

"So what can I fix you ladies?" Mona asked cheerfully.

"We're not here to eat. We're here to work," Kayla moaned.

"You mean you gotta hang out with the old folks today?" Jack chuckled. His pearl white hair was unlike any Skylar had seen on an old person before. It was the purest, prettiest color she had ever seen. Though she recalled Jack being around fifty, despite his white hair, he looked young for his age.

"Speak for yourself," Mona snapped playfully. "I'm very young. At least you girls get some relief from the heat. It's all day air-conditioned here."

Kayla and Skylar giggled.

"Well, I better show Skylar how to work the cash register, and then I'll help Mona wait tables," Kayla announced, tugging Skylar along with her.

"Go right ahead," Mona muttered, heading toward the table with a wet cloth in her hand. "Is it your first time behind a cash register, Skylar?"

"First job ever," Skylar said timidly, looking embarrassed.

As Jack prepared the food for the lunch rush, Kayla showed Skylar how to work the register—what to do when they paid cash or with a credit card. After several practice rounds, Skylar was set.

"Easy, right?" Kayla asked.

"Yup. Got it," Skylar replied enthusiastically. "Oh my God! This is so much fun. I love to punch in the keys. I could do this all day."

"You're such a cute dork. Let's see if your enthusiasm is still there at the end of the day." Kayla shook her head, giggling. Then she went to the back and came out with white aprons and hair ties.

"Here, put this on and tie your hair back. It's my mom's law." She rolled her eyes.

Skylar frowned in discontent, but she did as she was told. Looking at her attire, the long apron looked like a skirt on her, especially since she wore shorts. "Cute," she commented sarcastically. Struggling to pull her hair back in a ponytail, she turned her back.

"Remember, you offered to work here." Kayla reminded her, dragging out her last word. Laughing, she walked toward the back just as the door chimed.

"Welcome back to Kelly's Diner, boys," Mona greeted, leading the guests to their table.

After Skylar's hair was neatly tied, she turned to see the incoming customers and froze. Sure, her cousin had joked about it, but never in her wildest dreams did she imagine she'd see him here. Mortified, her eyes shot down to the buttons on the register. She didn't want to face him again after he had scolded her. *Stay calm. No big deal. Cops eat lunch too, but of all the places, why did he have to eat here?*

Skylar reached into her pocket and pulled out her cell phone to text Kayla, who was still in the storage room. *First day on the job and I'm texting.* She shook her head. This was not professional, but it was her aunt's diner after all. Keeping an eye out for customers, she placed her phone under the counter to hide it.

He's here!

Who?

The cop.

You mean the hot cop?

Yes!

I'm coming right out!

Skylar glanced toward his table. Her eyes flashed downward when his eyes met hers. As blood rushed to her face, she hoped he wouldn't recognize her. He didn't smile or acknowledge her, not that she should care. He was on duty when they met, so maybe he didn't remember her. Cops probably pull over so many people on a daily basis. What was another face to him?

Kayla burst out the door and then slowed her pace. Since Mona was already attending to them, she went behind the counter to observe, but pretended to be busy wiping an invisible mess. Feeling the vibration from her cell phone, Skylar pulled it out from her back pocket and read the text from Kayla.

Both are hot. Which one?

The one with the black T-shirt.

What? Both are wearing black.

Sorry. Only had eyes on my cop.

Which one? I get the other one. lol!

He didn't notice me.

I'll make him notice.

No!

Mona took the order and gave it to Kayla, and then Kayla gave it to Jack. After the sandwiches were made, instead of passing the plates to Mona, she took them herself, since Mona was attending to other customers that had just walked in.

"Hello...are you guys new to our diner?" Kayla asked with the most polite voice that she could conjure up, while placing their lunches in front of them.

"No, we've been here a few times, but I've never seen you before," the cop's friend answered, seemingly taken in by her charm.

"My mom owns this place. I help out once in a while. My name is Kayla." She pointed to the nametag pinned on her shirt. "And my cousin over there...." She pointed to Skylar. "Her name is Skylar." The guy's eyes glanced in the direction she pointed, but not the cop's.

Skylar let out a small smile and looked away.

"So, what are your names?" Kayla inquired.

"My name is Nicholas...Nick. And my brother's name is Mason."

Mason? Skylar was eavesdropping on their conversation. She was sure she'd read his nametag correctly, and it read "Officer Doug." Frazzled, she brushed it off. There was no choice. Clearly, his name was Mason. His brother Nick even confirmed it. Besides, in her opinion, the name Mason suited him better.

"We're having a party at the beach tomorrow night. Want to come?"

Kayla's face beamed brighter than the sun. "Sure, but can I bring my cousin?"

"Of course. You can bring whomever you like, as long as it's not your boyfriend."

"You're in luck. I don't have one right at this moment. So...when and where?"

"Meet at Point Beach at nine, and don't come too late. Look for the bonfire. Our group will be the only ones there. You don't need to bring anything. Just yourselves and a bathing suit if you want to swim, or maybe don't bring one and go skinny-dipping instead." He winked.

Kayla laughed the kind of laugh only Skylar could understand. It was a combination of a flirtatious and a nervous laugh. Then Kayla focused her eyes on Mason since she hadn't heard a peep from him. He gave her a short grin when she did.

"Well, I'll leave you two alone so you can eat. If you need anything else let me know."

Skylar saw her cousin flirting easily with the guys, and she knew if she could, Kayla would be floating in midair at that moment. Skylar wished she could flirt with boys like Kayla, but ever since she'd broken up with her ex-boyfriend, she'd lost her confidence.

She had felt things had been moving too fast, but what was fast to her was not fast to other girls her age. She had given him everything...well, almost everything—not her virginity, thank God. So, when he broke her heart, it broke all of her. Kayla had never liked him and told her many times that he wasn't good enough for her, but what did that mean, anyway? He was her first boyfriend, and for her, he was good enough.

After Skylar rang up a bill, she got bored standing behind the register. To keep herself busy, she turned to wipe off the counter behind her. She twitched when the sound of someone clearing his throat startled her.

"Umm...hi. Sorry, how can I help you?" she said, turning to see something black. She looked up. When she saw who it was, she froze, and wanted to hide.

"I'd like to pay our bill." His tone was low and soft as he handed the slip to her. The same, sexy tone went straight to her stomach, causing a tingling sensation.

"Sure, of course." She paused while looking at the screen. Feeling the weight of his stare, she suddenly forgot what to do as warmth flushed her face. *What do I push first?* Finally, it all came back to her. "That'll be twenty dollars and twenty-five cents."

When he handed her the exact change, his hand brushed against hers. She gasped inwardly from the mere touch of his skin. Then a millisecond later, she jerked back from the shock he had just given her, sending electricity down her spine. "Ouch." Startled, she looked right at him.

Flinching the same way as her, he frowned looking baffled and then annoyed. "I'm sorry," he murmured under his breath, and curled in his fingers to make a fist.

"That's okay," she accepted and lit a small, quick grin. After all, it was an accident, though she couldn't understand how it had happened. The diner had tile floors, not carpet, and it wasn't windy.

It was the hottest month of the summer, but what did she know about things like static electricity, anyway?

From the corner of her eye, she saw Nick stand and look their way, zeroing in on their conversation. He grinned slyly, and then sat back down. *Did he find Mason shocking me amusing?*

She contemplated whether to thank him for letting her go instead of giving her a ticket, since she still had no idea why she was pulled over, so she thought she'd ask before her shyness got the best of her. "I wanted to thank you for letting me go when you pulled me over. I mean, thank you for not giving me a ticket. It was nice of you. Though I still don't know what I did." She didn't know if she should have said the latter part.

Mason gave her the strangest look, as if she had just told him she was from outer space. He leaned in, making her pulse race. "You...remember me?" His words were slow and soft, almost mumbling, as if he didn't want others to hear. He even jogged his hand, gesturing to lower her voice as he looked over his shoulder to his brother.

"Yes, of course," she said flatly, but when he prolonged his stunned expression, she thought twice. Puzzled, she asked, "Shouldn't I? You pulled me over and looked inside my trunk as if I was a thief, hiding something. I mean...look at me. Do I look like a thief to you?" She couldn't believe she had found the courage to say those things to him. Mason being out of uniform looked a lot less intimidating. It was easier to speak up to him.

Mason gave a quick smile, seemingly amused, but shortly after, he looked distressed. Without eye contact, he spoke nonchalantly. "You must have the wrong guy. I didn't pull you over. If you'd like, you can pretend that I did." Then he walked out the door without his brother.

What did he just say? Skylar seethed with anger, if possible, fire would've blazed from her body. *What nerve. What a jerk.* Her eyes stayed rooted to the door he walked out of.

Recalling last night, she was almost certain his name was Doug, not Mason. Skylar began to wonder if she was losing her mind. Was it mistaken identity? It couldn't be. The voice, the face, the body, the same pull he held over her by his mere presence—everything was the same. So why did he make her feel like an idiot? *What a disappointment.*

"See you tomorrow," Nick waved to Skylar on his way out, chuckling as if he was in on some private joke only he and his brother knew about.

Nick was built similarly to Mason, with nicely toned muscles in all the right places, but his hair was a lighter shade, and he was apparently a lot nicer. Other than a slight resemblance, Skylar would have never guessed they were brothers.

Giving a forced smile to Nick, she turned to see Kayla practically tackling her. She wore a huge grin, trying to contain her excitement, knowing there were customers around. "Oh my God! Your cop was gorgeous, but so was his brother. Did Mason ask you out? It seemed like you two were hitting it off."

Skylar didn't want to burst Kayla's bubble. "No, I guess I was wrong. He's not the cop."

"Oh."

Skylar wanted to say she was as puzzled as Kayla seemed to be from the look she had just given her, but she kept it to herself.

Kayla brushed it off. "Well...looks like we have dates tomorrow night."

"You mean *YOU* have a date tomorrow night. I don't feel like going to a party with a bunch of strangers."

"But Nick asked both of us to come. Come on, please? Just go this once and see what happens. For me? Pleeeeze?"

"You know how much I don't like the water."

"It will be dark so you won't be able to see it. Besides, you don't have to swim. We don't usually swim when we go to the beach," Kayla tried to reason.

"True." Skylar pursed her lips. She could never say no to her cousin. They hardly spent time together, except during the summer and holidays, and those times were special to her. It wasn't worth the argument. Maybe he wouldn't be there. If he was, she would just ignore him and give him the cold shoulder—like he'd just done to her.

"Yeah, I'll go with ya." She suddenly became anxious to see him, just so she could give him a piece of her mind, maybe even a piece of her fist, though she wasn't prone to violence.

"Whoo hoo!" Kayla shouted. "I'm so glad Mom made us work today."

"Girls," Mona scolded, gesturing to keep their voices down. Then she walked over to Kayla. "Too bad I can't go with ya. Those boys were hot."

"You couldn't go even if you were young. You'd scare them." Jack chuckled at his own joke.

"Watch it, Jack, or I'll show you something to be scared of," Mona retorted.

"What do you mean? You already did by looking at me." Jack busted out with laughter.

More customers entered the diner, interrupting their teasing and joking.

FOUR

IT WAS A beautiful Sunday morning. The cloudless sky was nothing but an endless turquoise blanket hovering over the Earth. Since the heat was unbearable, with the temperature reaching over a hundred, the girls decided to head to the local mall. Sunday was their official day off from work, so they were ecstatic just to hang out.

When Skylar opened the main entrance door and stepped inside, the cool draft from the air conditioner blasted through her. The scorching sun had been beating down on them from the parking lot to the door, so any cool air would have been a relief. Since it was noon, they decided to have lunch before a fun filled day of shopping.

At the food court, there were too many places to choose from. The combined aromas from the variety of food confused Skylar as to what she wanted to eat. Finally, she opted for Mexican—two tacos, rice, and beans, while Kayla chose Chinese food. The two of them sat at the only empty table available, at the back end of the food court. Noting how crowded it was, Skylar guessed everyone had the same thought—go to the mall to escape the heat.

While taking a bite of her taco, Skylar looked around. She couldn't help but steal a glance at a couple of guys sitting at a table nearby who kept looking her way. Unsure if they were looking at someone behind her, she turned, but there was nothing there but the wall. If they thought she was cute, that would be a compliment, but if they were looking for some other reason...well, she didn't care to know anyhow.

One of the guys had dirty blond, shoulder length hair. His friend's dark brown hair was slicked back, exposing his forehead. They were both good-looking so she didn't mind too much, but when they acted suspicious—whispering, glancing at her and then whispering again—it gave her the creeps, so she turned away. If only she could hear what they were saying.

"So are you sure Mason wasn't the cop?" Kayla asked, taking a sip of her drink. "I mean...you were so positive it was him."

"I don't know. It was dark. It doesn't matter," Skylar muttered, although she was almost positive that it was him. She tried to recall that night, but after Mason's rude comment, the thoughts turned the hot cop into an ugly cop, and the excitement of seeing him again was no longer there.

"You're okay with going to the beach tonight, right?" Kayla asked hesitantly. "Because if you feel uncomfortable about it, especially being around people we don't know, I don't want you to do something on account of me. We can go see a movie instead, or just hang out at home."

Skylar took a bite of some beans she had just scooped up with her fork, then she poured more salsa on them. Her mind was so preoccupied with Mason's rude comment, she only heard half of Kayla's words.

"Skylar? Hey, Skylar?"

Skylar looked up, meeting Kayla's gaze. "Oh, sorry. I was just thinking. No, I'm totally fine with it. We can go. I was hesitant at first because we don't know them. But we'll be out in public, so I'm sure it'll be fine."

Kayla smiled, looking delighted. "Great. It'll be fun. This is going to be one of the best summers ever."

"Sure," Skylar agreed, but something in the pit of her stomach told her otherwise. She brushed off the feeling. She didn't want negative thoughts to get in the way of having fun. Then out of curiosity, she subtly turned her body and used her peripheral vision to check on the guys, but they were gone.

After the girls ate, they headed to the nearest store. Upon entering, excitement rushed through Skylar just from looking at all the clothes. Feeling carefree, she listened to the background music, skimmed through the racks, and picked out all types of clothing. So did Kayla.

With stacks of clothes draped over their arms, they headed to the dressing rooms together. The attendant gave them rooms across from each other. They had so much fun trying on different outfits, that it was like having their own mini-fashion show.

After spending about an hour in the store, they walked out with only one bag each. Skylar bought some shorts and T-shirts, and Kayla bought shorts and a light sweater. Then they headed to the next store. When they were finally tired of shopping, they decided to get some frozen yogurt.

Just before they entered the yogurt shop, Skylar noticed the guys from the food court standing a distance away. The thought of possible stalkers gave her goose bumps. Surely, she was overreacting. They had the right to be there, after all. They were sitting at their lunch table first. They might have been standing near the yogurt shop first as well. Either way, their persistent staring made her uncomfortable, so she entered a shoe store just to get away. When she looked again, they were gone. After a full day of shopping, she and Kayla went to the diner to grab some dinner.

As soon as Skylar entered the diner, she got a whiff of the delicious aroma from whatever Jack was cooking and the hunger pangs started. All that shopping had worked up her appetite.

The girls waved to Kayla's mom, Mona, Jack, and the weekend waitresses. Not wanting to interrupt anyone, they headed to a corner table and sat.

"What can I get you, ladies?" Mona beamed a smile. "Out of all the places you can eat, you came here on your day off? You girls must be desperate." Mona snorted.

"It's called free food," Kayla laughed. "With all the stuff we bought today, I'm going to have to sacrifice my stomach."

"You surely are sacrificing your stomach with Jack's cooking," Mona teased. "Last call."

Skylar giggled. "We're fine, Mona. I'd like to order Jack's famous burger with French fries, crispy thin. Don't forget the ketchup, please."

"That sounds good. I'll have the same...I think," Kayla said, looking undecided. "I'm so hungry. I could eat everything on this menu."

"Got it. I'll put your order through. Everything on the menu," she winked, then became serious. Mona leaned over as if she was going to tell them a secret. "By the way, I haven't seen the boys today." Then she walked away.

Skylar had finally stopped thinking about Mason, but after Mona's words? Well, now she was—again. He had already occupied her mind all day at the mall. She didn't want the thought of him to linger any longer.

After ten minutes, Kayla's mom brought dinner over and sat with the girls. "How do you like working here, Skylar?"

"I have to say, I was surprised how much I'm enjoying it."

"That's because you're with me," Kayla butted in. "Imagine working here alone and no one our age to talk to. Let's see what you'd say then." She looked at her mom, taking a huge bite of her burger.

Ignoring her daughter, Kelly continued. "Let me know if you decide you don't like it. I'm not going to force you to work for me. Do you understand?"

"Sure, Auntie Kelly." Skylar poured the ketchup on her plate and over her burger.

"So, what are you girls doing after dinner?"

"I think we're—" Skylar started to say with a mouthful of food.

Kayla kicked Skylar under the table. "We're going home. We're exhausted from shopping all day."

"Really?" Kelly looked surprised. "If you do decide to go out, make sure to stick together and be back home before I am. Well...." Kelly stood up. "I'd better get back to work."

"But you're the boss," Kayla pointed out.

"What kind of boss would I be if I didn't set a good example, right? Remember that girls." With a nod from Skylar and a roll of the eyes from Kayla, Kelly greeted the new customer that had just walked in.

"Why did you kick me under the table?" Skylar huffed. "That hurt."

"Sorry, but I didn't want you to tell my mom."

"Why?"

"She wouldn't let us go."

"How do you know? You didn't ask."

"Trust me. I know. And like she said, we just need to be back before she is. No need to tell her where we are going or whom we are going with." After they finished their meal, they headed home to get ready for the beach party.

FIVE

"THERE IT IS." Kayla pointed, focusing her eyes on the bonfire, which was blazing skyward, dancing with the colors of red and orange. Readjusting her bag, Kayla slung it over the other shoulder and walked side by side with Skylar along the path. Nick had told Kayla to look for a bonfire, and what a bonfire she'd found.

Seeing Nick, Kayla waved happily. He grinned as he watched them approach, wearing only navy blue trunks. Holding a bottle of beer in his hand, he gave the girls each a light hug, then turned to his friends. "Hey everyone, this is Kayla and Skylar."

Everyone waved without making eye contact, ignoring them to turn back to their own conversations. There were about ten of them. Skylar set her eyes on everyone when she greeted them, but she didn't see Mason, or Doug, or whatever his name was. Feeling disappointed and not knowing why, she settled on the sand when Kayla took out a beach towel and laid it down.

The night air felt comfortable and the bonfire kept them warm, though it wasn't cold out. Nick went to the cooler and brought back a couple of opened bottles. "Here." He handed one to Kayla.

"Thanks," Kayla nodded, taking a sip. Skylar gave Kayla a long stare, a look she used when she was not happy with her cousin, and Kayla understood. "What? It's okay," Kayla whispered and smiled. "I've had one before."

Then he gave one to Skylar.

"I actually don't like beer. But thanks anyway." She tried to sound as polite as possible. She didn't want to offend him, and she definitely didn't want to tell him she'd never drank beer before.

"Oh, no problem. More for me then." He chuckled and sat on the other side of Kayla.

As they sat there soaking in the perfect temperature, Skylar dug her feet into the sand. She loved the feel of the cool, soft sand seeping between her toes. Oddly, like Nick had said, there was no one else on the beach besides his group. This made Skylar uncomfortable, but she brushed off the feeling since they weren't the only girls there.

With her arms extending behind her, she laid back, enjoying the music blasting from the iPad, but the waves crashing on the shore took her in. It was somehow hypnotic, soothing. Turning her head toward the sound, she could see the moonbeams, flawlessly reflecting silver lights along the ocean, wrapping Skylar with a feeling of peace and comfort. Mesmerized by the view, she thought she could gaze at it all night. Though she was tired from shopping all day, somehow being there awakened her, providing a new vibe of energy.

Unfortunately, the peace was interrupted when Skylar turned her head toward the bonfire again. The guy with the yellow trunks was gawking at her. His stare was unlike anything she had experienced before. She couldn't tell if he was undressing her with his eyes, or if he wanted to hurt her, like a lion observing its prey, ready to attack. *Awkward!* Slowly, she turned without making it obvious she was uncomfortable.

Skylar wondered if she had a sign on her forehead that read 'Please stare at me.' First, there were the guys at the mall, and now this guy she'd barely met.

As always, though Kayla didn't know it, she came to Skylar's rescue. Relaxing as soon as she heard Kayla's voice, she honed in on her conversation with Nick. Kayla didn't waste time, and was not afraid to speak her mind, especially when it came to Skylar's interests. "Where's Mason?"

"He's around...somewhere."

"Are they all your friends?"

"The guy with the red trunks is my oldest brother. His name is Everett. And the guy with yellow trunks, my second oldest brother, is Remus. I'm the third one, and the guy that is missing, Mace...I mean Mason...is the youngest. Then the rest of the people are Everett's friends."

Remus was Mason's brother? *Great! What luck!* Skylar was already off to a crappy start, but for what? It wasn't as if she was interested in hanging out with Mason anyway, and it didn't matter what she thought about Remus or what Remus thought about her. Still, she didn't like the way he continued to glare at her, as if he was expecting her to do something horrible or suddenly turn into an alien or something. She couldn't begin to guess what his problem was. Then she looked at the girls. Their hands were all over the brothers. "Hmm...good friends I'm sure," she mumbled.

Kayla nudged Skylar with her shoulder, gesturing for her to keep her thoughts to herself. "So, you have three brothers. Any sisters?"

"Nope."

"Do you go to school?"

"Nope."

"Oh. So do you work?"

"Kind of."

"Kind of? Okay, so...do you do anything?" Kayla turned her head sideways in confusion.

"Nope. We inherited tons of money when our parents passed away, so we'll never have to work a day in our lives. Well, not really," he explained imperturbably. "We own businesses."

"I'm so sorry about your folks, but it must be nice not having to work, I guess." Kayla nudged Skylar again when she rolled her eyes.

Strange and odd. Parents passed away? How? Funny, he didn't mention Mason being a cop either. They kind of worked, but owned businesses? A huge red flag. They looked too young to own their own businesses. They were probably in their early twenties. Maybe if they inherited the businesses, then that would be a different story.

As horrid thoughts circulated through her mind, Skylar decided it was best to tune out their conversation. Speaking of parents reminded Skylar of her dad. He had left them when she was only eight years old, and she hadn't heard from him since. He might as well be dead, she thought.

What kind of dad would purposely leave his family unless he didn't care at all? It was difficult on Father's Day, his birthday, Christmas, and other holidays, but slowly she had gotten used to the realization that she didn't have a father. Though she tried to hang on to the happy memories of him, the older she got, the less the memories stayed with her. Then there was Kayla's dad, who had left her mom a while back for a younger woman.

"Do you go to school?" Nick asked, changing the subject.

"We just graduated from high school. We're both eighteen," Kayla said, emphasizing her age.

"Cool," Nick said, looking out into the ocean. His eyes dazzled in the moonlight. "Would you like to take a swim?"

"Sure." Kayla looked at Skylar, gesturing for her to come along.

Offering his hand like a gentleman, Kayla took it. With Kayla's other hand, she pulled Skylar and dragged her along. Though Skylar protested somewhat at first, she wanted to make sure Kayla was safe. Not only that, she didn't want to be left alone there with Remus. After all, they didn't know these people, and for some strange reason, she didn't think she could trust them.

She sensed danger, but didn't know why. Perhaps it was all the horrific stories she always heard on the news, or perhaps it was the way Nick didn't seem at all sad about his parents' deaths. Even more so, she didn't like the way Remus stared at her. Whatever the reason, she was going to keep her eyes wide open.

Looking out into the calm, dark water, Kayla dropped her bag, and she watched as Nick dove into the ocean. Wiggling out of her top and shorts, the fabric from Kayla's white bikini made her practically glow in the dark.

"Can you get any brighter?" Skylar teased.

"So you can see me better, my dear, said the wolf to Little Red Riding Hood," Kayla giggled.

Laughing at her remark, Skylar shook her head. "I'll be here, dunking my feet. You know I don't like going in the water."

"Okay, be careful. I'll be back real soon."

"Ya, right."

Though Skylar felt like a third wheel, she wanted to stay close, for Kayla's sake. Watching them go further in, Skylar took off her clothes, revealing a one-piece black swimsuit. Gazing to the right, she saw a pier, and did a double take when she thought she saw someone standing there. She dismissed it when there was no sign of anyone.

She was never fond of the ocean, the grandness and the strength of it frightened her. As long as she didn't go in deeper than her knees, she knew she would be fine. Coldness stung her legs when she first dipped her feet in, but then she got used it. The temperature grew on her, becoming comfortable. Bored to be doing nothing, she dug her feet into the sand again, and somehow, it gave her a sense of serenity.

Checking on Kayla, she looked into the distance. Seeing their bodies pressed together under the moonlight looked romantic, so she focused back on her feet, not wanting to intrude on their intimate moment. Watching them make out was not her idea of fun, so she headed toward the pier. Skylar respected her cousin, but she couldn't understand how she could kiss someone she'd just met.

Thoughts of her ex began to rush through her head. It had been several months since they'd broken up, but the pain re-emerged when she thought about what he'd done. They were together for almost a year, and after she gave her heart to him, he'd cheated on her.

Skylar swore she would be cautious with future relationships, and here she was, once again thinking about the cop, or whoever he was. Why did he have this effect on her? She didn't know him at all. It's pure lust, she thought. If he were there, she would kiss him, just to do something crazy, something she would never normally do. Maybe that was what her cousin was doing, something she just felt like doing. It wasn't anything bad after all.

Something shimmering like crystal caught Skylar's attention, changing in color from lavender, to pink, to gold under the water. Curiosity got the best of her and she inched her way toward it, now up to her knees in the water. As if she was spellbound, her whole being was sucked into the colorful tunnel of lights, and she couldn't peel her eyes from it. The glittering light was calling out to her. She was hypnotized by its exquisiteness, unaware she was drifting further in.

When the water was up to her chest, she snapped out of it. Realizing how deep she had gone in, she panicked. How was it possible she had drifted this far out? Ever since the time she'd almost drowned at the beach, she swore she would never go in this deep. Though she couldn't recall the full details, she could recall enough, as if they were etched in her memory. She had been eight years old, and it happened just before her father left the family.

Heaving, she felt like she was having an attack as her heart painfully hammered a mile a minute. Her muscles tensed up so tightly from fright that she couldn't move or breathe. It was dark, and Kayla was too far away to hear her cry for help. After telling herself to calm down, she turned back toward the land. After taking several long breaths, she moved forward, dragging her weight through the water and fighting the mild current.

Suddenly, she felt something wrap around her ankle. She didn't think much of it, figuring it was just seaweed or some kind of sea plant. She reached down under the water to pull it off.

Suddenly, whatever it was latched on to her wrist. With a yank, it flipped her and she was submerged as her body turned with the wave. Desperately, she pulled, tugged, and fought with all her might, but she couldn't get free. Managing to pop out of the water, she inhaled air with a loud extended gasp, only to get sucked back under again. Whatever this thing was, it coiled around most of her upper torso, and she couldn't move her arms. With no air left, she blew bubbles. Unable to escape the thing that held her captive, she had no choice but to accept death.

Skylar couldn't believe she was going to die. It wasn't fair. She was too young. Her life had just begun. Thoughts of her mother, her aunt, and Kayla—who would blame herself—flashed through her mind. Though she hardly ever prayed, now was the time to do it.

Skylar's eyes were already closed, but she could see a light, growing brighter by the second. Thinking it was an angel's light, she calmed herself into a state of tranquility. As her body became light as a feather, she drifted into unconsciousness, hoping she was floating to heaven.

SIX

MASON'S WHOLE BODY glowed brightly like a shooting star. He blasted through the darkness, and plunged into the murky, dark water so he could locate Skylar. The creature that held her captive in its vine-like tentacles had wrapped her up like a mummy and pulled her deeper into the ocean. Clutching one of its vines, Mason squeezed it forcefully and the intensity of heat from his electric-like power scorched it. When it unwrapped itself from Skylar's body, more vines came slashing through from below.

Bolts that looked like lightning, darted out from the palms of Mason's hands, but they didn't scare the beast away. It retaliated by extending more vines. One wrapped around Mason's waist when he dodged another that was trying to spiral around his ankles. He gripped it, sending blistering sensations through it. Sizzling, it uncoiled, but there were more around him.

Being a demigod, he could stay under the water as long as he liked, but Skylar could not. Knowing he needed to get her up for air, he shot multiple bolts as fast as he could. Finally, the beast disappeared into the abyss.

With incredible speed, Mason swam to shore with Skylar in his arms and laid her down on the sand to begin mouth-to-mouth resuscitation. Getting no response, he pushed onto her chest. With Skylar still unresponsive, he did it again...and again...and again. "Come on." Finally, water shot out from her mouth, followed by relentless coughing. Looking drained, her body went limp.

"Dou...g. Maccc....e," she mumbled, desperately trying to open her eyes.

Doug? Mace? Letting out a short chuckle, he realized she was recalling the nametag on the cop's uniform he had worn when he pulled her over, and by Mace, she must have meant Mason. Though Nick habitually liked to call him Mace, he couldn't recall him saying that name in front of her. He was most surprised to hear the name Doug. Mason was sure he'd told her that he wasn't the cop.

It was a good thing he had been taking a stroll on the pier. When he spotted Skylar, he watched her in fascination, but hid behind the wooden pole when he thought she had spotted him. He hid for only a moment, but when he turned to watch her again, she had disappeared. Frantically he had looked for her, but when there was no sign of her, he dove in.

He knew there was something different, something special about her the night he first looked into her eyes, but he couldn't determine what it was. Whatever it was, he liked the way she made him feel by her mere presence. Every cell in his body came alive and his heart burst with elation. Though he liked the feeling, at the same time it terrified him. Knowing she would be trouble, mostly for his heart, he had to dismiss her in every way, if he could. He had to. There was no room for her in his life, no room to care, and especially no room to love. He wouldn't let her in.

Skylar started to turn as her body shivered from the cold. Just before she did, he placed his hands on her forehead, willing the power within him to give her his warmth—one of his many powers.

He knew the heat would travel down her spine and immediately spread out to the rest of her, as if she had been wrapped in a heated blanket.

"Mmmm...." Skylar moaned, falling asleep, welcoming the heat.

Mason watched her as she lay, gazing at her innocent, beautiful face, from her closed eyes and high cheekbones, to her supple lips. Seeing a strand of hair flutter from a sudden breeze, he brushed her face to put it back in place. In accord, a small jolt from his finger sparked her. *What was that?* His eyes darted to his finger. This was the second time he'd lost control of his power, first when he touched her at the diner, and now here. Was it his doing or hers? He couldn't be sure. One thing was definite—something warm and pleasant ignited within him when he touched her skin. At that moment, he knew for sure he was in trouble.

Gazing back to her, one question remained. Who was she? The monster wouldn't go after a human, not only that, he had compelled her to forget when he pulled her over, but it didn't work. He would have to look into this, but for now, he'd keep it to himself. He didn't want to put her life in danger if he was wrong.

Trying to decide what to do next, he decided he had two options—one was to stay with her and wait for her cousin to find her, or two, walk away. He decided on the latter when he saw his brother and Kayla coming out of the water nearby. Mason hid behind a boulder by the pier and watched them run toward Skylar. Knowing she was safe, he swam away.

"SKYLAR! SKYLAR!" KAYLA shouted, running with a beach dress pulled over her bikini and her bag over her shoulder. Plunking herself down next to her cousin, she placed her hands on Skylar's cheeks, then her chest, making sure she was breathing. Skylar being wet from head to toe was evidence that she'd been under water, and her laying there almost lifeless indicated she had almost drowned. Oddly, Skylar's body felt warm, despite the circumstances. Unable to comprehend the contrast between them, Kayla forgot about it, thanking God Skylar was alive.

Skylar groaned, laying stiffly while trying to peel her eyes open. "Dou...g."

"Who the heck is Doug?" Nick asked, kneeling beside Kayla.

"I don't know." Worriedly, she refocused on Skylar. "Shh...shh...don't talk. Thank God you're okay."

"Let's take her home," Nick mumbled.

"Should I take her to the hospital instead?"

Before he could answer, Skylar mumbled. "No...no. Mom...go home."

Kayla understood. Skylar was right. Skylar's mom would insist on her going home. Their summer would be ruined for sure. "Okay, okay, but don't go in the water again. Why were you in the water? You don't like to go in that deep." Kayla was so mad at Skylar, but now was not the time to scold her, so she softened her tone.

"Let's help her up. I'll help you take her home," Nick said, already standing.

Kayla's eyes teared up, wiping them away before peering up to Nick. "Thanks." What she wanted to do was bawl. If anything happened to Skylar, she didn't know what she would do. She was more than her cousin. She was her best friend.

Effortlessly, Nick pulled Skylar up, and Kayla threw her beach towel around her. With her arms around Kayla's and Nick's shoulders, she looked like a rag doll being dragged.

"Monsssserr," Skylar managed to say.

"Skylar, don't talk. You almost drowned." Kayla was disturbed. She couldn't understand how this could've happened. Skylar was always careful—almost too careful. There were a few sports Skylar didn't like, and swimming was one of them, especially in the ocean. What the heck was she doing? Kayla blamed herself, and swore she would never bring her cousin near the ocean again.

"Dou...g," Skylar mumbled.

"Is Doug her boyfriend?" Nick asked, chuckling.

Kayla flashed a "be quiet" look to Nick. "We're almost there," she said to Skylar. "Rest. Don't talk."

The bonfire was out, and Nick's brothers and their company had gone. Smoke from the fire lingered, and a few empty bottles were buried in the sand. Nick grabbed his bag, slipped into his T-shirt, and wrapped a beach towel around his waist for privacy, quickly changing from his trunks into shorts. After they settled into Kayla's car, they drove to her house.

Not bothering to rinse the salt water off Skylar, Kayla helped her change out of her swimsuit into the shorts and tank top she always wore to bed, and tucked her in. Then she went to her bedroom where Nick waited for her.

He had spread himself across her bed, looking irresistible with his arms behind his neck to support his head. Kayla inhaled sharply, wondering if she should kick him out or ask him to stay until her mother came home. Being that it was past midnight, her mom was surely on her way and her decision was made.

Nick patted the bed, beckoning her to lie next to him. She did as told, but she suddenly became shy, realizing she was still in her bikini. She had taken off her beach dress, meaning to change into something comfortable after she had taken care of Skylar, but she had forgotten. Being shy rarely happened to her. She didn't know if it was Nick being in her room, or knowing her mom was on her way home, or if it was her cousin almost drowning tonight. Whatever the reason, she wasn't in the same mood he was.

"I think we should call it a night. My mom is on her way home." Kayla pulled in her lips, giving him half a smile, not wanting to disappoint him.

Nick frowned and pouted. "Okay, how about a kiss good-bye?" His fingers trailed from her cheeks, to the side of her neck, over the curve of her shoulder, and finally down her arm.

"Are you trying to seduce me?" Kayla moaned softly, taking in the pleasurable sensation, trying to suppress the heat that rushed through her body.

"You're still in your bikini. Easy access, you know. How am I to contain myself with a beautiful, half naked girl lying next to me?"

Kayla blushed. He'd called her beautiful. "You're containing yourself pretty well."

"You spoke too soon." Nick reached in, kissing the pulsating veins down her neck. At the same time, he positioned her right leg over his hips and ran his hand up her legs.

Maybe I won't be able to contain myself, she thought. Wanting more of him, she had to break away before things got out of hand. "Nick," she said, pulling away reluctantly. Still dazed from his caress, she had to clear her thoughts. "We need to figure out how you're getting home."

"I'm not going home. I'm sleeping here with you."

"What?" Kayla's pitch went up a notch.

"Relax, I'm just joking. I've already called my brother. He'll be here shortly."

"Which brother?"

"Mason, the reliable one, Mr. Goodboy."

"The reliable one? Then your older brothers are not reliable?"

"Sometimes."

"What about you?"

"I'm the bad boy kind." He pulled her in so fast she didn't have time to react. He conquered her lips passionately, letting her know he wanted her. His tongue danced with hers, tasting and sucking her deep within him. Kayla found herself on top of him again, as his hand ran smoothly over every inch of her curves. For a while, she forgot where she was, and the fact that her mom was coming home. Lost in his kisses, lost in his sensual embrace, she wanted to stop time.

Heat whizzed through from the tips of her toes to the depths of her mind as she vividly envisioned both of them naked. With that thought, every nerve in her body had awakened. Panting, wanting more of him, she knew she shouldn't, especially not right now. Not to mention, she didn't really know him that well. But no matter how hard she fought with her own free will, she couldn't pull away. He knew all too well how to get her high with ecstasy, pulling her into his world. He was experienced all right, that she knew for sure, and she knew from that moment that he would be hard to resist.

Just when she felt her top loosening, they were interrupted by the sound of the garage door opening. Still out of breath, Kayla climbed off him and re-hooked her top. "My mom is home. And...and you can't be here." She paced around, looking for a place for him to hide.

"Relax." Gently, he placed his hand on her shoulder. "Go downstairs and get her away from the door. I'll sneak out."

"Okay." Kayla took a deep breath. *No biggie. I can do this.* "Will I see you again, bad boy?"

"Of course. This Friday night at Starla. It's a restaurant and club. I'll text you."

"But I didn't give you my cell number."

"Don't worry. I have it." He twitched his brows. "Now go before I show myself to your mother."

Kayla slipped into her beach dress and ran downstairs. When she noted her mom was in the kitchen, she ran back upstairs, but Nick was gone. Strange...she didn't see him leave, and the front door was locked. He couldn't have gone through the window. She dismissed it, checked on her cousin, and went downstairs again to greet her mom. But she couldn't shake the hot sensation that still lingered from Nick's touch.

SEVEN

THE NEXT MORNING, Skylar woke up with a huge, pounding headache, and her lungs felt like an over blown balloon ready to pop. Not only that, she felt as if she'd swallowed half the ocean. Her muscles ached, especially her arms and legs, and her body throbbed like she had the flu. She wondered if last night was a dream, but when Kayla entered her room looking concerned, she knew it wasn't.

"How are you feeling?" Kayla sat on the edge of the bed.

"I feel horrible. I'm sore all over." Skylar suddenly realized how parched she was. Swirling her tongue to produce extra saliva didn't help. It felt as if she had swallowed a handful of sand. She noted she was in her shorts and a tank top, and wondered how she'd gotten home.

"Nick and I brought you home and I changed you."

"Thanks," Skylar said, feeling embarrassed she had caused trouble.

"You scared me last night. You were supposed to look at the water, not swim in it. What happened?"

"I don't know. I'm not sure. I know it sounds strange, but I can't remember how it happened."

"You kept saying Doug and monsters."

"I did?"

"You don't like to go in that deep. What made you do it?"

"I don't know. I saw a light. I guess I lost track of how deep I was going." Skylar was confused. She thought she'd seen something like a sea monster, and she was almost sure Doug...or Mason...had saved her. She blew it off, thinking she was delusional since she had been unconscious and sea monsters didn't exist. "Don't worry. I won't ever do that again."

"You better not," Kayla scolded. "You scared the life out of me. If something were to happen to you...." Kayla's eyes became teary.

"Hey," Skylar said, noting Kayla's sadness. "I'm okay." She pulled her in for a hug and changed the subject. "So, what happened after?"

Kayla blushed. Her eyes sparkled, telling Skylar about them making out on her bed. She also told her about the restaurant-club they were invited to.

Skylar rolled her eyes and shook her head. "I don't know if that's a good idea. We don't even know them."

"He didn't ask us to go to his house. We'll be out in public."

Kayla was right. Other people would be there. She guessed it would be fine. Not wanting to burst her cousin's bubble, she agreed. Watching Kayla's eyes twinkle the way they did when she talked about Nick, she knew Kayla was in trouble.

To Skylar, Nick and his brothers were out of their league. Not only were they mega rich, they seemed more experienced, and they were the type that didn't mind breaking young girls' hearts. They fell under the category her mom termed bad boys.

"Sure, I'll go with you. Someone's gotta watch over you," Skylar teased.

"Well, you won't be near the ocean, so at least I'll know you're safe."

Skylar smiled. "Let's get some breakfast. I need to take something to get rid of this awful headache. Does your mom know what happened last night? You didn't call my mom, did you?"

"You think I'm crazy? No way. You would've been out of here by now. Your mom would personally come and snatch your butt."

Skylar's tense body relaxed. "Just checking. Speaking of which, I'd better give her a call."

After Skylar showered, got dressed, and called her mom, she went downstairs to greet her aunt and eat breakfast, then they were on their way to the diner.

As usual, it was empty when they walked in. The breakfast rush was over.

"Hey, Jack. Hey, Mona," the girls greeted.

"Hey, girls. Back again, huh?" Mona cheered. "To eat or to work?"

"To work," Kayla replied.

"How are my two Barbie dolls?" Jack asked from the kitchen.

The girls giggled. "Just peachy," Kayla answered. "Get it, Jack? Peach pie is our special today, right?"

Jack chuckled. "It's Monday." Jack's tone was cheerful like it was every day. He was always carefree and full of life.

"So how was the beach last night?" Mona asked.

The girls flashed their eyes to each other and busted out laughing.

"That good, huh?" Jack said.

"Sorry, it's just that...," Skylar started to say and lost her words. She didn't know what to say without providing too much information.

"Yup, we had the best time ever." Kayla turned to Skylar and winked.

WITHOUT WARNING, KAYLA jumped like she had just sat on tacks, then pulled out her cell phone from the back pocket of her shorts. "My cell phone. It vibrated." Kayla laughed out loud, playfully sticking out her tongue, mostly embarrassed by the way she'd leapt off the floor. Looking at her text, she beamed a huge smile.

Hey good girl.

Hey bad boy.

What cha doing?

I'm working.

Shall I come over and be a bad boy?

No!

How's your cousin?

Skylar is fine thx for asking.

See you Friday at 9.

Will Mason be there?

Don't know. Wear something hot.

Haha...in your dreams. I'll wear my PJs if I want to.

Frown.

Or nothing...giggle.

Oh, I like. I'm already picturing you.

Gotta go. Customer.

No!

SEEING KAYLA ENGROSSED in her text and giggling to herself, Skylar had a hunch it was from Nick. After Kayla placed her phone back in her pocket, she caught Skylar's eye. "From Nick," she mouthed and turned to look at Mona, who was scowling at her.

"Put that away, young lady," Mona scolded, pinching Kayla's cheeks. "Ahhh...to be young again. When I was your age—"

"Don't scare the girl," Jack laughed, and the other customers joined in on the humor.

Mona shook her head, giggling, and went to greet more customers. "Hello, boys."

When they walked in, all eyes turned to them. With their swaggering cool steps, they looked like four male runway models. Skylar's eyes grew wide and she was stunned. Mason was there again, but this time he was there with all of his brothers. The oldest, Everett, was the tallest. Remus and Mason looked similar, with dark hair and sensual greenish-blue eyes, while Everett and Nick had light hair and dark eyes. They all wore shorts and black T-shirts that had different designs on them, except for Mason. He wore a sky blue T-shirt, which brought out the enticing color of his eyes.

Surprised Kayla hadn't warned her, Skylar gave her a questioning look. Ignoring Skylar, Kayla lit up like the sun and took them to their seats. Besides Nick, who greeted Skylar with a smile, none of the brothers looked her way. After Kayla took their orders, she headed to Jack.

Skylar tried her best not to look, but she couldn't help herself. Every time she glanced Mason's way, as if he knew she would, he would catch her gaze. But once their eyes met, he too would drop his, as if he didn't want to get caught looking at her either. Many times, she'd replayed in her mind how she was going to tell him off, but seeing him now, her anger had tapered.

Something about that family was different. Skylar could feel it to her core, but she didn't understand why. What made her most uncomfortable was their brother, Remus. Sometimes she could sense him glaring at her, and as if his stare could burn her, her muscles would tense up, making her unpleasantly hot. He definitely gave her the creeps. Trying to focus her attention elsewhere, she glued herself to the cash register. Distracted by customers paying, she was glad for the chance to stay busy.

Skylar loved to watch Kayla serving. She could hold four plates at once, as she was doing now, balancing them perfectly. Skylar wondered if she could do the same, or if she would accidentally drop one. Perhaps she should try. Laughing to herself, she was soon distracted by another customer who brought her their bill.

"Here you go." Kayla brought the guys their lunches, setting the plates down one by one.

Curious to see what they'd ordered, Skylar placed herself on the other side of the counter. After getting a peek at their sandwiches and French fries, she went back to the register. The brothers held a conversation with Kayla as they ate. Kayla was at ease, speaking her mind, laughing, and looking like she was having the time of her life. How Skylar wished she could feel at ease too, not so much with Remus, though. Maybe she could one day. She just had to be bolder.

After an hour had gone by, the brothers flipped a coin and Mason stood up. Skylar guessed he lost the bet and had to pay the bill. As if she was spellbound by him, her eyes held Mason's, unable to look away even as he came toward her, looking dreamy. Every nerve in her body tingled, awakened by him. She couldn't deny the magnetic pull, and she was unable to explain the hold he had on her.

"Here," he said, placing the bill on the counter.

"I guess you lost the bet, huh?"

"I never lose."

So you wanted to pay the bill and come see me? Skylar flushed brightly. "Oh."

"So are you're going to the club Friday night? It's more of a restaurant actually."

"I think so. I mean...my cousin really wants me to go, but—"

"But not your crowd?"

"No, not really. I've never been."

"How do you know you won't like it if you've never been?"

"That's true. I guess I'll know Friday. Will you be there?" She couldn't believe she'd asked. *Be bolder.*

"Yes. See you then."

Was that a direct invitation from him? She didn't know, but he'd said, "see you then." *Must mean something, right?* Just from a perceived invitation, she felt like her whole essence levitated to the ceiling and her eyes followed his stride back to his brothers. Then, the brothers stood up at once. On their way out the door, Mason gave a sideways quick smile. Nick waved, looking directly at her. Remus raked his eyes over her, and Everett didn't even bother to look her way. *Strange, but good-looking family.*

Skylar jerked. She was startled by her phone vibrating. Ahhh! She hated when that happened. If people saw her, she probably looked like a girl startled by someone smacking her in the rear.

It was a text from Kayla.

Did he ask you out?

I don't know.

What do you mean?

Kayla raised her brows in confusion. She could have just walked over, but they were getting busy, and she didn't want Mona reprimanding her again.

Like I said, I don't know.

What did he say?

He asked me if I was going Friday & then said see you then.

Ahhh! That's a date!

Don't be silly. Gotta go. I'm working you know.

EIGHT

"**Y**OU'RE NOT SERIOUSLY going to wear that, are you?" Skylar asked, stunned to see her cousin dressed in a skintight black, short dress. It had a cowl loop in front and showed major cleavage. She did look sexy and alluring, but it was not the type of dress Skylar would wear.

"Why not? All the girls will be dressed like this. I want him to see only me. Here." She pulled a similar dress out of her closet and handed it to Skylar.

Skylar gasped, shaking her head. "I don't think so. I won't be able to breathe."

"Just try it on. It's not as low or as short as mine, I promise."

After Skylar slipped it on, she stood in front of the mirror. It didn't look as bad as she thought it would. She felt older, more attractive.

"See? It looks great on you." Kayla tugged Skylar to the bathroom and fussed with her hair and face.

"Natural...I like it natural. Light on the makeup. Don't make me look like a clown."

Kayla giggled. "A clown? Are you serious? Please, don't insult my expertise or I *will* make you look like one. Now turn around, Miss America."

"Miss America? Yeah, right." Skylar turned to see herself. "Wow. I like it. I look...different."

"I told ya so, beautiful clown. He better ask you on a real date, or else he is either blind or gay."

Skylar laughed aloud. "Thanks."

After slipping on black high heels, they both grabbed their purses, got into Kayla's car, and drove away.

The live music blasted as they entered. Skylar felt overwhelmed by the ambiance, but Kayla radiated with excitement. It was dark, but the lights above the bar and the candles in the middle of the tables gave off enough light. Being tugged to the other side of the club, Skylar knew Kayla had spotted Nick.

Zipping along, Skylar observed the bar. All the stools were taken except for one. As they zigzagged through booths and tables, she saw the empty dance floor. Standing tall towards the back, waving, was Nick. With a hug, he gave each of the girls a kiss on their cheeks. Disappointingly, he was the only one at the table.

As the girls scooted into the booth, Skylar saw Nick was dressed in black slacks and a lavender dress shirt. Not only did he smell nice, he looked quite dashing, and part of her felt guilty for thinking he looked hot. Sitting there, she wondered if Mason was around, but she didn't want to ask Nick. Her question was answered when she saw Mason across the dance floor looking straight at her, but he was with a girl.

Skylar's heart sank, and her face stung as if she had been slapped. She tried to justify his actions. He didn't ask her out directly. It was her fault for not thinking straight, her fault for jumping to the conclusion that he had asked her out—sort of.

Kayla followed Skylar's gaze. "Oh no he didn't," she mouthed, turning to get her cousin's attention. "Hey, Skylar. Want a drink?"

"What?" Skylar's eyes were already on the bar, trying desperately not to look toward Mason and his date. It was difficult when they were right across from her. And it was totally not fair that he looked so debonair with dark slacks and a gray dress shirt.

"Nick will get us drinks," Kayla suggested, looking at Nick.

"No." Skylar snapped, taking her anger out on her cousin. She didn't mean to. Upset with herself for allowing Mason to crawl under her skin the way he had, she was determined to prove to herself that she was strong. "I mean, I'll get them." Her tone was softer. "What can I get for the both of you?" She smiled. She wasn't going to let him get the best of her. *Jerk.* He wasn't worth her time. She was here to have fun with her cousin, and fun she would have, even if it meant faking it.

"Get me any beer. I drink all kinds," Nick said.

"Get me the same." Kayla looked at Skylar with concern.

Skylar ignored Kayla and grabbed her purse, walked over to the bar, and sat at the open seat. "I'll take two beers. No, make that three," she said to the bartender, who acknowledged her with a nod and a smile.

"What kind?" he asked. He was tall, slim, and attractive. He needed a shave, though.

"The best you have."

"I'll need to see your ID, miss."

Shoot! She forgot she couldn't buy beer because she'd never bought one before. Skylar looked over her shoulder to get her cousin's attention, but froze when a body brushed against hers. Then she heard his voice—the voice that called to her, the voice that made her go all crazy inside, the voice that could probably make her do just about anything if he asked nicely.

"It's okay. She's with me."

The bartender nodded and walked away.

Skylar's breath got caught in her throat and she couldn't move. She didn't know what to do. On the one hand, she was furious with him, but on the other hand, she didn't have the right to feel this way. He didn't ask her out. She kept repeating those thoughts to make herself feel better. With no other option, she had to be polite.

"Thanks." She didn't look at him. Looking at him would be dangerous. In fact, she kept her eyes rooted on the bartender, but she could smell his musky scent, and wanted to get lost in his eyes.

"You know you can't buy beer. You're only eighteen," he scolded lightly.

How did he know my age? Then she recalled Kayla telling Nick they were eighteen. Either that, or he really was the cop he denied being, and had seen her driver's license. "I'm almost nineteen. I don't even drink beer. I was getting it for your brother. It's my first time buying it, and I forgot I couldn't."

"Well, that explains it."

Frowning at his remark, she kept her vision straight ahead.

"But you bought three?"

She paused, trying to think of something clever to say, but failed. "I thought I would try it tonight."

"So no fake ID?"

"What? No. I'm not that kind of girl" She scoffed. From the corner of her eye, she could see Mason wearing an amused smile. Then she swiftly shifted her eyes to his left, thinking she saw the same dirty blond haired guy she'd seen at the mall. After doing a double take and catching no sign of him, she gazed to Mason's strong ripped chest, unwilling to look him in the eye. Though he had a shirt on, she could clearly see the firmness of his muscles, making her blush.

"Looking for someone?"

"No. I thought I saw...." She paused, looking dismayed. "Never mind."

"Do you have a habit of conversing with shirts?"

"What?" She knew why he made that comment. She hadn't looked him in the eye once since the conversation started, and now she was staring at his chest. For goodness sake, she didn't mean to make it obvious.

"If you prefer, I can take off my shirt and give it to you, since you seem to like it so much."

That wouldn't be such a bad idea. No! What was she thinking? "I don't think so."

Thankfully, the bartender came back at that moment with the beers, breaking their conversation. "That will be eighteen."

Eighteen bucks for three beers? What do they put in it, gold? Skylar reached into her purse to get her wallet out, but when she reached to give the bartender a twenty, her hand collided with Mason's. Clearly, he was trying to pay. Once again, some kind of exhilaration sparked down her spine.

"Ouch. You shocked me again. What are you, like the static king?" Her hand jolted back to her side with the bill.

"Sorry," he mumbled, cursing under his breath.

"That's okay," she replied without making eye contact. Then she turned her attention to the bartender before he could walk away with Mason's twenty and placed her bill in front of him. "Wait. I can pay for it. I'm treating them."

Mason's hand was slightly on top of hers as he carefully pulled it back. Even though his touch was gentle and light with hardly any pressure, her hand followed obediently. "You *can* pay for it, but you need to be twenty one. Are you?" His tone demanded attention.

He was right. Submissively, peering up to answer his question—which was a big mistake—she saw his supple, kissable lips. They spread across, giving her a smile she could die for. With her eyes fixated on his, she pulled her hand away slowly. At that moment, every sound, every movement seemed to blur around her. Swallowed up by Mason's world, she was breathless. His powerful body just inches away from hers, caused a longing feeling to surge that she could not control. She hated how he could make her feel weak all over. "Thanks. I'll let them know you bought it."

"There's no need for that. Do you need help carrying them over?"

"Nope," she snapped, and then twisted her neck to where his date was sitting. With a compact mirror in front of her, she was checking herself out. The woman reached into her purse, pulled out her lip-gloss, and glided it across her lips. Her beautiful blonde hair cascaded down, blocking one side of her face. "Shouldn't you go back and entertain your date?"

"My date? You think I should?" He chuckled.

What kind of answer was that? She suddenly felt bad for his date. "You should do whatever you want." She grabbed the bottles of beer and walked away as if she didn't care, never looking back.

"I was beginning to worry," Kayla whispered. "What was going on over there?"

"I'll tell you later, but now we need to toast." Skylar clinked Kayla and Nick's bottles. "To you, and you, and me." Then she took a sip and almost threw up. Squirting some out of her mouth, she quickly apologized and wiped her chin with a napkin. She didn't know why people liked to drink something she imagined pee would taste like.

Nick laughed. "You'll get used to the taste really fast."

After several sips, Kayla wanted to dance. With Kayla's persuading and tugging their hands, Skylar and Nick were pulled onto the dance floor. They were the first to break the ice, and more people joined in. Skylar was enjoying herself, but in a way, it was forced. She wanted to prove to Mason, and herself, that he didn't affect her at all.

Soon, after a few more sips of beer, she found herself dancing alongside Kayla with a complete stranger. Once in a while, she would steal glances at Mason. Though he never fully looked at her, she could tell he was watching, and that made her happy, like she'd won a contest or something.

As the music continued to blast, the crowd got bigger, surrounding them, and she lost sight of Mason. Not just him, she lost sight of Kayla, too. Thoroughly enjoying dancing, the not so bad looking guy she was dancing with was all smiles. By now, thoughts of Mason vanished, and she disappeared into the crowd as she danced like she'd never danced before. The vibration from the bass pumped through her body, enticing and fueling her with energy that was buried within her. With both of her hands up in the air, she moved in ways she'd never dared to do—seductively. Certainly, she was having the time of her life.

Skylar felt carefree, and at the same time, she felt light headed from the alcohol. Now she knew what feeling buzzed felt like. Though she didn't know if she liked the feeling, she knew it made her feel braver, more daring, like the way she was dancing with a total stranger. As they continued to sway to the beat, sweat trickled down her forehead. Blood rushed to her face, making her feel hot from all the movement.

Unexpectedly, her dance partner placed his hands around her hips and pulled her in. Not only did he reek of alcohol, he was sweating so much he looked like he had just gotten out of the shower. His hands were all over her, uncomfortably. Wanting him off her, she pushed him, but he didn't budge and continued to hold onto her. Then he pulled her arms behind her back to lock them in place. It happened so fast she didn't have time to react.

"Stop!" she yelled. The people around her were so hypnotized by the sound of the music. They were unable to hear her cry for help. Skylar desperately tried to push him off, but with all her pushing and yanking, and him moving to her sway, it looked like they were just dancing together.

"Get off me!" she yelled again. Thank goodness, her mom had made her take a self-defense class. *Think. Think. Think.* Recalling the demonstration she'd observed and practiced during a class session, she thought to try it. With the only part of her body that was free, she jabbed her heel on top of his shoe as hard as she could, and kicked him on his shin to push him away.

Stumbling several steps backward, and looking like he was in great pain, he moaned loudly. With piercing eyes that held a look of rage, he pulled his hand back to swing at her. Just before contact, he was thrown across the floor, knocking people down who happened to be in his path.

"She said no!" Mason looked at Skylar. "You okay?"

Feeling humiliated and stunned, tears streamed down her cheeks. Unintentionally, she darted to Mason and threw her arms around him. She couldn't help herself. She didn't plan to do it—it just happened. Skylar only did it for one reason—to thank him.

NINE

"SKYLAR? SKYLAR!" KAYLA shouted, sounding concerned.

Hearing her cousin's voice, she pulled herself from Mason. "Sorry," she whimpered, looking up at him as she wiped her tears away. His eyes gazed into hers with a look of concern, or was it a look of annoyance because she'd hugged him? She didn't know. Whatever the reason, his hands were straight down and his muscles were tense, so she was all too glad to have Kayla come to her rescue.

"Are you okay?" Kayla asked, pulling Skylar away from the dance floor and toward the exit.

Looking over her shoulder, Skylar had a clear view of Mason still standing there stiff as a board. Her body continued to tremble as tears dampened her cheeks again.

Kayla pushed the door open and led them half way down the block. "What happened?"

After Skylar explained, Kayla thought it was best to go home. Not wanting to ruin Kayla's night, Skylar convinced her to stay. She told her to ask Nick to drive her home, and she would take Kayla's car.

"Are you sure?" Kayla asked, letting out a conflicting heavy sigh.

"Yes. I'm a big girl. Please go back and have fun. I don't want Nick waiting for you too long, and I don't want to be the cause of you going home early and ruining the night for both of you."

"Wait. This is like your first beer. Are you feeling buzzed?"

"I'm not sure what feeling buzzed feels like, but if it was what I was feeling a while ago, then I'm fine now. I don't feel that funny feeling, like you're floating on clouds, anymore. I only drank half the bottle of piss water."

"What?" Kayla laughed aloud. "You won't be saying that after several more rounds."

"That's because I'd be too drunk to even notice."

"Ha ha. Let me at least walk you to my car."

"I can drive her home," said a male voice, handing Skylar her purse.

Where had he come from? Skylar wanted to ask if his date would mind, but thought twice about it. Since she didn't know what to say, only that she needed to be polite, she said what first popped in her mind. "Thanks, but...." She took her bag. "I can drive home."

Skylar recalled how Mason didn't hold her after the altercation with the drunk. His arms had remained rigidly down at his sides. Not that he should have embraced her, but he could have comforted her at least. A pat, a smile, or any little gesture would've been fine, but no. His body was so uptight it was as if she was the plague.

"You still smell like alcohol, and if a cop pulled you over, you would get arrested. Unless you prefer to spend some time in jail."

Skylar wanted to sniff herself. Did she really smell like alcohol? Unsure, she looked at Kayla, but Kayla was too busy rummaging inside Skylar's purse. She pulled out her car keys and handed them to Mason. "Skylar drove my car," she explained. "Thanks Mason. I feel much better knowing she's in good hands." Kayla turned, gave her cousin an encouraging smile, and strutted back into the club.

Since she hardly knew him, and the times she had been with him were weird and awkward, Skylar felt a bit uncomfortable. Walking behind him, she took two steps to every long stride he took. With a click of a button, he opened the passenger side door for her. It was the second nice thing he had done so far, but how did he know which car to unlock?

"Thanks," Skylar said, sitting stiffly as he unexpectedly tried to pull the seatbelt strap, but found it was stuck. With one forceful yank, it finally budged. Letting out an irritated sigh, he reached over and wrapped the straps around her as he spoke. "Do you have a habit of dancing with strangers?"

Skylar paused, taken aback by his rude question. Glaring at the side of his head, she fired back just as she heard the "click" sound. "Do you have a habit of asking people what their habits are? Apparently, according to you, I have many habits. And my answer is yes."

Locking her in, he looked right at her, face to face, lips to lips. She gasped. Though he was way too close for comfort, she enjoyed the proximity, yet at the same time, was frightened by his angry eyes penetrating through hers. "Well, you shouldn't. It's dangerous. I should put you in the naughty corner."

What did he mean by the naughty corner? "I'm not a child."

"Then stop acting like one."

Startled by his tone and not wanting him to think she was the reckless type, she decided to tell him the truth. "No. My answer is no. I don't have a habit of conversing with shirts, and I don't have a habit of dancing with strangers, especially drunk ones. In fact, if you must know, this was my first time even drinking that awful piss water."

"Piss water? First time, huh?" His face relaxed, his lips puckered. She could tell he was trying to hold in his laughter. "You must have enjoyed it somewhat. You sure showed it on the dance floor."

"Do you have a habit of watching people dance?"

"Only the ones that demand attention."

What was that supposed to mean? Embarrassed he had been watching her dance, she didn't respond. Though she hated to admit it, he was right. As childish as it may seem, she was trying to get his attention.

"Lost your tongue? If you want to make me jealous, don't dance."

Skylar felt her face burn, knowing he knew what she was trying to do, and from his rude comments. "I wasn't."

"Uh, huh. You can keep saying that to yourself. I'm not buying it."

"And I don't belong in a naughty corner," she added.

"We'll see about that."

With an exasperated sigh, Skylar's eyes fell in the same line as Mason's gaze, to where her dress had gathered up, showing more of her thighs than it should. His eyes moved up to hers again with a slight flush on his cheeks. He turned away from her and stood up. His obvious stare made Skylar hot. It had almost the same effect as if he had run his hand up her thigh. She felt her face flush too, knowing that he took notice of her, but she couldn't help but smile inwardly, because he found her attractive enough to look at.

Skylar watched him enter his side of the car, but just before he got in, she saw him sweep the perimeter with his eyes, as if he was making sure no one was around. Maybe he didn't want to be seen with her. Mason started the car, pressed the gas pedal, and took off. His hands held tightly onto the steering wheel, he drove without uttering a word for several blocks. Finally, he spoke. "Would you like to hear some music?"

"No, thanks. Well, actually, you can turn it on if you'd like," Skylar replied, trying to sound polite. She didn't know why her heart was pounding with nervousness. He was just taking her home. It wasn't a date. He didn't say anything. Instead, he looked over, gave her a quick sideways smile, and turned back to look straight ahead.

Skylar didn't give him the address or tell him how to go, but oddly, he was going in the right direction. She didn't bother to ask how, though it was creeping her out. Instead, she kept her eyes glued to the familiar streets and the street signs, to make sure he wasn't taking her anywhere else. Finally, unable to hold in her curiosity, she had to know. "Do you know where you're going?"

"Yes, I picked up my brother at your cousin's house."

"You did?"

"The night when you almost drowned, my brother and Kayla took you home in Kayla's car. He left his car at the beach and asked me to pick him up at Kayla's house."

"Oh." Now it all made sense. She began to relax, breathing easily again. "I never got to thank you for saving me."

He gave a short laugh and a quick grin, still looking ahead. "Which time? I mean...tonight?"

Which time? Was there more than one time? "Yes, tonight. Do you remember throwing a guy across the room?"

"Yes. He deserved it." Mason sounded angry.

"Were you at the beach?" She didn't know why she asked this question. It just slipped out.

"Nope," he said flatly, gluing his eyes straight ahead. "Why would you ask that?"

"Cause I could've sworn I saw—"

"You were delusional. It happens when people are in a state of unconsciousness. But thanks for thinking of me before you almost drowned."

What? I didn't want to think of you. You would be the last person on Earth I would think of before I died. And how did you know I was unconscious? When Kayla found me, I wasn't. Skylar blazed with anger. Being that his tone was flat, she didn't know if he was being serious or if he was joking. Regardless, he was arrogant and rude. Not knowing what to say, she didn't respond. Instead, she looked out the window.

The hot puffs of irritated breath Skylar blew out her mouth fogged a small section of the window. After she wiped it clear, she focused on the dim streetlights, thinking this was going to be one heck of a long ride. It was only a twenty-minute drive, but to Skylar, it felt like an eternity.

When he pulled onto their street, it was dark. It was close to midnight, and the streets in their neighborhood had hardly any street lamps. Relieved she was home, she couldn't get out of the car fast enough.

Skylar unlocked the seatbelt and pushed the door handle just as he pulled into the driveway, but before she had the chance to step out, Mason opened the door wider and yanked her out in a hurry with a look of fury. Skylar gasped sharply. A scream for help reached her throat, only to get cut off by Mason's hand. She was locked in his hold with his hand over her mouth. Twisting and fighting, she tried to escape, but to no avail.

"Shhh...." Mason whispered. "They'll hear you."

Is he crazy? And how did he get to me so fast? Skylar's eyes were wide and confused.

When he noticed her expression, Mason gestured his head to her house. "Something is in there."

Sure enough, the front door was wide open. Skylar shook her head and muttered some noise. Unable to hear, Mason released his hand and lowered both of them beside the car.

"That's my cousin's house," Skylar whispered, panicking. Why did he say "something" instead of "someone"? As sounds of crashing objects and loud inhuman groans filled her ears, she trembled. She had never witnessed a break-in before. "We're being robbed? Call the police."

"The police can't help."

"What do you mean 'the police can't help'? We can't just stand here." Skylar narrowed her eyes at him, thinking he was out of his mind. "Listen." She stood up.

Mason yanked her down. "Shhh...they will hear you."

"I don't care if they hear me. Then maybe they'll leave."

"Trust me, they won't."

"Trust you?" Skylar scoffed.

"They aren't what you think." Mason sat on the cement with his back against the car. "How did I miss them?" he mumbled, raking his hair back and then standing up.

"How did you miss them? Are they your friends? What's going on?" Skylar's voice was loud. She didn't care that he'd asked her to keep her voice down. Maybe if her voice were loud enough, they would be scared off and just leave.

Mason rolled his eyes. "Great. Now you've got their attention. Run!"

Two men suddenly stood outside the doorway, obviously searching for where the voices came from. They turned and spotted Skylar dead on. What they did next seemed impossible, but it was real. They morphed into beast-like forms.

She stood frozen, unable to believe her eyes. Incapable of moving by her own will, a powerful yank pulled her arm, forcing her out of her trance. Mason had seized her wrist as he began to run. Wobbling and unable to run as fast with her two-inch heels on, she swiftly took them off one by one as she ran, and hooked the back straps over her fingers.

Looking over her shoulder to see who—or what—she was dashing madly away from, she saw two hideous creatures on their tail. Skylar was glad Mason made her run. Their body structures were grotesque. They appeared to be half beast and half human. Their arms and legs were bulky, like steroids gone wrong. With distorted heads and bulging yellow eyes as bright as headlights on a car, their humongous mouths were too big for their faces. They roared with vengeance through their shark-like teeth, charging ahead, both with a look that showed no thoughts of mercy.

What the hell? Am I dreaming? She wasn't sure, but the way her heart painfully pounded out of her chest brought her back to reality. Not only that, her bare feet hitting the cement sent searing pain through her legs. She was sure she would have blisters on the bottoms of her feet. Thank God, it was night, but she wondered if the neighbors could hear them. Mason was much faster than she was. He practically dragged her. As she ran as fast as her feet would allow, she looked over her shoulder to see them closing in.

"Faster," she yelled, but it came out inaudibly since she was out of breath. Wanting to lose them, they turned right, jumped over low bushes, darted through someone's backyard, crossed the street, and then crouched behind some tall bushes.

"We can hide here for now," he said, releasing his grip, catching his breath.

Skylar's legs were extremely sore and her lungs were about to explode. She had never run so fast in her entire life. Slumped over with her hands on her knees, air frantically rushed in and out of her body. Something damp on the bottoms of her feet caught her attention, and she realized she was standing on wet grass. The coolness from the contact eased the burning sensation on the soles of her feet.

Still panting, she snuck a peek through the bushes and dabbed the trickling drops of sweat with her hand before they could fall.

Parched and needing water, she smacked her lips and tongue. Finally, when her heart rate was steady, she spoke. "Did...umm...did you see what I saw?"

Mason arched his brows in an "as if" fashion. "Yeesss. It was the reason why we were running."

Having him confirm what she saw validated that she was not going out of her mind, but she didn't like his mocking tone. She turned to him and stuck her finger into his chest. Yup, it was firm alright. Then she dropped her hand. She hadn't meant to touch him. "What were those things? And who are you?"

Mason raised a brow, giving her an incredulous look, and then placed his finger over his lips. "Shhh....not so loud. Is this the first time you've ever seen them?"

"Is this the first time?" Suddenly, Skylar's anger went up a notch. "I've never seen what I just saw ever in my entire life. In fact, right now, I'm not even sure if I'm dreaming or if this is real. Things like that don't exist. It's nothing near normal."

"What a minute. They were in your house. They're after you, so who the hell are you?" he whispered sharply.

Skylar scoffed, irritated by his apparent accusation that she was to blame for them showing up. "Are you kidding? I was perfectly fine until you showed up. I would've gone home, straight to bed, and that would have been the end of my night, but noooo. You came along, and now these creatures are following you. So, let me ask you again. Who are you?"

Skylar thought about what she'd said. The monsters were in Kayla's house. Logically speaking, they were after her or Kayla, or even perhaps her aunt, but not him.

Mason placed his hands on her shoulders, as if his touch could pacify her. "Keep it down. You really don't know who you are, do you?" His tone was softer than a second ago.

Skylar peered up to him in mystification. "I know who I am," she stated, giving him an attitude, but she couldn't help but notice how close they were. She wanted to melt into him. *Focus...focus...not on him, but on why we're here.*

"Then tell me why I couldn't make you forget I was the cop?"

Because you were so darn cute. "What do you mean? How the hell do I know? So you *were* the cop that pulled me over? Why did you try to make me believe it wasn't you? I don't understand." Skylar placed both palms of her hands on her face, hoping this mess would go away, and just be a nightmare she could wake up from.

Why was this situation so complicated? Meet a cute guy. He likes you and you like him back. Go out on several dates and fall in love. Sounds so easy. So why? Why couldn't that happen, instead of meet a cute guy and monsters chase after you, and you have no idea why all the craziness is happening, making you feel like you're insane.

Mason was sweeping the street thoroughly with his eyes. Since there was no sign of the monsters, he turned to Skylar. "Look, I'm sorry, but now is not the time to explain. I only dressed up like a cop for that day because I was told those ugly creatures—we call them vultures—were in town. I thought they were in your trunk. I got a strange vibe from your car, so I had to check."

"What? In my trunk?" Skylar finally understood why he'd wanted her to pop the trunk. She thought it was an odd request, but she'd done it anyway. "So I was right. You're my Doug. I mean, you were Doug, right?"

"It's not my name. I borrowed a friend's uniform. Obviously, his name is Doug."

"Isn't that illegal?"

"It is, but apparently I got away with it."

"Whatever. Is Mason even your real name?"

"No. I mean, yes. Mason is my name."

"Explain to me why you would think one of THOSE would be inside my trunk. There's no way that...that thing could fit in my trunk."

"It's complicated. They can be in human form. You saw them earlier. A human body can fit in a trunk, and they're not the only kind of vultures. They come in different forms and sizes. I—"

"Wait a minute. If they can take on human form, do they live among us?"

"No, they don't. At least I don't think they do."

"Who told you these vultures were in town? How do you know?"

"I can sense their presence, and they smell worse than anything you've ever smelled before. I'll explain later."

"You've got a lot of explaining to do, but my cousin and my aunt are most likely home already. I'm not going to tell them what happened. They'll think I'm crazy."

"Okay, let's wait five minutes, and then we can head back."

"Okay," Skylar agreed, looking up at the full illuminating moon. Casting the brightest yellow beams, it almost looked like the sun, but not quite, and it brightened the dark sky. Now that was reality. She would hold on to that. It was mesmerizing and peaceful in contrast to how she was really feeling—deathly terrified.

TEN

THREE POLICE CARS were parked in front of the house. Red lights were flashing and neighbors peered out through their windows with curiosity. Skylar saw her aunt standing by the wide-open front door with the cops. When she saw Skylar, she pulled her into a tight hold, turning her back on the officers. "Thank God, you're okay." Her tone was urgent. "Why didn't you answer your cell phone? Kayla and I were worried about you. We thought you had been kidnapped. I was just about to call your mom." Her eyes went to Mason, then to the shoes Skylar was holding in her hand.

"I'm sorry. I left my phone in the car. We were taking a walk." She didn't know what to say, but she knew she couldn't tell her the truth. Her aunt looked at her with scolding eyes, most likely not approving of her late night walk with a guy she'd neither met, nor given her approval of.

"At this time of night? You need to be back before I get home. That is the rule here."

"I'm really sorry I worried you. It won't ever happen again." Skylar dropped her eyes, feeling terrible for making her aunt worry. She could only imagine what had gone through her mind.

"I'm just glad you're safe. Please don't ever do that to me again. I'll be telling your mom about the robbery, but I won't tell her you were out late. I don't know what she'll decide to do. She may want you to go home. I'll do my best to convince her to let you stay."

"Thank you," Skylar said softly. She turned her attention to Mason. "This is Mason. He's a friend."

Mason extended his hand to her with a warm smile.

"It's nice to meet you, Mason. Next time make sure to bring her back before midnight, even if you're just a friend."

"Yes. I'm so sorry. I lost track of time. It won't happen again."

"Skylar." Kayla ran toward her, almost knocking her down, grabbing her tightly. "Thank God, you're okay." She turned her attention to Mason, releasing her hold. "Oh...hi, Mason. I'm glad you were together at least." Kayla gave Skylar a questioning look.

Interrupted by Kayla, she was glad to be out of her aunt's line of fire. Not meaning to ignore Kayla, her eyes were fixated on the living room, which was the first place one spotted upon entering the house. The furniture had been turned over, and picture frames were shattered. It was shocking to see the mess. It wasn't even her house, but it didn't matter. It was Kayla's house, and though she didn't cause this, somehow she felt responsible. Her eyes pooled with tears. "I'm so sorry," she muttered to Kayla.

Kayla was trying to hold it together, but lost it when she saw Skylar's tears streaming down her cheeks. Kelly was still talking to the policemen by the porch. Her arms were crossed and she looked tense.

Mason gazed around too, but he mostly stood by the door. "Did they take anything?" he asked.

Skylar sniffed and wiped her tears. "I don't know. I'm afraid to look upstairs." She turned to Kayla, who was also wiping her tears away. "Do you know if they took anything?"

"Nothing down here that I can see, but I didn't go upstairs yet. I'm afraid too."

"I'll go with you." Skylar looped her arms around Kayla's shoulder as they headed for the stairs.

"I'll escort you both, just in case." Mason followed behind them.

"Skylar, why are you holding your shoes?" Kayla questioned.

"My feet were sore from wearing these heels." Skylar felt bad for lying, but it was partially the truth.

"Oh." Kayla continued to climb.

Skylar took several strides up the stairs, and then stopped. Her legs wanted to give out. The bottoms of her feet were still achingly sore. Holding onto the rails, she ascended forward, limping again. "How did you get home?" she asked Kayla.

"Nick dropped me off, but he got worried when he saw my car was parked in the driveway and you two were nowhere to be found. He went looking for you guys, since there was no text back from Mason and he couldn't reach him by phone. I should text him to let him know you're both okay." She pulled out her phone. Skylar watched Kayla's speedy fingers as they entered her room.

Mason took his cell phone out from his back pocket. "I have several missed calls and texts from him. Tell him I had my phone on silent."

Skylar didn't hear a word Mason said. With a look of horror, she started to tear up again. Her heart had been ripped apart, and a feeling of being violated rushed through. Her stuff was scattered everywhere. Drawers were pulled out. Clothes that had been neatly hung were yanked off their hangers, and even her mattress was flipped over.

"What the hell?" Kayla exclaimed. Her eyes swept the chaotic room. "I'll be right back." Kayla ran to her room.

Skylar was stunned and speechless. She couldn't get her body to move. Why would they do this? What were they after? Her thoughts were broken when Mason rested his hand on her back. "Are you okay?"

"They can't be real. Monsters don't exist," she stated numbly. Her eyes were glassy, looking straight ahead, out the window, too overwhelmed with everything that had happened. "I think I'm going out of my mind."

Mason spun Skylar toward him. "Skylar." Skylar snapped out of her trance. "They are real. They were looking for something."

"But I have nothing. I don't own anything expensive."

"Think. It could be an object."

Ignoring Mason, she spoke. "Thank you for taking me home. I think I want to be alone. I'm...." Her tone was soft and hardly audible, sounding more like an echo in her head. Suddenly, the room started to spin. She took a step forward, trying not to fall. Looking at Mason with uncertainty, wondering why this was happening, she saw three of him. Bewildered, she shook her head as white spots appeared in her vision, looking like fireflies dancing in her room. Her unsteady legs gave out and her body went limp. Just before she fell, she felt the weight of strong arms across her chest as she slipped into darkness.

SKYLAR OPENED HER eyes and saw Mason sitting beside her bed. Startled to see him still there, she blinked her eyes and jolted upright. Strangely, there was no sign of him. Odd! It had to be a dream, or her eyes were playing tricks on her.

Recalling last night's incident, she thought about the mess she had to deal with, but when she looked around, to her surprise, the room was spotless. There was no evidence of a robbery. How could this be? She couldn't remember falling asleep or even saying good-bye to Mason. Did it even happen? As these thoughts ran through her mind, there was a soft knock on the door. "Come in."

The door cracked open and Kayla stepped in. She stood by the foot of the bed. Still in her nightgown, she looked like she had been through hell.

"Did what I think happened last night really happen?" Skylar asked, hoping Kayla would give her the answer she was hoping for, that it was just a dream.

"Yup, it's real." Kayla plunked her body on the bed and tossed her hair to the side. "You know you fainted last night, right?"

"I did?" Trying to pull it out of her memory, she paused to think.

Kayla giggled. "You fainted right into Mason's arms. He carried you to your bed. Actually, he fixed your bed first, then like a prince, he carried his princess to bed. He even placed the blanket over you."

"He did not," Skylar said, blushing, thinking it did explain why she was still wearing the clothes she had worn last night.

"Oh yes, he did. I saw the whole thing. You know me. I was spying. It was easy since your bedroom door was open, but what I can't figure out is how your room got cleaned up so fast. Hmmm...that, I don't understand. Anyway, are you missing anything?"

"No, are you?" Skylar asked, looking around, though she couldn't remember. She didn't bring anything of value with her. In fact, she didn't possess any expensive items that were worth taking.

"Nope."

"I'm sorry this happened to you." Skylar pulled Kayla in for a squeeze and let go.

"It's okay. The police said the robbers are going from house to house and doing the same thing—breaking in and escaping without taking a thing. There has been a break in every single day for the past week. They all report that nothing is missing. The funny thing is, it started the day you arrived in town." Kayla laughed out loud, teasing.

Not liking her remark, Skylar's brows angled into a hard line, while her lips pursed crookedly.

"I don't get it," Kayla continued. "Why go through all that trouble, knowing there's a possibility that you could get caught, and not steal a thing? I mean, they could've taken my computer, the television, or the camera that was on my desk. I even had a twenty inside my desk, and they didn't take that. What kind of thieves are they?"

Skylar shrugged her shoulders and shook her head. The only clear picture that came to mind was the image of the hideous monsters as they came after her. She thought it was best not to mention them to Kayla for now, until she investigated further. The only person who could clarify anything was Mason. She needed to talk to him. "How's your mom?"

"She's fine. She already spoke to your mom about it. I'm sure you'll hear from her. From what I've been told, your mom gave the green light for you to stay. My mom said we were lucky we weren't home when this happened. Material things can be replaced, but we can't...which, I totally agree with. You know me and my smart mouth. I told her you and I needed to go out more often then."

Skylar pushed Kayla playfully. "Do keep your mouth closed."

"Sure, I can do that, but I'll keep my lips ready for Nick," Kayla giggled.

"I'm sure you will." Skylar nudged Kayla and stood up. "We have work today, right?"

"Ugh...don't remind me. Okay, I'll go get ready."

"I better call my mom. She'll want to hear my voice and hear my side of the story."

After Kayla walked out of her room, Skylar carefully, achingly got out of bed. Her leg muscles were sore and the blisters on the bottoms of her feet looked unattractive. Moving toward the closet, she stopped when she saw the same shadow figure in the window next door, just like the last time. However, this time she noted the length of his hair to the shoulders. Dirty blonde guy? As she moved closer to the window, the figure disappeared. Was she hallucinating? "What the...?" This had happened twice. She kept forgetting to ask her cousin about it. Making a mental note to ask Kayla, she headed for the shower.

"GOOD MORNING." JACK sprang cheerfully from the kitchen. The diner was empty as usual since the morning rush had just ended.

"Good morning? You mean good afternoon," Kayla said, throwing herself on the stool. Skylar did the same.

"Did you just wake up?" Jack asked.

"Yes," Kayla replied, feeling embarrassed that he knew.

"Then, it's good morning."

"Oh, stop pestering the young ones," Mona said, walking out from the storage room. "Sorry about last night, girls. Your mom filled me in. That's just awful. Some people are crazy. You just never know."

"Thanks," Kayla said softly. "We were in shock, but I'm not going to let those assholes ruin my week."

"Hey, watch that mouth of yours," Jack reprimanded. "Pretty young girls don't talk like that."

"Sorry, Jack." Kayla shrugged sheepishly.

"Did they take anything?"

"Nothing...nada...zip." Kayla rested her head on the table.

"How about you, Skylar?" Mona asked.

"Nothing from me, either. I didn't have anything worth much. Just my clothes."

"Good thing you girls are safe," Jack said. "Or else I'd personally hunt them down."

"What are you going to fight them with, your wrinkles?" Mona teased.

Jack laughed aloud. "Now that was funny, but you would do a better job scaring them with your looks."

Mona scoffed playfully. "Well, you wouldn't get much of a punch with your flabby muscles."

"Speaking of muscles, I guess all you have to do is sit on them."

Skylar and Kayla gaped back and forth, giggling from the banter going on between them, until Kayla jumped high off her stool. "Darn this phone. I forgot I put it in my back pocket." She glanced at it, heading to the back of the diner.

WHAT YA DOING?

"It's from Nick," Kayla said to Skylar.

Hello. Getting ready for rush hour. What're YOU doing?

Thinking of you.

What kind of thoughts?

Bad, naughty thoughts.

Giggle

What are you doing after work?

I have a hot date.

You better be talking about me or I'll have to get rid of him.

Ha ha! Yes, it's you silly. I like your jealous side. It turns me on.

I'll have to do it more often. What else turns you on?

Just you. I gotta go. Some of us work you know.

Meet me at the theater Monday after work at 8.

Monday?

I'm busy tomorrow. Bring your cousin!

Bossy, bossy. And why the exclamation mark?

Mason needs to get out more.

Kayla walked out of the storage room to see Mona frowning at her.

"Sorry." Kayla batted her eyelashes and got back to work.

ELEVEN

"I DON'T THINK I should go," Skylar said, sitting in the passenger seat.

"See?" Kayla placed her phone in front of her. "Read the text. 'Bring your cousin.' I think Mason will be there. This is great. It will be a double date."

"I do need to talk to him. What are we going to see?"

"I don't know. You're okay with any movie, right? I know you don't like to watch scary movies."

"I'm sure it will be fine. Just keep your eyes on the road," Skylar said, feeling nervous, driven by the thought of seeing Mason again, but she needed answers. Something paranormal had happened that night, and though she tried to pretend that it didn't just to stay sane, she couldn't help thinking about the beasts. "Vultures" was what Mason called them, but to Skylar they were monsters—hideous, freakish, stinking, straight from hell creatures.

After Kayla parked, they got out of the car and headed into the theater. The parking lot was pretty empty, but then again it was Monday night. From what Skylar could remember, Monday was the slowest night for moviegoers, even during the summer, especially in this small town.

Skylar spotted the flashing sign of red and blue neon lights. It sparked a little excitement in her. It was good to get out of the house. Speaking of houses, Skylar remembered the question she'd wanted to ask many times before. "I've been meaning to ask you. Does the old lady still live in that house next door?"

"Yeah, why? You miss her?" Kayla giggled, nudging her shoulder playfully.

"She does?" There had to be an explanation.

"But you can't visit her because she's on vacation," Kayla continued.

Icy chills ran down her spine. "Is anyone watching her house?"

"No. Why are you so interested?" Kayla asked, walking faster. Her skinny jeans fit firmly down her long legs. She wore a black ruffled tank top and held tightly to her small black purse.

Skylar had dressed plainly—shorts and a T-shirt with tennis shoes. She wasn't going to dress to impress, especially on a hot night. Even if he took interest in her, he'd have to like her for who she was.

"Just wondering." She didn't want to tell her cousin she saw someone inside the house. She doubted herself a lot lately, and thought it was best not to mention it.

Nick waved his hand, his face bright with a grin. When they approached, he gave Kayla a kiss on her cheek and to Skylar's surprise, he did the same to her. "I've got the tickets." He fanned them out.

Skylar saw three. *Great! I'm the third wheel.*

"What are we seeing?"

"*Zombie World.*"

"Great," Skylar hummed softly, cringing, walking through the entrance.

Nick halted abruptly and turned to Skylar. "Oh, I forgot to tell you. Mason will be coming soon."

"Oh, okay." Skylar gave a faint smile, but she was hiding behind the giant one she gave herself secretly.

They arrived just in time, missing all the credits. As they climbed the stairs, the girls followed Nick. They passed a couple sitting smack in the middle of the theater. Besides them, it looked like they were the only ones there. Nick kept on climbing until he reached the last row of seats.

"I don't like anyone kicking me in the back." He took sideways steps to the middle seat, and Kayla sat between him and Skylar.

Soon after, Skylar excused herself. "I'll be right back," she whispered. "I have to use the restroom."

"Okay," Kayla whispered back. "Want me to go with you?"

"No. Stay here. I'll be fine." Skylar quickened her pace down the stairs, rooting her eyes on the florescent lights below. Not wanting to miss any more of the movie than she had to, she swiftly turned left. She hated finding her seat in the dark, especially during a suspenseful part.

Entering the restroom, she saw four stalls with dark gray doors that were all shut. Not knowing if they were occupied, she looked underneath the stalls for feet.

Seeing no one around, even while heading to the restroom, she had a bad case of goose bumps. She disregarded her thoughts, deciding she was scared for no reason, but her heart thumped faster by the second. She finished her business as fast as she could, pumped soap in her hands, lathered it up, and placed her hands under the sensor.

As thoughts of when Mason would meet them flowed through her mind, she dried her hands and pushed the door to exit. She pushed again, but the door didn't budge. *What the heck!* She pushed again. Nothing.

Suddenly, a pipe burst and water started gushing out. She turned, leaning her back against the door, wondering what to do next. Her breathing became jagged as she started banging on the door with all her strength. "Help!"

A second pipe burst and water poured from it just like the first. Skylar couldn't fathom what was happening. Even the toilet water was overflowing. Seeing the water rising, she screamed for help again, banging on the door in desperation. Recalling that no one was around, she was sure that no one could hear her cries for help. Her cell phone was in her purse, which she'd left with Kayla. Surely, she would be fine, she reasoned. The water would seep out through the tiny opening at the bottom of the door. She soon realized as the water level was rising, it wasn't happening as she expected.

Think, think, think. Assuming she could turn it off at the pipe, she trudged through the cold water and she thought it felt like the ocean. It was now up to her knees, pricking painfully at every nerve in her body. She was already starting to feel numb. Wanting to survive, she touched all the knobs, buttons, and anything else she could put her hands on to shut the water off, but it was useless. There was nothing she could do. The pipe seemed to take on a life of its own.

Skylar was drenched from her waist down. Shivering, she scanned the room and noted there was no way out. Of all the ways she could die, this was the way it would happen—drowning in a bathroom with toilet and sink water.

It happened so fast she didn't see it coming. A vine, like seaweed, slithered through the broken pipe, grabbed her ankles, and dragged her into the water. She recognized it as the same slimy something that had attacked her at the beach. She once again tugged, yanked, and pulled for her life, but to no avail.

Running out of breath, she managed to hang onto the sink and push herself up for air. With a loud, sharp gasp, she took a breath and sunk back under from the force. She went through the same cycle several times, catching a few breaths, but then it became impossible when the water level rose higher.

Just when she thought all hope was lost, the seaweed released its grip. The water flowed back to where it had come from, as if someone had pushed the rewind button on a DVD remote.

"Thank God," she mumbled, collapsing on the ground from sheer exhaustion.

Unexpectedly, she felt arms cuddling her, carrying her out the door. Immediately, she knew it was him. Being in Mason's arms left her breathless, and she didn't want to move a muscle. He laid her down on a wooden bench and bent down on his knee.

Skylar held her eyes closed, but opened them slowly when he brushed the strands of her hair away from her face. Surprisingly, when his hand slid down tenderly to her cheek, she felt a slight tingling sensation around the area that he touched. Whatever it was that she felt, definitely came from him. It was something between heat and a mild shock, but it wasn't painful. In fact, it felt warm, pleasurable, and soothing, but she didn't understand how he was doing it.

Peering up, she caught his eyes as they held hers, through space, through time, through her soul. Sparks flew, and some kind of connection Skylar didn't understand erupted through her. Though she didn't want to feel this way, she had no other choice. Her heart longed to know him even more.

Mason blinked his eyes, looking frazzled and concerned. "Are you okay?" His tone was softer than usual.

Anchoring her trembling hands on the bench, she raised herself up and rested her back against the wall. "I think so. I'm drenched." *My mascara. Great! I wonder how I look.* "You opened the door and saved me. How did you know I was in there?"

"I just got here. Nick told me you were in the restroom. He asked me to check on you."

"Good thing you came, but...but...?" Tears pooled in her eyes. She buried her face in the palms of her hands. Looking up, her glassy eyes shone as pearl drop tears trickled down her face. She was mad at herself for being weak in front of him, but she was more afraid of how he would react.

Though he showed a tender side of himself tonight, she couldn't help recall the times he was rude to her. What puzzled her most was that these supernatural encounters, things that happened only in books, television, and movies, were happening only to her. Somehow, he was always there to save her, but why wasn't he flipping out like her?

How was it that he didn't find what had just happened to be anomalous? Either he had had extraordinary encounters of this kind before, or he was good at hiding his true emotions in front of her. Regardless, she needed answers. "Am I going crazy? I don't know what's happening to me. If you know something, please tell me."

To her surprise, he was calm—too calm. He didn't answer her. Instead, his eyes revealed sadness, and she couldn't comprehend the reason for it. Her stare was broken when he stood tall. "You're wet. You should take off your clothes."

What a way to avoid a question! Skylar blinked her eyes in disbelief. Did she hear him correctly? "Excuse me?" Not wanting to assume he was really asking her to strip off her clothes, she didn't move a muscle, but the way his piercing eyes laid on her, she might as well have already been naked. She gasped when he started to unbutton his shirt. Her eyes shot to the floor, then back to him, and then to the floor, wondering what she was supposed to do in this awkward moment.

"Here. Go change in the restroom. You don't want to catch a cold." He placed his shirt in front of her.

She looked up to see him shirtless for the very first time. With all the right curves and tightness, he looked like a chiseled statue of a god. He was beautiful and perfectly toned, with satin-like skin, which looked like it would be smooth to the touch. Then, there was the small tattoo shaped like a lightning bolt on his upper right arm, toward his shoulder. Way too sexy!

As warmth flushed her face, she tried not to stare, but there was no way around it. "You won't have a shirt," Skylar said, thinking that was the most idiotic thing she had said so far, but she couldn't think when he was half-naked in front of her.

"I'm not cold, but you will be."

Mason was right. Skylar didn't realize she was shivering until she placed her hand out to take his shirt. The adrenaline from the initial shock had kept her warm, and now it was wearing away. The blasting air conditioner didn't help, either. "Thanks."

Just as she pivoted right toward the restroom, even though she was deathly scared to go back, Mason gripped her arm. "Wait. Don't go in there without me."

His sudden protectiveness surprised Skylar, but then again, he had saved her. With a nod, he gestured for her to lead. Walking back into her nightmare, her blood pressure soared faster than she expected, but when she entered, surprisingly, she was calm, for two reasons. First, Mason was with her, and second, the restroom was in one piece, as if it had never happened. After she'd had enough of looking at the sinks and the stalls, she turned to Mason.

"Oh, I'll turn my back." He turned away from her. "I have a really nice view—white ceiling...mesmerizing. And a clear view of myself from the mirrors. So many mirrors. Mirrors everywhere I look."

Skylar giggled and her face lit with a small smile. Underneath that stiff heart of his, he had proven he had a sense of humor.

After slipping her arms into the sleeves of his shirt, her eyes followed her hands as she buttoned it quickly from bottom to top.

"Okay, I'm done." She looked up expecting to see Mason's back, but he had already turned and faced her.

Skylar turned red. "You...you just turned, right?"

He pointed to the left, to the right, and to all the mirrors in the bathroom. "Do you girls need all these mirrors? Can't get enough of yourselves? I thought you were done."

"You could've closed your eyes," Skylar scoffed, feeling embarrassed.

"What would be the fun in that?" he smirked.

He was right. Every direction he turned, he had a clear view of...her. Whatever. She justified that seeing her in a bra was like seeing her in a bikini top. "Well, next time, make sure you do."

Unsure whether he was uncomfortable by her remark or he was simply ignoring her, he didn't say a word. "Let's get out of here," he suggested, opening the door, looking as if his mind was deep in thought.

"Are you going to tell me what's going on?" she asked, folding her shirt to hold as she stood by the doorway.

"Later."

"No, I need to know now," she demanded.

"Let's go. It's not safe here."

Cold chills pricked along her spine from his words. First, Skylar gazed around cautiously. Then she glared at him, walked out, and headed to theater number ten.

Suddenly, Skylar jerked back when Mason grabbed her hand. She couldn't believe he was holding her hand. Not only that, he pulled her close to his chest—so close, almost into a hug.

Her eyes drifted to his, unable to look away, as if he held a spell over her. She could see so much love, tenderness, and the possibilities behind his rude, egotistical, arrogant attitude. She blinked and retreated a few steps when he released her abruptly, as if he finally realized he was holding her longer than he wanted to.

"We're not going there," he stated, as if his words were final.

"We're not going there?" *When did I become a part of "we"?*

"No. We need to talk."

You got that right. I've been asking you like constantly. It's about time. "Yes. We need to talk. Where should we talk then?"

"At my house."

Skylar gulped nervously. "At your house?"

"Are you going to repeat everything I say? I should just call you Echo."

There he goes again, back to Mr. Rude. "I'm not repeating. I'm just asking."

"If you don't want answers to your questions, then fine with me."

"What? I've asked you so many times, but you won't answer them. I'm not going to beg."

"Umm, that might be interesting." He arched his brows giving that tantalizing smirk he did so well. The kind that made butterflies dance in her stomach, the kind that made her want to just pull him in and plant her lips on his.

"Are you kidding? Just take me to your house." She couldn't believe she'd just said that, but enough was enough. "I need to tell my cousin and get my purse."

"You don't need your purse. I've already told Nick." Without her permission, he snatched her wrist and tugged her out the exit door.

After a few strides, she yanked her arm back to her chest and stood her ground. Gritting her teeth, she peered up to him angrily. "I can walk by myself. And next time, ask me first before you make a decision for me."

With a nod from him, not knowing if that was an answer to her request, he led the way to his car.

TWELVE

MASON OPENED SKYLAR'S side of the car. When she stepped out, she was still holding onto her T-shirt. Mason placed his hand out, asking for it. After she reluctantly gave it to him, he placed it on the passenger seat. "You don't need to carry that around. I'll leave it right here in the car."

Skylar nodded and looked past him. She didn't want to freak out from the grand size of his house, but her eyes gave her away. Passing the long, enormous steel gate upon entering the circular driveway, she should have known she would be setting her eyes on a mansion. She had seen big houses in magazines, but never had she been this close to one.

As she followed Mason's footsteps to the front entrance, her eyes were still glued to the house, admiring the elegance of it. Though it was dark, the surrounding lights were enough to reveal the beauty. Red rose bushes edged the cobblestone path leading to the front door. To the right was a huge water fountain with an ivory statue she thought looked like Zeus, lounging in the middle, but she wasn't sure if it was him. He looked majestic and proud.

Upon entering, her eyes got even bigger when Mason hit the lights. Standing on the caramel marble floor, her eyes went straight up to the crystal chandelier, shaped like an upside down umbrella. It sparkled like diamonds reflecting from the lights above. Underneath it, a grand vase was centered on a tall, round mahogany table. Filled with stargazer lilies, the fragrance permeated the house with a heavenly scent.

"This way," he directed, reaching for his cell phone from his back pocket. "Excuse me," he said, making eye contact. He turned his back and spoke into the receiver. "What?" He sounded upset, pausing for what seemed like a minute. "Tell them I'll be there in half an hour or so." He paused again. "Don't say anything. Just wait for me, got it?" Then he hung up.

Seeing two staircases, Skylar wondered which way he would go. She followed when Mason pivoted to his right, heading up the stairs, stepping onto the lush, beige carpet. Lagging behind, she marveled at the elegant furniture and the paintings on the wall. Then her eyes shifted to the white walls as she walked down the long hallway.

"This is my room." Mason opened the door.

Skylar tried her best not to be overly excited, but she couldn't help it. His bedroom was three times the size of hers. The first thing she observed was the illuminating moon peeking through the slightly opened velvet curtains, and a feeling of warmth immediately encased her. Then she saw the neatly made, king-sized bed with several plush pillows by the headboard. With a huge flat screen television mounted to the wall and the elegant furniture, Skylar thought his room was designed for a prince.

"It's not much, but I hope you'll find it comfortable. I'll get you a change of clothes." Mason opened another door and entered.

Not much? Was he serious? Surely he was being humble. Skylar didn't know where to sit. Her shorts were still damp. Not wanting to leave a wet spot on the expensive comforter, she stood instead. As she waited for Mason to return, she noticed there were no picture frames adorning the walls or on the dresser.

"It'll be a bit big on you, but at least you'll feel comfortable," Mason said, walking out from the closet with a T-shirt on. T-shirt on or off, he still looked the same—hot. Walking past her, he placed a T-shirt, a pair of thin sweat pants, and flip-flops on his bed. "You're welcome to take a shower if you like."

Her thoughts returned to what happened in the theater, and she blankly stared into space.

"Skylar, what are you thinking?" Mason asked with a tender tone, closing the gap between them.

"Before I do anything, can you please tell me what's going on? I feel like this is all a dream, or a nightmare. I don't understand how those things appeared in the ocean, and it tried to kill me, and...and those things...vultures you called them...they look like monsters. Monsters are not real. And...how does water just overflow from the sink and the toilet and fill a room? You act like this isn't weird, like it's normal to you." Skylar mumbled frantically, trying to make sense of it all, trying to tell herself that she was not crazy.

Mason placed his hand on her back, guiding her closer to the bed. "Sit down."

"My shorts are still damp, I think." She patted her butt.

"It's alright. Please sit."

Skylar did as told. Mason sat beside her, looking at her with a weary expression, and placed his hand on his lap. "You have to promise me you won't speak a word until I'm finished. What I'm about to tell you will be unbelievable. You may even think I'm crazy. Will you listen and not freak out?"

Skylar nodded, having no choice. She needed to know.

"What we call gods, like Zeus, Poseidon, and Hades, ruled the world once upon a time. As religion progressed, people stopped believing and praying to them. When prayers are no longer received, the gods are forgotten, and unfortunately they vanish."

"What?" she muffled, arching her brows, wondering if he was joking, but when she saw the look on his face, she knew he wasn't.

"That's actually putting it mildly," he continued. "They just...die. Knowing their deaths were inevitable, Zeus, Poseidon, and other gods thought it was best to continue their bloodline, so they massively reproduced with mortal women and men. At least then, a part of them would live through their children and in the generations to come. Being born from mortal mothers or fathered by mortal men, the half-blood children were able to live on Earth.

"Unfortunately, Hades found out, and was mad as hell. He believed it was unfair that his brothers were about to continue their family lines, whereas he was forbidden to. Hades swore he would get rid of all the half-blood children. The sea creatures and the vultures you saw were Hades' creations. Are you following me?" Mason asked sternly, looking at Skylar's impassive expression.

"Then, you are...whose bloodline are you from?" Skylar asked slowly, feeling flabbergasted by what she was hearing, trying to soak in his words.

"Our ancestor line comes from Zeus. We didn't have the honor of meeting him, of course. This was ages ago."

"Was?"

"Yes, was."

"How about Poseidon and Hades?"

"They are gone too. As I said before, people stopped believing. From what I've been told from Nick's mom, all the gods are dead, even the minor gods. Unfortunately, Hades' monsters are still out there, carrying out his revenge. They have been for decades. My brothers and I are born from different mothers, but the same father. So we are technically half-brothers.

"From what I've been told, our father was attacked by the vultures, but he managed to find Nick's mother first and confessed his infidelity to her the night he was attacked. He confessed everything. His purpose was to procreate, to father more children like himself. You see, our kind was dying. The vultures, sea creatures, and others yet to be seen, have taken their vengeance, just as Hades had planned.

"Fortunately, Nick's mother knew what was going on and found out just in time. She was the one who told the other moms about the gods and the monsters, but she was a little late telling my mom. Remus's and Everett's mothers suffered the same fate as our father. Hades' monsters killed them.

"My mom found out last, and I learned I was one of the god's children the night she died. Nick's mother took care of me, along with Remus and Everett. Before Nick's mom passed away at the monster's hand, she made sure we were taken care of financially, and that is how our little family of four grown boys came to be." He paused and took a deep sigh. "But we'd rather have our moms back instead of all this wealth."

Though he tried not to show it, his eyes were filled with pain. Skylar knew that expression all too well. She had shown that look many times before when people would ask her about her dad.

"There are more of us out there," he continued. "This I know for sure. We like to keep to ourselves so we've never tried to contact the others. That way, we don't attract too much attention and the vultures stay away. If there are any suspicious activities, we move on to another small town or go away for a while, but we try to come back because this is where we all grew up. It's been a while, but we haven't had any activities until you came along, and that is the reason why I believe...you're one of us."

Skylar busted out laughing, not that it was something to laugh about. She just couldn't believe what she was hearing. Standing up, she paced back and forth "So, you're telling me my mom had sex with one of the god's descendants? Does my mom know?" Then she stopped pacing when she recalled Nick telling Kayla that his parents were dead. He didn't give reasons on this morbid topic, and they had never asked the question "how?" "No, it can't be true. My dad—"

"Left you and your mom." Mason finished her sentence.

Skylar froze in place, recalling that day when her dad never came home. Being only eight years old, she never understood the reasons why, and her mom seemed reluctant to discuss that specific topic. It took her a long time to get over the hurt. Eventually, the hurt grew into hatred, and then her heart became numb. It was the only way to deal with the loss of him, but now knowing that her dad could be special and that there was a possibility that he could be dead, it was too much to bear. But this all depended on whether Mason's story was true. "I don't understand." Skylar focused on the floor, trying to grasp his words.

"I know this is a lot to take in, but if it makes you feel any better, there is a chance I may be wrong about you. I'm not sure. You're quite complicated."

Skylar shook her head in disapproval of his words. She didn't want to be complicated. "What do you mean?"

"You can't defend yourself. You have no powers, so for sure you wouldn't be one of us. But these water creatures came after you, and they don't attack humans, so in that case that would make you one of us. You can see the vultures. Humans can't see them when they morph into beasts, and they don't go after humans unless they've been touched by a god or one of the descendants."

"Touched by a god?" she asked, confused, needing more explanation. Kayla had been touched by Nick. Was she in danger?

"I meant sexually. I hate to ask you this question, but have you...lately?"

"What? No." Skylar was appalled. What kind of girl did he think she was? She had almost done it with her ex-boyfriend—thank God she hadn't. But from the way he was so casual about it, and by using the word "lately," she assumed he did.

"Good. I mean, you can do whatever you want. I'm just asking. You know, just ruling things out, making sure you're not pregnant."

"Why does that matter?"

"Reproduction. Supposedly, when pregnant, or having given birth before, the mortal being produces a special scent only Hades' creatures can smell. I don't know too much about this. I've only been told. That is how our mothers were found."

"But they didn't go after my mom. I mean, if what you say is true, and my dad is...or was...a descendant of a god, she would have been attacked by them a long time ago. Unless they couldn't find her? Or, maybe *she* was one of the descendants." Skylar suddenly got worried for her mom's safety, but she was mostly baffled as to which parent was one of them.

"I don't know. I don't have all the answers. But I'm almost positive she is fine. Like I said, your situation is complicated. All I know is the fact that they trashed your room, and barely touched your cousin's, means you have something they want or need."

"I promise I don't have anything of value, or god-like." Having powers would've been great, only then it would have meant she was definitely one of them, and she didn't know if that was a good thing—most likely, not. "So then, let's say I'm one of you guys. Will I have special powers like you?"

"Most half-bloods have some type of supernatural abilities. For example, we are faster and stronger than an average human being, but only to a certain degree. Depending on our DNA structure, some of us have other abilities. Nick and I are similar. We can create heat and produce an electricity-like current at will by the simple touch of our hands. Unfortunately, Everett and Remus are normal, at least by godly standards. However, Remus can heal faster than any one of us, and they both are very strong."

"Create heat? Electricity? Really?" Skylar's eyes grew wide, wanting to see what that would be like, but she didn't ask. The word electricity made her revert back to the times she'd been shocked by him. Electricity equaled static, which would create a shock. Now she understood. She had been shocked by him several times before. "That was you. It was from you. I got shocked from your energy, or whatever you call it."

Mason raked his hair back, looking apologetic. "Yeah, sorry. I didn't mean to. I think I got a little...I don't know why that happened."

"Oh." That was all Skylar could mutter. Got a little what? Excited by her presence, she hoped.

He gazed down, apparently deep in thought. "Wait a minute...." He looked at her. "You made me do it. It never happened before until I touched you."

"So now the shock is my fault? You shocked me, I didn't shock you," she retorted. Since he didn't respond, she changed the subject. "If I'm supposedly one of you, and if I have supernatural something, how will I know?"

"The night my mom died, Nick's mom was there. She explained everything, but I didn't want any part of it. I didn't trust her. Who would believe a crazy story like that, right? One night they came after me. Since I had been to Nick's house several times with my mom, I ran to his house. That is when I discovered I could run faster than I had ever imagined. And when Nick's mom was attacked by them, Nick and I did our best. We discovered something else we could do, but it was a little too late. What I'm trying to tell you is that I don't know. It could just happen, but I really think your situation is unique."

Skylar's eyes glowed with a sudden revelation. Perhaps the light she thought she saw at the beach wasn't an angel's light, but instead was from Mason's heat. He was the light, but was that even possible? He said he created heat, not light. What did that mean?

She didn't know whether to feel grateful that he saved her at the beach, or be angry that he lied to her, making her think she was going out of her mind. "You were at the beach. You saved me. I wasn't hallucinating."

Mason shrugged his shoulders nonchalantly. "Sorry, but I didn't know if I could trust you at that time."

"Trust me?" Anger boiled inside her. Of all the nerve. He had the audacity to say those words? She dismissed it when she thought about the reasons why the monsters would be after her. "I don't have anything they would want. I don't understand."

"I don't either, but I need to find out why this is happening to you. I'm not sure who to trust, so it may take a while to get our questions answered. Until then, I need to look after you. I guess I'm stuck with you."

Was that such a bad thing? He didn't have to make it sound like she was a nuisance. "Oh."

"But right now, I need to take care of an emergency at work. The phone call earlier was from one of the employees. Stay here. Change and relax. I'll be back within an hour or so. Do you think you can do that?"

"I don't know. Maybe I should go home."

Mason lifted Skylar's chin with his fingertip, forcing her to look into his eyes. They were infused with longing.

"Ouch." Skylar jolted from the shock. Though it wasn't as strong as the last few times, she was quite surprised that it happened again.

"Sorry. I don't know why that happens only with you." His eyes moved to his fingers. "Anyway, you can trust me."

"Okay," Skylar said reluctantly, nodding her head. She wanted to trust him. He hadn't given her any indication that he was a threat to her. After all, he was the one that saved her from almost drowning, not once, but twice. Before he could take a step toward the door, Skylar gripped his wrist. The moment her hand touched his skin, she felt a kind of pleasant energy, but not a shock, thankfully. Their eyes met. Swallowed up by him, she had forgotten why she stopped him in the first place.

The way Mason held her eyes with such care made her almost crumble, making her weak. If only she could break through. She knew there was a kinder side to his arrogant, rude personality, and he definitely had shown it tonight.

"You'll be fine," Mason finally said.

Skylar nodded to agree, then asked a question. "My cousin, Kayla, is she—?"

As if Mason knew what she was going to ask before she could finish, he answered her. "No. I'm almost positive that she's not."

"Does Nick care for her in a special way?" Skylar wasn't sure about asking this personal question about his half-brother.

"I don't know. I don't get into his personal business. Let's just say, he likes to play around, and he's never been serious with any girl in his lifetime. I'm quite surprised Kayla is still around. In fact, we don't take any relationship seriously. So if you're wondering about Kayla's heart, it will likely be broken sooner rather than later."

Skylar's heart sunk in her chest. Though she had hoped that Mason might take interest in her as more than a friend, hearing his sharp, cold words felt like a stab to her heart. What was even worse, he'd admitted Nick would end up hurting Kayla.

She knew these boys were up to no good the moment she met them, so why did she even bother to give them her time? Besides the obvious, of course, like Mason saving her from death a couple of times, she knew the answer. Kayla was head over heels in love with Nick ever since she'd first laid eyes on him. As for Skylar, she was drawn to Mason in ways she couldn't explain.

Mason placed his hand on the doorknob, twisting it while keeping his eyes on Skylar. "I'll be back in an hour. Stay here." He closed the door behind him.

Knowing she was alone in this giant, empty house at night gave her goose bumps all over. Feeling a cool draft, she grabbed the extra clothes and changed. The sweats were too long and too big at the waist, and the long T-shirt could almost be a dress on her. Folding them at the waist and the hem helped. Though the flip-flops were big, she'd rather slip on a pair of big slippers than feel the wetness from her soggy tennis shoes.

THIRTEEN

AFTER A WHILE, Skylar got bored. One hour wasn't that long, but with nothing to do, it seemed like an eternity, especially when she was alone. Debating whether to leave the room, even though she was instructed to stay, Skylar decided that maybe he meant to stay in the house. Curiosity got the best of her, and she turned the knob.

It was deadly silent in the house. The only sound she heard was her own steps, sinking into the plush, thick carpet. Carefully and slowly she moved, step by step. Though it was dark in the hallway, the light from downstairs was enough to light her way. She thought about opening the other doors, wondering which rooms belonged to Nick and his half-brothers. As she was about to open one, she stopped when she heard the front door open.

Skylar quickened her steps. With her back against the wall, she peered downward. Remus had entered with two women, his arms draped around their shoulders. They were talking, laughing, and walking as if they were drunk. Remus was dressed in jeans and a T-shirt, but the ladies were dressed like they wanted to be noticed.

Suddenly, he stopped, sniffing the air, walking closer to the stairs with the ladies still in his arms.

"I smell something sweet and delicious," he said cunningly.

"Are lou...ungry?" the blonde lady slurred.

"No," Remus snapped, pushing them out of his arms. The ladies toppled over, falling to the hard floor.

"Ouuuch!" the blonde lady huffed, pushing her friend's legs off her.

"What the hell is the matter with you?" the brunette yelled angrily, becoming more aware of the situation. She got up, stumbled toward him, and flirtatiously ran her hands down his chest. "Come on big guy. You promised me the time of my life."

Skylar wanted to gag. The blonde was on the other side of him doing the same thing, but she could hardly hold herself up.

Looking annoyed, Remus effortlessly gripped the backs of their dresses, one in each hand, lifting them up so their feet dangled, and carried them to the door. "Get out," he yelled callously.

Under normal circumstances, Skylar would have freaked out, but now, knowing who Remus was, his ability to hold up two grown women like that didn't surprise her at all.

"Put me down!" the brunette screamed.

"Vat do lou meeen?" the blonde girl mumbled, seemingly unaware she was lifted off the ground.

"Out!" Remus didn't give them time to register his words. He dropped them, opened the front door, pushed them out, and slammed the door behind them. Then he dropped his car keys on the table by the vase.

Skylar swallowed a frightened lump in her throat. Quietly, she tiptoed back to Mason's room. Her pulse raced for unknown reasons. Remus didn't know she was in the house, and Mason wouldn't have told her to stay unless he thought she was absolutely safe. Besides, even from the way he'd treated those girls, and those times he had stared her down, she didn't know why she felt threatened by him. He'd never indicated he wanted to harm her.

As these thoughts flooded her mind, she tried to calm herself, but hearing the loud, hard thumps of Remus's footsteps as he climbed the stairs gave her icy cold chills. Suddenly, the sound of his footsteps dissipated. Most likely, he'd gone straight to his room.

Her heartbeat became steady again, and she exhaled the breath she didn't realize she was holding. Sitting on the edge of the bed, she relaxed and thought watching television might be a good idea.

Just then, the door flew open and Remus stood there, looking like he was ready for a kill.

Skylar stood up and took several steps toward him so he could clearly see her, ready to defend herself with words. "It's me, Skylar. I'm Mason's friend. He told me to stay here and wait for him to come back," Skylar said loudly and quickly.

Remus advanced toward her, while Skylar took small steps back, thinking all the while that she was scared for no apparent reason. After all, this was Mason's half-brother, which made him a demigod. Her self-assuring thoughts ended when he suddenly stood right in front of her with a look of hatred in his eyes.

"I know what you are. You are the keeper of death, aren't you? You're here to kill us."

"No, no, no." Skylar shook her head. "I don't know what you're talking about."

"That's what they all say. They act so sweet and innocent, and when you're not looking, they attack. How do you do it? Do you have a special weapon?"

"I don't understand what you're talking about. I'm not what you think I am," Skylar said aloud, thinking by raising her voice it would get through his thick skull, but it didn't.

"Liar." Remus backhanded Skylar across her face. From his strength, her body swept across the floor like a mop, sliding to the other side of the room and crashing against the wall with a loud thump.

Indescribable pain erupted through her body, like sharp razor cuts. It took Skylar a few seconds to realize what had just happened. The ache from the impact of his hand to her face and her body being thrown across the room made it difficult for her to stand. Wincing, she started to pull her achy, wobbly body up, and she felt a small pool of blood streaming down the side of her lower right lip. There was no way she could fight him, especially when he held such powerful, god-like strength.

By the time she was standing upright, Remus was already by her side. His fingers wrung her shirt, dragged her across the carpet, and tossed her on the bed. "I'm going to beat it out of you if I have to. Talk. Who are you?"

Trembling, she could hardly speak, but she managed to bounce off the bed and run. Remus immediately stood in front of the door, blocking her way out. "You can't outrun me," he snickered. "You talk now, or die holding your tongue."

Again, Skylar was glad her mom had made her take self-defense classes. It had helped her at the nightclub, surely it would help her again. Without heels this time, the impact would be less effective, but she thought to try it any way. She slammed her foot on top of his, but the mocking expression he showed was as if she had just brushed it. Seeing that it had no effect at all, she ran the other way.

Remus yanked the back of her hair and dragged her like before. When they reached the bed, she twisted her body and jabbed her elbow into his stomach with all her strength, then aimed lower and hit his private area with her fist like a hammer. With a loud growl, he released his grip. She guessed god's descendants or not, when it came to the male parts, they were all just as sensitive.

He wasn't in pain for long. Skylar's strength was no match for his. Managing to crawl to the top of the bed, she curled her body in. Tucking her knees close to her chest, she hugged a pillow as if somehow it would create a barrier between them. The only way she could leave here alive was to talk some sense into him.

"Remus, I'm just Skylar," she whimpered as her lips quivered. "I'm nobody. Look at me. Do I look like I can fight you back?" Tears trickled down her cheeks.

Remus looked confused at first, raising his hand to let her know he was coming toward her in peace. "You're not a keeper?" His tone was soft.

Skylar shook her head. What she really wanted to do was give him a hard sock in the face and call him a dumbass, but she didn't have the energy to move.

Remus sat on the edge of the bed, looking almost apologetic. He raised one hand and slowly ran it down the side of her hair, making Skylar cringe from his touch. "I see why Mason has taken an interest in you. All this time I thought he was trying to get close to you, thinking you were a keeper." With the back of his hand, he glided over her soft, red cheek where he had smacked minutes before.

Skylar turned her face away from him and pleaded. "Please, get out. I want to be alone. Mason will be here soon."

"Where did he go?" Ignoring her request, his hand traveled down her arm. "You feel so soft. How is it that you can resist me? I see you're wearing his clothes. What belongs to Mason belongs to me."

Does Mason know? Skylar wanted to vomit. Was he for real? She wanted him out, and since he wasn't leaving, she was going to leave. "I'm going to the restroom." Skylar turned her aching body, crawled out of bed, and headed for the door. But before she could get there, Remus had beaten her to it, blocking her way again. "Do you mind? You're going to watch me take a piss now?"

"Not until I get what I want." His tone was low and demanding.

"Excuse me?" She tried to sound polite, but she was scared out of her mind. "Please—"

Before she could finish her words, Remus ripped opened Mason's T-shirt, exposing her bra. He picked her up like a rag doll and threw her on the bed. At that moment Skylar knew what he wanted, and the human need to survive kicked in.

Remus's strong hands gripped both of her wrists, pinning them to the bed. She wiggled and pushed with all her human strength, but to no avail. His tongue ran down from her face, to her neck, to the base of her breast. Feeling violated, Skylar screamed as tears poured down her face. "Get off me!" she yelled.

Remus continued to take pleasure in his actions, disregarding her shouts. In order to keep her quiet, he covered her lips with his, taking her in, and started to pull down her sweat pants. Though her body throbbed in pain, she wasn't going to let him have her. Pinned beneath his weight, she did the best thing she could think of. She bit down hard on his lips, so hard that his blood seeped out of his mouth, but he still continued, as if it had no effect on him. Unintentionally, she swallowed his blood, so cold and sour, and she was sure he swallowed hers.

"Don't bother fighting back. You can't hurt me. I heal fast," he gritted through his teeth with a malicious tone, seeming to enjoy the control he held over her.

Skylar didn't care what he said. Just when she was ready to bite him again, without warning, he jolted upright like a puppet pulled by its strings and looked like he was having a seizure.

"You...you...what did you do?" he murmured under his breath as he continued to convulse. His eyes were wide with disbelief. Stumbling backward, he coiled to the floor as if all his energy was being drawn out of him. His hair and tanned skin were now as white as the sheets. What looked like thick spider veins began forming on his face, and like poison, started spreading to the rest of his body at an incredible speed.

Skylar covered her ears to block the loud cry that escaped from Remus's mouth. Was he in pain or frightened by the change? As she stood there and watched the transformation, she wanted to help. But then again, he deserved whatever was happening to him. Regardless, she didn't want him to die. After all, he was Mason's half-brother, and that was the only reason she needed to help, but how?

Afraid Remus would attack her again, she backed away. She wasn't sure if he was going to change into a monster. She couldn't believe she was thinking this way. It wasn't normal to have such thoughts, let alone see what was happening in front of her.

Remus kept staring at Skylar with a look of revulsion, as if she was to blame for what was happening. Finally, his body curled into a fetal position and became still, like a statue. When he stopped moving, she advanced toward him to get a closer look, to see if he was all right. Without thinking, she peered lower to his face. He looked unidentifiable—hideous, like some kind of ugly creature.

"Remus," she whimpered.

When there was no answer and he didn't show any indication he was alive, she tapped him and jerked back just in case he reached out to grab her. Instead of seeing a movement from him, he crumbled into ashes.

Remus was simply gone. He turned into dust right in front of her eyes. She covered her face with the palms of her hands and frantically paced around the room.

"This was a dream. This isn't real." She tried to calm herself, but it wasn't working. How could this have happened? She had no weapon. In fact, he'd attacked her. All she could think about was what Mason would say when he came home. Not only that, she had taken a life. Why should he believe her words when his brother was dead?

Tears welled up and her heart thumped out of control. What to do? She had no other choice but to run. It would be much too far to walk or run to her house. Suddenly, she remembered Remus had flung his car keys on the table. She was sure he had an expensive car that would undoubtedly have a navigator to help her find her way. Closing the bedroom door behind her, she ran downstairs. With the car keys in hand and her arms crossed to cover Mason's ripped shirt, she went out the front door.

FOURTEEN

SKYLAR PARKED REMUS'S car around the corner, where it was out of sight, and trudged her aching body the rest of the way home. What she really wanted to do was run, run as fast and as far as she could from all this madness. It was insane to even imagine what she had been through, and without anyone to talk to, she felt so alone. She couldn't confide in her mom or even in Kayla. They would think she was crazy. Perhaps they would even get her some psychiatric help. But what would happen when Mason found out his brother was in ashes, dead in his room, knowing she was the last one who saw him?

Wanting to go inside, she realized she didn't have her purse. Without the house keys, she had no way to get inside Kayla's house. All the lights were off and nobody was home. Kayla must still be out with Nick—that no good Nick, who would end up breaking her cousin's heart. And Auntie Kelly was still at the diner. Then she remembered Kayla telling her about the spare key under a rock by the front door.

There were many rocks. Which one? She lifted each one frantically until she found the key. Relieved, she opened the door and placed the spare key back under the rock. Shutting the door behind her, she went upstairs, straight to the bathroom.

Looking at her cut lip, strangely, it wasn't as bad as it felt, as she winced from the pain. It was more on the inside than out, but she was sure it had been bigger from the amount of blood that had swirled inside her mouth. Wanting to forget about tonight, she took a shower and changed into her sleepwear. Afterward, she scrubbed her teeth vigorously, as if she could wash away the fact that Remus had stuck his tongue in her mouth. Then she took out a plastic bag that was underneath the sink cabinet and placed Mason's T-shirt inside it.

Exhausted, she tucked herself into bed, thinking about what she could have done differently, but there was no answer. It didn't make sense. Maybe he'd had a stroke, but that didn't explain why he'd turned into ashes, unless that was just how they died? Skylar's thoughts were broken when she heard Kayla's steps on the stairs.

"Skylar, are you up?"

Skylar was relieved it was nighttime. The dim, small lamp on the nightstand was still on. Hopefully Kayla wouldn't notice her lip, or at least she could try to hide it by purposely cascading her hair down toward it. Then she wiped away any evidence she had been crying. "Come in."

Kayla peered in. Happily, she walked through the door, placed Skylar's purse down, then plopped herself on the edge of the bed. "Where did you and Mason run off too?"

"Tell me about what you did first," Skylar asked, trying to move the topic away from her.

"We watched the movie. Well, we were in the back. There was hardly anyone around. So...you can say we saw some parts of the movie." Kayla giggled. "Then we went out for some ice cream." She giggled again, her eyes beaming blissfully.

"Sounds like you had fun." Skylar tried to sound cheerful. Though she was glad for Kayla, she couldn't help but recall Mason telling her how they were the types of guys that didn't take relationships seriously. Not only that, if Kayla decided to give all of herself to Nick, then she would be touched by a god. Her life could be in danger, but only if she got pregnant. She had to do or say something. "Are you serious about him?"

Kayla gave her a side-glance, most likely wondering why she had asked such a question. "I don't know. It's summer. I'm just having fun."

"That's good. You *should* think like that. I don't want you to think that this relationship could go anywhere. I mean, just don't rush into things, okay?"

"And why not?" Kayla's tone sounded defensive. "Maybe I will be the one who dumps him." She paused, frowned, and exhaled a deep sigh. "Most likely not. Why? Do you know something I don't know? Did Mason tell you anything?"

"Yes...I mean, no." This was way too complicated. Kayla was a virgin, just like her. They had made a pact they would wait until they fell deeply in love. "Just remember our promise, okay?"

Kayla looked like she was thinking, most likely trying to figure out which promise Skylar was referring to. There were so many—a promise not to do drugs, a promise to be each other's maid of honor, and many more.

Skylar just needed to say one word. "Sex. Remember?"

Kayla turned red, giving her a giddy smile. "Oh, yeah."

"You didn't, did you?" Skylar raised her tone.

"No." Kayla squinted her eyes, giving her a "why are you raising your voice" look.

"Just promise me that you won't, okay? Just wait. Give the relationship some time."

"Don't worry. Nick has been perfect. He hasn't tried to. He knows I'm 'V', okay? So, you never told me how your date went."

"We—" Skylar started to say, but they were interrupted by loud knocking on the front door.

Skylar's heart leapt out of her chest. At this point any sound made her jumpy.

"Who's banging at my door after midnight?" Kayla bounced off the bed.

"If it's Mason, can you tell him I'm not home?" Skylar said impassively. She wanted to disappear now that Kayla knew something went wrong.

"I want details. First, I'm going to tell him off. I'll be right back."

Before Skylar could tell her not to, Kayla stomped downstairs and opened the door.

"YEEESSS." SHE NARROWED her eyes on Mason with a look of disapproval. Letting him know he wasn't welcome, she opened the door one third of the way.

"Could I speak to Skylar?"

"Do you know what time it is, Mason?" Kayla placed her hands on her hips and tried to look upset, but when she looked into his eyes, her rage softened.

"I know it's late, but it's important or else I wouldn't be here."

"Skylar isn't home right now."

"Really? I wonder where she could be this late at night?" he asked sarcastically, letting her know he wasn't buying her story. "Her bedroom light is on." Mason pointed upward.

"That's...that's because I was just in there looking for something."

Mason shot his eyes to the floor and then back up again. "Could you please tell her I was here, and that we need to talk? It's very important."

"Sure. But whatever you did, I hope you're sorry. My cousin is one of the sweetest, most wonderful people I know, and I know a lot of people. You mess with her, then you're messing with me. I hope you know that she deserves the best." Kayla slammed the door, not giving Mason an opportunity to defend himself, and stormed back upstairs to Skylar's room.

"Did he say why he came?" Skylar asked. She had been eavesdropping on their conversation, but quickly tucked back into bed when she heard Kayla approaching. She'd heard Kayla's voice clearly, but it was difficult to hear what Mason was saying.

"He said he needed to talk to you. He seemed really sorry. What did he do?"

"I don't want to talk about it right now. Could we talk tomorrow? I'm so tired."

"Okay, but I want details. I'm tired too. We have work tomorrow. See? This is the reason why I don't like to work during the summer."

"Okay, I kind of agree with you there."

"Want me to turn your lamp off?"

"No. I'll turn it off later." In a way, the light was comforting. After tonight's trauma, she knew she would have a hard time falling asleep.

"Alright, see you in the morning." Kayla closed the door behind her and headed to her room.

After Kayla left, Skylar nestled into her pillow, but not for long. She was startled by a humming sound from her phone. Letting out a heavy, irritable sigh, she reached into her purse and took it out. There was a text message.

It's me, Mason. We need to talk.

Staring at it, she read it three times just to make sure she'd read the name correctly. How did he get her number? Before, it would have been a thrill to get a text from him, but not tonight, when she knew the reason why. And right now, she just wanted to be left alone.

Skylar started to text back, but then she deleted it. What could she say? After pondering if she should reply, she decided to go to sleep instead. Placing the phone on the floor, she snuggled back, only to find herself unable to sleep, tossing and turning. A brush of air swept over her, and suddenly she got a strange feeling, as if someone was watching her. Surely she was imagining it. She was just feeling antsy from today's crazy, astonishing incidents. After all, she had closed the window earlier.

Lights flickered in front of her closed eyelids. Wondering what it could be, she turned away from the wall and jerked back from fright. Seeing a body in front of her, her heart skipped a beat. Her scream for help could not penetrate the hand that covered her mouth.

"Shhh...it's me, Mason. Don't scream." He released her after she nodded to comply.

Skylar was irate, but a part of her couldn't help feeling a bit happy to see him. "What are you doing here, and how did you get in?" she whispered, trying to sound mad, but it was almost impossible when he looked so irresistible. He found a way to see her, even if he wasn't invited. And knowing who he was, she guessed anything was possible.

"I had to see you."

Sweet words to Skylar's ears, if only it was for the reason she hoped for, but she was sure it wasn't. Assuming she knew why he was there, before he had a chance to ask, she confessed. "I'm sorry. I don't know what I did. Remus kept saying I was the keeper of death, and he hit me." Her tone was low, trying to explain everything that happened while whispering, afraid Kayla would hear. "Then he tried to...." Skylar got up, ran to the bathroom, and came back, holding up Mason's ripped shirt. "He tore this when it was on me."

Mason looked livid when his eyes set on his T-shirt. His brows angled inward, creating a pinch at the center. He looked tense, his shoulders raised, and his whole body tightened as if any minute now, he was going to explode out of whatever was holding him together.

Seeing Mason's facial expression and holding the T-shirt brought back the memories, and she lost it. Tears poured down her checks as she remembered how scared she was. With her back against the wall, she slid down and curled her knees into her chest. With her hands covering her face, she sat there and wept.

"I believe you," Mason said, holding out his hands at first, but instead of reaching for her, they went straight down. As Skylar continued to sob, he lowered himself to her and copied her position. "Skylar, I just want to know what happened. I'm not blaming you. I don't think you could hurt a fly."

Skylar finally managed to lift her head. She wasn't sure if she heard Mason correctly from the sobbing sounds she was making. But the fact that he wasn't mad at her, and the fact that he believed her, helped her to calm down. After several gasps and the lingering tears subsided, she breathed with ease and told him the whole story. She didn't leave any details for the imagination.

"I'm sorry for what happened to you. Though Remus was my half-brother, I have no emotional attachment to him. I've never really liked him. What puzzled me the most was how he died."

"I don't know. Maybe it wasn't me? Maybe it was a coincidence?" Skylar hoped. "I've never hurt anyone before. I didn't do anything. He...he...just turned to stone and then he transformed into ashes right in front of my eyes. This isn't normal. Things like this don't happen."

"I don't know if you knew, but his ashes disappeared too. I knew it was Remus because of the leftover residue. But don't worry, I cleaned it up. That's what happens to gods and half-bloods when they die. It's as if they never existed. I'm not going to tell Everett or Nick about this, and you shouldn't say a word to anyone. Pretend like it never happened. It wasn't your fault, but I'm going to look into it. I should've never left you. I didn't know he would or could do this. I'm sorry."

Mason's voice was sweet and caring. It was this side of him that made Skylar forget about his rude self. She always knew there was a wonderful side to him. She could just feel it when she first looked into his soulful eyes. "What will you say to them? Won't they be looking for him?"

"I'll figure something out. But that is not the reason I came here. I came to make sure you were okay, and since you weren't answering your text, I thought...actually, I didn't know what to think. I knew Remus went out and when he does, he's out pretty late. I'm actually appalled. I never thought he could...well, he did have anger issues, but that's not an excuse for what he did. I didn't want you to think I left you there so Remus could do what he did, even though I had no idea what he did at first. You didn't think that, did you?"

Skylar couldn't remember if that ever crossed her mind, and since she didn't want to make him feel bad, she shook her head. "No, I didn't."

"Good, because even though you may think I'm what you would call a 'bad boy,' I would never hurt you physically. I'm not that bad."

Skylar gave a short smile and almost giggled, but stopped when his finger traced the cut on her lower lip.

"Remus did this to you, didn't he?" For a brief moment, he closed his eyes and inhaled a deep breath, as if he was trying to suppress the anger that seemed to have crept up on him. Delicately, he brushed it again. "I'm sorry."

The small gesture of his simple touch drove Skylar into a whirlwind of heated emotions. He was already sitting way too close, and every time she turned her head to speak, all she could do was think impure thoughts. In order to avoid something she might regret doing, she nodded to answer and pulled back, making Mason drop his hand.

"You should smile more often. It makes me smile," he said unexpectedly.

Blushing like she'd never blushed before, she looked away shyly.

"How did you get back home? You didn't fly, did you?"

"Nooo." Skylar took in his teasing. "I...well, I kind of...*borrowed* Remus's car."

"Borrowed, huh? I think it's more like stealing."

Unsure if Mason was joking again by his tone, she tensed up. "I—"

"I think I need to call the cops. Maybe I should call Doug. What do you think, Ms. Rome?" Mason chuckled.

He had called her Ms. Rome the night they met. Skylar couldn't believe his sense of humor tonight. Laughing like a schoolgirl, she held on to the moment. After what had happened just a couple of hours ago, his presence gave her comfort and put her mind and heart at ease.

"If you don't mind, I'm going to drive his car home."

"Yes, of course. The key is on top of the dresser. Then, what about your car?"

"I didn't drive here."

"Then, how did you get here?"

Mason leaned over and whispered, "It's my little secret."

The small breeze from his warm breath in her ear sent tingly awareness all over her. Brushing away the thought of his lips on hers, she tried to focus on other things. Knowing he had super abilities, it didn't surprise her that he ran there. Most likely, he figured out she'd taken Remus's car to get home, so he came to retrieve it.

"It's way past your bedtime, and you have to work tomorrow. I should go." He got up and gave her his hand. The force of his pull made her leap into his arms. Inhaling a small gasp, she immediately drowned in their tangled bodies. In his arms she felt small, but safe for the very first time. From that moment, she knew without a doubt that she could trust him.

Mason finally released Skylar after gazing into her eyes longer than usual. "Umm...I should go now." His eyes scanned her from head to toe as he guided her to her bed. "So, is this what you wear to bed?" He gave a mischievous grin, twitching his brows.

Warmth flushed to her cheeks. She suddenly realized she wasn't wearing a bra, and immediately got into bed and pulled the sheet above her chest.

"Why?" She examined what she wore—short shorts and a tank top. "What's wrong with what I'm wearing? Should I be wearing something else?"

"Kind of skimpy, don't you think?"

Great! He was back to being himself again. "Kind of skimpy? It's hot," she stated. Suddenly, she felt like she was exposing herself.

"It's hot alright. Wear something longer next time, or else I may not be able to control myself."

Skylar flushed with warmth again. He was actually flirting with her.

"Close your eyes," he said, guiding her lower until her head was on the pillow. Then he sat on the edge of the bed. Flexing his muscles, he pressed his hands on either side of the pillow, and the intensity of the want and need in his eyes as he looked at her left her breathless. His eyes traveled to her lips, then back up to her eyes, and stayed there as he slowly moved to close the distance.

Withering beneath him, Skylar's breath was still caught in her chest. His close proximity aroused every inch of her, and undeniable desire brewed in the energy between them. In anticipation of the sweetness of his lips on hers, the pitter-patter of her heart made her chest rapidly rise and fall. Parting her lips, she was ready for him as he lowered toward her...closer...closer. Though it seemed to take a great amount of effort for him to turn away, he nuzzled the side of her neck instead.

"Close your eyes." He huffed out a heavy, rough breath, as if he was trying to restrain himself from something he wanted to do. His hot breath brushed against the side of her neck, making her quiver in all the right places.

Frozen in place, Skylar had to gather herself before she could speak from the letdown. "Close my eyes? But, you're still here." Her words barely escaped her lips. Snuggling into her pillow, she tried to shake off the heated daze.

Raking his hair back, he sat up, looking overcome. "Stop talking, Echo, or you're going to the naughty corner." His lips stretched into a smug half grin. That grin he does so well, frisky and sexy at the same time.

"And if I don't? What are you going to do, spank me? No, wait...are you going to shock me?"

He arched his brows playfully. "You really want to know? We can do both and see how that feels."

With no comeback, she sank deeper into the mattress, hiding beneath the sheet, secretly thinking how hot but twisted that sounded.

His hand reached over, covering her eyes. "Go to sleep, Echo." His authoritative tone was final, but she was up for the challenge.

"My name isn't Echo, and you're still here," she yawned, feeling extremely lethargic, waiting for his response. When she didn't feel the light weight over her eyes, she opened them. There was no sign of Mason, or any evidence he had gone out the door.

FIFTEEN

"**H**EY, PRETTY LADIES," Jack greeted. "Why do you look so tired, especially you, Skylar? Rough night, huh?"

"You could say that," Skylar replied, putting on her white apron and tying her hair back. Rough night was an understatement. Rough week and a half was more like it.

"You girls get to work the late shift today?" Jack asked.

"Yippee," Kayla said sarcastically, twirling her index finger up in the air.

"Oh, cheer up. Your mom is interviewing waitresses."

"Really? I hope she finds a replacement for us soon."

"She will. She already has a few in mind."

"Perfect," Kayla said with a smile. "What's the special today?" Kayla moved behind the counter.

"Today is Tuesday. Chicken soup," Mona stated, walking out of the storage room. "Good to see you girls. Tuesday is one of our busiest days, so let's get ready for the lunch and dinner rush."

"So bossy, Mona," Jack muttered. "Aren't we in a bad mood."

"I have to work with you every day. Yeah, that would do it," Mona joked, straightening the chairs around the tables.

"Yeah, yeah, yeah, that's why you never leave. You can't be apart from me after all these years. I can't even make you leave me."

"Whatever you want to think is fine by me," Mona scoffed.

Their teasing was interrupted by the sound of a bell chiming as a customer entered. Everyone went back to their post. It was extremely busy during the lunch hour, until they finally had a break. As they got ready for the dinner rush, Skylar noticed Kayla standing near the kitchen, smiling, holding her cell phone.

Skylar went behind the cash register and took out her phone to text.

What are you doing?

I'm texting with Nick.

Mona will get mad.

I don't care. You're texting, too. lol!

Lol!

Nick is on his way and so is Mason. I'm glad you two talked it out over the phone last night.

Me too.

Hugs hugs!

Hugs back!

You end.

No, you end.

Mona coming. End.

During the drive to work, Kayla had asked about her cut lip. Skylar told her she accidentally bit it. It was almost the truth, but since the cut was hardly noticeable, which was odd, it was believable. She also wanted details of their fight. Skylar didn't know what to tell her, so she made up a story, telling her they argued about where their relationship was headed. Feeling bad about their fight, Mason had called her on her cell phone. Kayla took the bait and didn't ask any questions after that.

Skylar wanted to see Mason, but for some reason she felt nervous to see him after the heated moment they'd shared last night. Not knowing exactly what she meant to him, she didn't know if he was playing with her emotions. She kept herself busy, wanting to keep her eyes away from the clock. Anxiously, she waited as customer after customer came and went. Finally, at about 7 p.m., Nick entered.

Kayla beamed a smile, escorting him to his table. Skylar wondered where Mason was, but about five minutes later, he walked in with a girl by his side. She was the same blonde that was at the nightclub. Skylar's heart dropped. He might as well have stomped on it. She looked just as Skylar remembered—too pretty and too blonde. Her attire was casual, but it didn't matter what she wore. She was naturally gorgeous.

Nick raised his hands to let Mason know where he was seated, and the two of them walked side by side toward him. Not wanting to see him, Skylar ducked where she stood, hiding behind the cash register. How could he bring her here after last night? Was he that cold and heartless? But she knew she had no right to feel that way. They weren't going out. Come to think of it, they weren't even dating.

He was just her knight in shining armor, and that was it. The fact that he flirted with her a little and took care of her, obviously didn't mean anything to him, but it did to her. From the corner of her eye, she saw Kayla taking their order and giving it to Jack. While waiting, she pulled out her phone. From the look Kayla gave her, she knew the text was from her.

What the hell! Who in the hell is she?

The same girl he was with at the club.

What is she doing here?

I don't care. We're not dating. He can go out with whomever he wants.

But I thought you two made up?

I guess it meant nothing to him.

Forget him!

I will!

Ass!

Yeah, heavy sigh...but a gorgeous one though.

Nowhere to run, Skylar took a deep, painful breath and stood up to face him. *Be brave!* Skylar could tell Mason was trying to make eye contact with her, but she would not give him the satisfaction. She kept on repeating to herself that he didn't care about her, and that she deserved better. When she thought she could make it, Mona stood in front of her.

"Skylar, could you please take these plates to that table over there?" She pointed straight across to Mason.

"Can you ask Kayla?" Skylar whispered. "I should stay here in case a customer needs to pay."

Mona chuckled. "You've been eyeing that table ever since Mason got here. Now, take these and go say hello. That's an order," Mona whispered back.

Skylar swallowed a nervous lump down her throat as she anxiously headed to Mason's table holding the two plates. Not knowing who ordered what, she didn't need to ask, since they'd ordered the same thing: steak, mashed potatoes, and asparagus. *Great! They even like to order the same food.* Carefully, she placed the plates in front of them, when she really wanted to smash them in their faces. Nick was already eating dinner since he'd gotten there first. He was never good at waiting.

"Hey, Skylar," Nick said. "Nice to see you on this side of the diner. You're usually stuck behind the register."

"Thanks," she said, desperately trying not to look Mason's way, or at the girl sitting next to him, but she failed. When Mason gave her a sweet smile, she couldn't help but smile too. *Why do you have to be so darn cute? Why do you make me feel like I'm walking on air when you're around?*

"By the way, this is our cousin, Amanda. She's visiting us from out of town," Nick introduced.

Cousin? The pang that twisted her heart a second ago disappeared with Nick's words. Skylar gave her the biggest smile. That Amanda was Mason's cousin was the best news she'd heard in a long time. No wonder his manner was odd at the restaurant when she asked him about his date. She also recalled Mason telling her there were more like them, but he'd never mentioned having a cousin. "It's nice to meet you."

"Same here," Amanda muttered. "I've heard a lot of things about you."

"You have?" Skylar didn't know if her tone meant good or bad. "I hope good things." She smiled again. "Let me know if you need anything else." Then she backed away, heading to the register.

"Skylar," Mason called.

Skylar's heart skipped a beat from the sound of Mason's voice. "Yes?"

"We're going to the mountains this weekend. We have a cabin up there. Would you and Kayla like to come?"

Skylar blinked her eyes in surprise. "I'll ask her, but yeah, sure." Then she thought about what she'd said. She answered without thinking it through.

"We'll pick you up Friday after work. At Kayla's house. Is that okay?"

"Sure. We get off early on Friday, about three."

"We'll pick you guys up at 3:30." Mason looked at Nick to confirm.

"Okay." Skylar turned on her heel, and walked away.

When she headed to the cash register, her phone buzzed inside her pants. Knowing who was texting, she didn't answer. Just to be playful, she looked across the room to Kayla and produced a devious grin.

"Pick up your phone," Kayla mouthed, pointing to her phone and sending it straight back into her pocket when Mona steeled her eyes at her.

Skylar knew it was driving her nuts. She waited a few seconds for Mona to head to the other side and texted her back, since she couldn't take the excitement any longer either. Mason asked her out for the very first time. Even though it wasn't a one on one date, it didn't matter.

Mason asked us to go to their mountain cabin this Friday.
What? Really?
Just kidding.
Shut up.
Okay, NOT just kidding. Yes!
What did you say?
I said, I'll think about it.
What? Really? Are you nuts?
I said yes.
Stop messing with me. Yeah!
What are we going to tell your mom?
Don't worry. I know what to say.
Are you sure?
I'm going to tell her we're going with a bunch of girls.
And she'll buy your story?
Why not? I'm a good girl.
Yeah right. Go back to work. Lol!

Skylar put her phone away and glanced toward Mason's table. They looked like they were in a heated conversation. She wished she had supersonic hearing so she could hone in on what they were saying. Whatever it was, she hoped Mason wasn't talking about Remus. Every time she thought about Remus, it freaked her out, so she tried to think about other things. Going to Mason's cabin would be a great distraction. She couldn't wait.

SIXTEEN

THERE WERE TWO cars parked in front of Kayla's house. Both boys had the passenger side doors opened. Kayla hopped into Nick's silver Mercedes and Skylar slid into Mason's black BMW. As soon as Skylar settled herself in, Mason pulled her seat belt to lock her in.

This was the second time she had been in the car with him and both times, he had belted her in. She wasn't used to this kind of attention, but it felt nice. It was something her ex-boyfriend had never done—acting chivalrous. As soon as Mason closed the door, Skylar practically jumped out of her seat, startled by an unexpected voice. Skylar turned to the sound of a cheerful greeting.

"Hello, Skylar," Amanda said, smiling.

"Oh, hey, Amanda," she replied, smiling back. Assuming it would only be the four of them, she was quite surprised to see her, and wondered if Everett was in the other car. After that, things were quiet until Mason got in.

Skylar enjoyed the scenic route they passed through—nothing but mountains, valleys, and trees. The conversation was minimal. Amanda asked Skylar many questions, but mostly focused the topic on herself. She did tell some funny stories about Mason, which seemed to break the ice as their laughter rang out in the car.

After a couple of hours of driving on many winding roads, they finally reached their destination. The place was bigger and more modern than Skylar had expected. Though she had been to the mountains a few times before, she had never seen a nice place like the one in front of her. With a huge, beautiful yard full of trees and flowers, this was obviously a private vacation home. She didn't spot any other cabins nearby either.

The warm fresh air brushed softly against Skylar's skin as she stepped out of the car, giving her a tranquil feeling. Inhaling deeply, she exhaled all her worries away, as if they could be carried off by the wind.

When Mason grabbed the bags and led the way, Skylar turned to look for Kayla, but instead she saw Everett stepping out of the car. Seeing him reminded her of Remus, causing her stomach to tighten into knots. She wondered if he knew his half-brother was missing. Her thoughts were distracted when she saw Nick and Kayla walking side by side toward her. Then Kayla linked arms with Skylar, walking ahead of Nick.

"Pretty nice," Kayla muttered, grinning from ear to ear. "We're gonna have so much fun." Then she leaned closer. "What's Amanda doing here?"

Skylar shrugged her shoulders. "I don't know what's going on with Mason and me, so I'm glad she's here. Amanda is a great distraction."

"Exactly." Kayla's tone was sharp. "You two need to figure things out. Get to know each other and not have a third wheel tagging along."

"She's not tagging along. Plus, you could say the same thing about Everett."

"True, but at least he's cute to look at," Kayla giggled.

"He's alright, but he makes me nervous."

"Don't worry about anyone except Mason."

"I don't know what I'm feeling these days."

"Don't think so much. Just have fun." Kayla took several steps up to the front door and her eyes grew wide as she unlinked her arms from Skylar.

Skylar felt her eyes widen, just like Kayla's. "It's so beautiful here."

The fresh smell of pine and the summer breeze whizzed through the air. The first thing Skylar spotted in the house was the tall vase filled with beautiful flowers. It was situated on a round table that looked just like the one at Nick's home. Then her eyes moved to the elongated windows that reached up to the second floor, surrounding the house, allowing plenty of natural light in. The house was elegant, modern, yet it still felt like a cabin. It was furnished with only the best, as far as Skylar could tell, but it was simple, warm, and felt like home.

After the guys gave a tour of the house and directed the girls to their bedrooms, they settled into the dining area where the food was already prepared. Mason sat to Skylar's right while Kayla sat across from her. Plates filled with steamed tilapia, balsamic rice, and mixed vegetables were placed in front of them.

"Delicious," Kayla muttered, taking a bite. "I wish my mom could cook fish like this."

"Amy, our housekeeper, is a great cook," Mason said matter-of-factly.

"You have a cook here when you come?" Skylar asked, gazing at the utensils, plates, and glasses that were arranged as if they were in a five-star restaurant.

"Yes, she lives nearby. She takes care of this place when we're not around. She doesn't work during the weekends and she leaves right after she makes our dinner. This was already prepared before we got here," Nick informed, scooping a spoonful of rice into his mouth.

Everett got up and took a bottle of wine out of the wooden cabinet. "Let's drink a toast to our new friends." He went around pouring wine in the wine glasses that were already placed on the table. Then he picked up his glass and held it in the air. "To our new friends and Remus. Where ever did he wander off to?"

Skylar glanced at Mason, but he didn't look her way. Anxiety was building up and she wanted to run—run away from there, and run away from Mason and his brothers. The sound of the clinking of glasses brought her back to the present. She realized everyone was waiting for her to toast with them. "Oh, sorry. I don't drink wine."

Kayla kicked her under the table, making Skylar jerk back.

"Oh, here," Skylar said, glaring at Kayla and lifting her glass to toast. Then everyone took a sip. Skylar pretended she did, and placed the glass back on the table.

"Where is Remus?" Everett asked. "I hope he's not creating any problems."

"You know Remus. He's always up to no good," Amanda stated.

"I know, but he's not answering his cell phone. That's not like him."

Skylar's muscles tensed as she listened to their conversation. Her eyes were glued to her plate and her appetite vanished.

"Can we talk about something else?" Mason murmured. "I don't think our guests really care."

"Yes, you're right. Where are my manners?" Everett gave a quick grin, but he narrowed his eyes at Mason.

"Anyway," Nick said, breaking the silence. "I'm taking Kayla for a walk after dinner before it gets too dark. Would anyone else like to join us?"

"I would love to walk," Kayla exclaimed.

Skylar didn't want to be the third wheel. Since Mason didn't ask her, she didn't respond.

After dinner, the guys got up to clear the table. Itching to get up and help, Skylar was only asked to sit back down again. She was not used to having someone else clean up after her. After the dishes were put away, Kayla and Nick went out the back door with flashlights in their hands. Though Skylar was uncomfortable without Kayla, she tried her best to fit in as they gathered in the living room.

The sun was starting to set, but it was still light out. Everett poured his fifth glass of wine, sat on the sofa, and looked like he was a mile away. They sat there as the sun disappeared and the stars came out. Darkness engulfed them, and having no curtains or blinds gave Skylar an eerie feeling. She tried not to look out the window. She could imagine something popping out just like in the scary movies, so she focused her eyes on the television instead.

"Let's watch a movie," Amanda said, flipping through the channels. "There's nothing to watch on a Friday night."

"Forget the movie. Aren't you worried about Remus?" Everett looked frustrated. His eyes pierced through Mason's and then to Skylar's. "Where the hell is he? He said he had something important to tell me. He wouldn't disappear like that."

Skylar sank into her seat. She already felt small against Everett's physique, but his tone and the way he looked at her made her feel tinier. Though she knew Everett had no idea what happened, feelings of guilt took over, and her pulse shot up.

"Maybe he doesn't want to be found," Mason blurted.

Angry, Everett grabbed Mason's shirt, lifting him from the sofa. "What are you not telling me?" he yelled.

"Stop it!" Amanda bellowed. "Let him go. What the hell is wrong with you?"

Mason pushed Everett off him, straightened his shirt, and focused on Skylar.

"He knows something. I can tell," Everett grumbled.

"We have company. Can we please behave?" Amanda mumbled. "This is so embarrassing."

"She knows something too, doesn't she?" Everett accused, pacing to Skylar.

Mason pulled Skylar off the sofa and protectively hid her behind his back. "Don't you dare touch her. She has nothing to do with Remus."

"Our blood binds us. I can't feel him anymore. Either he went somewhere far away or something is wrong. You should be able to feel that too, or do you not care?" Everett sneered.

"Mason?" Amanda called softly. "What's going on?"

Skylar couldn't take it anymore. She didn't want their brotherly bond to break because of her. Without thinking, she blurted out, "It was an accident. He tried to...he hit me...and...." Skylar didn't know what she was saying anymore. She was confused and couldn't explain any further when Everett and Amanda looked at her accusingly.

"Stop!" Mason raised his hands. "You all know what Remus is like. He knew I was dating Skylar. He tried to take advantage of her. We had a fight and he took off."

Everett let out an irritated sigh and stormed away.

"You have some explaining to do, Mason. I'll go calm the big guy." Amanda chased after Everett.

Skylar couldn't believe what she'd heard. Mason said they were dating, but he had a funny way of showing it, unless he really didn't mean it.

"Are you okay?" Mason asked, tenderly.

"Yes," Skylar answered, but she wasn't.

"I had to lie about the dating part to throw them off."

"Yeah, of course. I understand," she replied, feeling disappointed.

"We'll be leaving in the morning. I need answers and staying here won't help. I didn't know Everett would tag along. Like I said before, I'm not very close to my brothers, but I think I can trust Nick. But even then I'm not sure. Let me take you to your room. I'm suddenly feeling really tired." Mason led the way.

After Skylar tucked herself into bed, she lay there thinking about all that had happened. What was supposed to be the best summer of her life was turning out to be the worst summer ever. She had a crush on a guy who had turned out to be a demigod, meaning half human and half god. This concept was difficult to grasp. His half-brother tried to rape her, and somehow, he died in Mason's room. And here she was alone and mystified, and she couldn't even tell Kayla.

Kayla had been gone for two hours. Though Skylar knew she was fine, she had wanted to stay up and wait for her, but slowly her eyelids closed against her will.

SEVENTEEN

SKYLAR WAS GROGGY when she woke up. Her eyes were still closed. She didn't want to open them, sensing that it was still late at night, but something was out of place. Startled by the sound of someone rifling through her duffle bag, she lay motionless. Too scared to move, she listened for any clue as to who it might be.

Desperately, she wanted to turn her body and face the intruder, but she was immobilized by her terror. When it became deadly silent, she knew the intruder had stopped digging through her bag. Frightened, every nerve in her body was alert and her heart hammered faster with the sound of creaking steps approaching the bed. When her bed sunk from the weight of the person, afraid of what he or she would do to her, Skylar turned swiftly and sat upright.

"Amanda?" Relieved that it was someone she knew, her pulse steadied somewhat. Though she didn't know her that well, she figured she could trust her. "What are you doing in my room?"

"Skylar, come with me," she demanded, dropping Skylar's shoes in front of her. "It's very important. We need to straighten this out once and for all."

"Straighten what out? It's the middle of the night. What time is it?" Rubbing her eyes, she looked down at her shoes, debating whether to put them on.

"I don't have time to explain. Just hurry."

From Amanda's urgent voice, Skylar got up, slipped into her shoes, and huffed an irritated sigh. Wearing nothing but cotton shorts and a tank top, she put on a light sweater and left the house with Amanda. Though she wasn't cold, following Amanda to the woods gave her the shivers. "Where are we going? And why were you digging through my bag?"

Amanda didn't answer. She was too busy trudging along a crooked path, holding a mega flashlight—a spotlight—leading the way, heading further away from the cabin. The fresh scents of the evergreens awakened Skylar, but the eerie darkness took away all the beauty. As the dirt shuffled underneath Skylar's feet, the sound of a broken twig made her jump. When Amanda noted Skylar lagging behind, she gripped her wrist and forced her to keep up with her.

"Amanda, please. Where are we going in the middle of the night? I'm getting cold." She wasn't really cold, but being out in the dark caused her to tremble as her imagination got the best of her. She could envision wild animals roaming about, and who knew what else could happen in the complete darkness, in the middle of the woods, without any protection.

Amanda finally stopped. "We're here. I'm sorry, but we have to know."

From out of the darkness, Everett suddenly appeared. Stunned to see him, Skylar scurried back and bumped into a tree. As if she could disappear into it, she pressed her back against it as her eyes locked onto Everett, who was coming toward her.

"What's going on? Where's Mason?" Her timid tone hid behind the fear.

Everett towered over Skylar, looking down on her with a look of conviction. "Tell me the truth and I'll spare your life. Are you one of the keepers of death?"

"What?" Skylar asked, befuddled. She recalled Remus asking her the same question. "I'm nothing. I don't understand. Why did you bring me out here to ask me this question?"

"Liar!" Everett's tone startled Skylar and even Amanda. "You killed Remus, didn't you? And you convinced Mason you didn't. My blind brother may not see, but I can. Who sent you to kill us?"

"Please, you've got to believe me. I didn't do anything. Remus tried to kill me. He tried to...." Knowing they wouldn't believe her, Skylar frantically looked for a way out. With no sense of direction and without a flashlight, where would she go?

Everett lost his patience. He extended his arm and grabbed Skylar by her throat. "Tell me who sent you," he sneered through his gritted teeth.

Pinned against the tree by Everett's hand, she tried to pull him off.

"Everett. We're not sure who she is. Don't kill her. Mason likes...I mean, she's Mason's friend," Amanda pleaded.

"Since when do you care who I kill or not?"

"Since now, since Mason. You've never killed anything in your life besides the vultures. If you're wrong, well, I don't want to think about what Mason will do to you."

"Let. Her. Go," Mason demanded, having a difficult time getting his words out. Wearing shorts and a white T-shirt, he rested his hand on the tree for support. Looking extremely lethargic, his movements were sluggish as he held loosely onto a small flashlight. Though he looked somewhat aware of what was going on, he seemed to be struggling to stay alert.

Everett released his grip and stepped away. Letting out a dreadful cough and taking in breaths of fresh cool air, Skylar composed herself. Ecstatic to hear Mason's voice, she knew she would be fine.

Mason continued to confront his family. "Who...drugged... me?"

"I did," Everett confessed. "I drugged your wine. I needed to know who she really is."

"And exactly what is she? Do you even know what you're talking about? Now I have to explain everything to her. How...why we exist. She can't even defend herself from you. How could you assume she killed Remus?"

Skylar already knew how and why they existed. She knew he only said those words to throw them off.

"I can feel some kind of energy from her I didn't feel before. I don't understand. If she isn't one of us, she must be something. I'm almost certain she is a keeper of death. Can't you feel it? Or are you blindly in love?" Everett laughed out loud.

Mason didn't answer. He shook his head, seemingly trying to stay in focus.

"Oh, joy. My little brother is in love with a killer," Everett continued.

"I'm not in love and she is not a killer. You're too obsessed, thinking a keeper is on our trail." Mason turned to Amanda. "How...could...you?"

Amanda locked her eyes on the ground to where her flashlight shone brightly, and then she looked up. "This is totally your fault, Everett. I'm not helping you again." Then she turned to Mason. "I'm sorry, but I was only thinking of you. You know what the prophecy says. Something as critical as this, we can't wait around and find out." Then she turned to Skylar. "Sorry. I didn't mean to scare you. Now you know we're...different. Welcome to our crazy world." Amanda headed back to the house.

Everett offered no apologies and stormed off angrily. Skylar looked distraught, her back still against the tree. Too terrified to move, she felt as if her legs were planted to the ground like the roots of the tree.

"I'm sorry," Mason mumbled, stumbling toward Skylar. "I didn't know he...she...had...or would do this. I knew something was up...so sleepy, but couldn't control it. I tried to fight it off." Mason shook his head, trying not to fall asleep. "We should get out before I crash on the ground. Here...take this flashlight. Go straight this way." Mason pointed ahead.

"Let me help you." Skylar did as she was told, and draped his arm over her shoulder to hold him steady. The weight of his body caused Skylar to bend low. Dragging her feet, sometimes stumbling, she managed to find her way back with Mason's directions.

Without a word, Skylar took Mason straight to his bedroom. She accidentally fell on top of him when she tried to ease him onto his bed. She tried to wiggle off, but Mason's hold was too strong, even for someone who could barely control his mind and body.

"Smell...nice," he sniffed her hair, and then his arms dropped down to his sides.

"Thanks, but right now you have no idea what you're doing."

"Stay...lay...to me," he mumbled. "I'll...keep...you safe." His words were soft and sluggish. His right arm reached for her, then he rolled over to his side with his eyes closed.

"Okay, I'll just lay here next to you," Skylar agreed reluctantly, taking off his shoes then hers. Not wanting to keep her sweater on, she took it off and placed it on the edge of the bed. Though she didn't feel comfortable sharing his bed, she felt safe just from his presence, even though he was almost asleep. Thinking it was an opportunity to ask him questions since he was drugged, she asked freely. "Mason."

"Hmmm?"

"Do you blame me for Remus's death?"

"No."

"Are you and Amanda close?"

"What? Close? Amanda...yes."

"Do you have a girlfriend?"

"No. No more...no questions. Go sleep. Tired." He snuggled against the pillow.

Did "no more" mean he'd recently broken up? "Are you mad at me?"

"No...but...I will." He moaned.

"What if I hurt you?"

"You won't."

"How do you know? I don't even know what I did to Remus. I—"

"I know. Echo...sleep."

"Why do you care?"

"Trouble."

"Trouble?"

"Trouble...I think...like...Echo."

EIGHTEEN

SOMETHING HOT LEANED against Skylar's body. Slowly, she peeled her eyes open to settle on Mason's beautiful face. She loved the scent of him, faint musky spice from his after-shave that still lingered from yesterday. When her eyes glanced over what she could see from her position, she knew she wasn't at her cousin's house. Then suddenly, vivid images of last night's events merged to the forefront of her mind, making her aware this wasn't a dream.

Shock from seeing their bodies tangled sent exhilarated tingles through her, but she didn't know what to do. His arms and legs were on top of hers, snuggling her as if she was a body pillow.

Breathe. No, don't breathe. No, breathe. She was afraid to wake him up. She wanted to stay snuggled into him as long as possible, but she couldn't help but wonder how he would react when he saw their bodies positioned in such an intimate way.

Though she enjoyed being in his arms, she knew he wasn't aware of what he was doing. Instead of pulling him out of his sleep, she studied his facial features. With her eyes, she traced the curves of his eyebrows, to his thick eyelashes, moving her gaze to his strong cheek bones, to his nose, and last, down to his kissable lips. How she wondered what it would feel like to press her lips on his.

When he snuggled tighter, she held her breath and held it longer when he leisurely rubbed his heavy leg against her bare skin. Simultaneously, his hand slid down her back to the hem of her shirt, lifting it with his fingers while mumbling words she couldn't understand. Gliding upward, warmth produced from the palm of his hands, and erotic heat spread through her whole body.

Skylar gasped when his hand started to move again, caressing her in a circular motion. The same electric feeling, between a mild shock and the subtle heat that emanated from him, aroused her in ways she had never known. The heat started from her belly button, igniting with pleasurable sensations, spreading to the rest of her body, making her hot and quivery. *Oh Mason, what are you doing in your sleep and with whom?* She desperately wanted to know.

When the motion stopped, she wondered if he was dreaming or aware of what he was doing. Slowly, she tilted her head back to see if he was awake.

Mason's eyes were wide open, and he looked flabbergasted. Startled, she jerked out from his hold, almost falling on the floor. Mason sat up and raked his hair back as confusion showed on his face. "Did we umm...did 1 try to...did something happen last night?"

Embarrassed he would ask such a question, Skylar got out of bed. "No. What kind of girl do you think 1 am?" She suddenly realized she was wearing what she had worn to bed last night, and she was braless. Embarrassed at the thought, she crossed her arms without making it obvious.

"You're in my room. On my bed," he said matter-of-factly.

"You told me to stay here last night."

"I did?" He paused, deep in thought as his brows angled crookedly.

"Don't you remember anything that happened last night? Your brother Everett tried to kill me in the woods." Skylar was irritated. She didn't want Mason to think she was trying to take advantage of him.

"Okay...now I remember. Sorry. I just woke up and saw you here."

Would it be such a bad thing?

"So, we should...you should...," he started to say.

Skylar didn't know what to say or do. She knew he was baffled and most likely still dazed from being drugged...or maybe he wasn't. She didn't care anymore. "I'm going to go back to my room. Obviously, I'm safer there than here." At least her heart was.

"Stop. Hold on a minute. I didn't mean to offend you." Mason tumbled out of bed. "I need to think. Please, keep your voice down. They may hear us."

Skylar's hand was on the doorknob, already turning it. "*They may hear us,*" repeated in her mind. Did he not want the others to know she'd spent the night in his room? "You need to think? Think about what?"

Mason chuckled lightly. "Here we go again, Echo."

"I'm not repeating your words," she snapped. Or was she?

"We should leave. I'll take you to your room to pack," Mason said, heading to the door. Skylar stepped aside for him, knowing she had no choice. As soon as Mason placed his hand on the knob, the door automatically thrashed open. He flew across the room as if he had been punched in the stomach, bounced off the bed from the impact, and tumbled to the floor. Stunned by what had just happened, Skylar hid behind the door. Unexpectedly, a claw gripped her shirt and yanked her out.

STILL ON THE floor, Mason shot his eyes up to find Skylar, but she was gone. Dashing out the door with lightning bolt speed, he saw her in the arms of a vulture as it sprinted down the stairs. She was desperately trying to fight him off, kicking and punching, but her size and strength was no match for the beast.

Looking to the right, he saw Nick was a step ahead of him. He had already flung himself down to the first level near the front door, and gestured for Mason not to make a move. Knowing Nick was waiting for the vulture, he positioned himself, ready to jump. When Nick dashed forward, Mason made his move and landed behind the vulture.

Nick tilted his head back and looked at his opponent with revulsion. "You're one ugly, giant dude, and you stink like hell. What planet did you come from?"

The vulture hissed loudly, reaching for the door, but Nick stood in the way.

"Where do you think you're going? I don't think she's your type, and you're certainly not my type with those long nails."

The vulture growled, holding Skylar with one arm. It swung with the other and missed Nick by a hair's breadth. Given the opportunity, Mason jumped on its back and grimaced from its body odor. It stunk with the smell of sewer and urine. Its' cold, leather-like skin was hard to grip, and Mason's hands were slipping.

In anger, the vulture twisted its body, swatting its free hand to get Mason off its back. Ineffective, it weaved from side to side. With one wild twirl, Mason's body knocked the tall vase over, sending it to the floor where it shattered into pieces.

Losing his grip on the monster, Mason tumbled to the floor and struggled to get up. A broken piece of the vase had pierced his upper arm. He yanked it out to see scarlet liquid soaking through his T-shirt as it trickled down his arm. Though he was in throbbing pain, he could feel his arm slowly healing.

Just before Mason got back to his feet, the vulture gripped his shirt and tossed him with one hand. The weight of the impact caused Mason to fall on top of Nick. Before Mason had time to adjust, the vulture picked him up and tossed him again.

Everett and Amanda rushed out of their rooms at the same time to see Mason sliding across the floor. His body swept the broken vase pieces like a mop, leaving a clear path.

"What are you two looking at? This isn't a free show. We could use some help here," Nick said aloud, ducking another blow. He saw two more men charging from the other side of the cabin, morphing into vultures right in front of him, advancing toward him. "What the hell? Where did they come from?"

Everett stayed where he was with an impassive expression on his face. With elbows on the banister, he didn't budge. As for Amanda, she ran to her room and came back with a sword in her hand. Looking eager, she flung herself over the rail and landed gracefully on her feet.

Mason grabbed a long broken piece of vase off the floor and stabbed it into the back of the vulture who was still swatting at Nick. It screeched in pain and lost its hold on Skylar. Pulling Skylar out of the way and heading to the corner, Mason stood in front of her protectively.

"Amanda, go back upstairs. Nick and I've got this handled," he demanded, moving from side to side, contemplating what the vulture would do next.

"And let the boys have all the fun? No way." Amanda twirled her sword and missed. She leapt to the left, swung, and missed again.

"Dang, they're fast for being so chubby." She rapidly flipped over the vulture in front of her, confusing it, but it caught onto what she was doing and turned.

When Amanda jolted back, she scraped her sword across its chest. Black fluid squirted out. The wounded vulture turned away from her. "Where do you think you're going?" Amanda huffed and chased after it.

The other vultures continued to make ear piercing, horrendous sounds, as they angrily fought back. Mason knew that one way to end the beasts' lives was to use his power, but their swift movements made it difficult. He could have easily bolted deadly light out of his hand, but he would be taking a risk if he missed. Not only that, he worried about what Skylar would think of him.

An opportunity finally arose when Nick knocked one to the floor. Mason gripped its shoulders and zapped it with volts of electricity that flowed out from within him. Bright light emanated from Mason's body as if he, himself, was lightning. Then the vulture's body seared and fizzled, looking like a barbecue gone wrong.

The beast bellowed in pain, burning from the inside, before turning back into human form. Suddenly, as if it was a torch, fire blasted out of it and it flailed its arms in a fanning motion. As black smoke circulated through the air like a magic trick, it emitted a giant puff of smoke and crumbled into ashes.

"Well, that was very toasty," Mason said, turning around to see Nick zap his power into the other vulture. Wondering where the third beast was, he turned to Skylar to make sure she was safe.

Skylar was shivering in the corner where he had left her, bent down with her back flat against the wall. Black ooze mixed with red liquid was seeping out of her hands. Looking as pale as the white wall behind her, she looked frightened and fragile.

At the sight of her, Mason's heart dropped. His emotions were filled with empathy and a feeling he couldn't quite understand tugged at his heart. He'd promised himself he wouldn't let her in. Had she been peeling away a layer at a time and unknowingly found her way in?

Sure, he flirted with her, big time, but what guy in his right mind wouldn't? She was attractive, but there was more to her than a pretty face. He had never met anyone like her before—innocent, strong willed, spunky, and her heart beat purely.

It was getting more difficult to fight the feeling he had been trying to conceal since the day he first met her. All he could think at this moment was to take her away from all this madness. He wanted to comfort her, and a part of him wanted to kiss her. Wait...what was he thinking? He had to wipe that thought from his mind. He had told himself many times over he wouldn't let her in. He had to remain strong.

Peeling his eyes away from her, he saw the motionless beast flat on its stomach. Oddly, it hadn't turned back into human form, which they always did before they died. Decapitated, a long sharp piece from the shattered vase was sticking out from its back. Next to it was Amanda, holding up her sword dripping with black liquid. With one foot on the vultures back, she looked proud and victorious.

Soon after, the vulture turned into stone, just like Skylar had said Remus had done, and transformed into ash. Amanda, Nick, and Mason were alarmed to see the transformation. It had turned into stone, which was not normal, before it burst into ashes, which was. The other two flashed their eyes to Mason with questioning looks.

"Not a word. I don't want to hear it," Mason stated, then turned to Skylar. "Skylar," Mason said softly, disregarding the ashes on the floor. "You're bleeding. Let me clean that up."

Seeing that she was unable to move, Mason swept her off her feet and took her to the kitchen. There, he ran her hands under the water at the sink. The wounds were not as deep as he had thought, but there were long gashes across both of her palms. It was most likely not the cause of her bleeding that much. The black fluid indicated that she had the vulture's blood on her hands as well.

Opening a cabinet to his right, he pulled out an emergency bag. With cotton balls, he dabbed the cuts with antibacterial ointment, then wrapped them with bandages for extra protection. "It's not too bad," Mason said, cradling Skylar's hands as if they were wounded doves.

SKYLAR COULDN'T TAKE in air. Mason was standing too close. When she caught his eyes, they stared back at her. Then he blinked and looked away. She couldn't believe what she was seeing. Mason was so sweet, taking care of her, but she was so awed by watching him use his powers, that she was completely speechless and couldn't stop gawking at him.

"Don't stare at me," he said, making sure the swathe wouldn't come undone.

"I...I...." Skylar couldn't muster up a sentence. It was caught in her throat.

"What happened?" he asked, peering up under his thick eyelashes to catch her eyes.

"You...your hands...they...the monsters turned into ashes by your hands," Skylar rambled. "I saw lights. I mean flashing, lightning lights, like the ones you see up in the sky. They came out of your hands, or fingertips, or somewhere...and your eyes too. And you move...you all move so fast...and how did you...oh my god! I can't even believe I'm saying all this." Flabbergasted, she was so caught up with what Mason was able to do, she didn't answer his question.

"You do remember me telling you that I can do things like that, right?"

Skylar nodded, looking like she had seen God himself. She recalled being told, but hearing was one thing. Seeing lightning bolts flash out the palms of his hands, and seeing him move with such great speed, was a whole different story.

"I'm still me, okay? You're not afraid of me, are you?"

Skylar shook her head. "No."

"Good. Now you've just seen some of the things I can do first hand."

"Why didn't you fight them off when they were trashing Kayla's house? If you could do what you just did, why did we run?"

"I had just met you. You would've thought I was a freak and tried to run away from me too. It would also have been two against one, not that I couldn't take them on my own, but I would be putting your life at risk. I'd rather hide and protect you than try to kill two of those. Enough about me. What happened?"

Ignoring his question, she looked at him. "You're hurt," she said, looking at the patch of crimson on his torn white T-shirt. Starting from his right shoulder, it was ripped diagonally across. She stared at his exposed tattoo, remembering how it had lit up when the lights shot out of his fingertips. Slowly her hand reached out to touch it, but dropped it when Mason stiffened and retreated a step, seeming to anticipate what she was doing.

"I'm fine. I'm healing. Now...what happened?" His tone was sharper, demanding, wanting his question answered.

"The thing came at me. I picked up whatever was in front of me and jammed it through it, and Amanda chopped its head off. My hands...." Skylar gazed at her hands. "I cut my hands when I jabbed the broken pieces into its back, but the thing turned and I accidentally touched the bleeding wound on its chest. It was already bleeding from whatever Amanda had done."

"So your bleeding hand touched its open wound?"

"I guess. It happened so fast. That is how I think it happened. Why do you ask?"

"Nothing. I'm just trying to figure out—"

"How it turned to stone?" Skylar assumed what he was thinking.

"No." His eyes fell to her chest, looking surprised.

Skylar followed his gaze and realized again that she was braless. Her face flushed with warmth. Too busy trying to survive, she had forgotten. When she crossed her arms, he looked away shyly and continued.

"Don't be so brave next time. You could've gotten killed," he said in a scolding tone, changing the subject.

Did he seriously say that to me? "What do you want me to do next time? Let it kill me instead of defending myself?"

"No, of course not. Nick and I were there. You should've let us handle it."

"Amanda was right there. She—"

"Doesn't matter. Amanda thinks she can do anything."

Anger was boiling to the surface, but Skylar kept it at bay. After all, he was right. Her human speed and strength were not comparable to theirs, but his hot and cold personality infuriated her. First, he's so sweet and tender, and then the next minute, he's arrogant and back to himself.

Just when things were getting awkward, Nick entered. "That was fun. Amanda and I cleaned up the mess. Breakfast anyone? I'm cooking."

"Sure," Skylar faked a smile.

"No. We can't stay," Mason said, standing in front of Skylar, blocking Nick's view, apparently covering Skylar with his body.

"Where are you going?" Nick inquired. "And just so you know, Amanda told me everything."

"Whatever she said is wrong. You need to hear it from me," Mason stated.

"Whenever you're ready."

Skylar turned red, wondering how Nick felt about Remus's death. She tried to read his facial expression, but he had none. Either he was good at hiding them, or he didn't care, like Mason. And how much did Amanda know?

"I was going to tell you," Mason said, looking sheepish. "I told Amanda parts, but not all."

"I know, and you don't have to do this alone. Let me help you," Nick muttered, standing in front of Mason, looking deeply into his eyes. "You can trust me."

Mason paused, inhaling a deep accepting breath. "Okay. But I don't know where to start."

"My recommendation is to seek the Oracles." Amanda entered the kitchen, talking as if she was already part of the conversation. She looked at Skylar with a quick smile, as if to apologize for what she had done the previous night.

"Are you nuts?" Mason snapped. "We tried before, but they didn't appear."

"Amanda is right," Nick interrupted, walking toward the stove. "They would be the ones that could answer all our questions. They may appear this time, especially since we'll be bringing an unknown along."

"The unknown has a name," Mason snapped.

"Mace...chill. I didn't mean it that way."

"Okay, sorry. The road ahead could be dangerous. I don't think we should take Skylar there."

"Why is it dangerous?" Skylar asked, wondering if she had any business butting into their conversation.

"It somehow limits our powers," Mason explained. "I won't be able to protect you like I can here."

"I'll have to agree with Mason. Going really could be dangerous," Amanda seconded. "So, no problem. I'm coming with you guys. Someone has to protect you."

"No. You can't go," Mason protested.

"And why not? Because I'm a girl? I can handle myself. There is strength in numbers. I'm going, Mason, and you can't stop me."

Mason let out a heavy, defeated sigh. "Fine. When do we leave?"

"After breakfast. I'm starving." Nick took out a frying pan from the bottom cabinet and poured oil into it.

"I'll help." Amanda opened the fridge, took out the eggs, and handed them to Nick.

"What are you going to tell Kayla?" Mason asked.

"She'll have to come. I can't just ditch her."

"You're putting her at unnecessary risk," Mason said.

"Bringing a human may help. You know they won't show themselves in front of humans," Nick reminded, cracking the eggs into the frying pan.

"True, but...alright," Mason agreed.

"Hey, it won't be like the last time," Nick said. "We know better."

"The last time we went for fun, and that was stupid."

"But it was fun," Amanda giggled.

Using the spatula as if it was an extension of his hand, Nick rattled it as he spoke. "Like I said, since we know what we're up against this time, we know better."

Amanda clapped her hands once, breaking up their conversation. "Okay boys, don't forget to bring camping gear. We need to pack lunch and dinner. This is going to be so much fun."

Skylar stood there, gaping back and forth between their conversations, having no idea what they were talking about. Just when she wondered where Kayla was, she entered, yawning and stretching.

"Good morning," she cheered, heading to Nick. "Did you put these ear plugs in my ears?" She held them out. "I slept like a baby. I need to get me some. It was the best sleep I've ever had."

Nick turned to Kayla, giving her a quick peck on her cheek, and then turned to Skylar with a wink. "I like to have them around just in case."

She bet he did, wondering how many girls he'd slept with. "Would you like some help?" Skylar offered, looking at her hands, then remembered she was braless and thought twice about what she'd said. Oddly, her wounds that were throbbing a minute ago were now painless.

"Why don't I help you pack instead?" Mason suggested, guiding her out the door. "You also need a few more layers on you."

Skylar looked over her shoulder to see Kayla give her a big smile. Skylar knew that look. She wanted details. There was so much to tell her, but she couldn't.

NINETEEN

AFTER DRIVING ALONG the highway for a while, the road became unfamiliar. Skylar didn't know where they were headed, but she knew they were going higher into the mountains. After a couple of hours, they finally arrived at their destination.

"This is our stop." Mason pulled off to an unpaved road.

"There is nothing here." Skylar gazed at the surroundings.

"We need to hike the rest of the way," Amanda informed, opening her side of the car.

When Skylar got out of the car, she saw Kayla stretching her long arms and legs. She rolled her eyes to Skylar, indicating she didn't like it there. Then she turned to link her arm with Nick's. When Everett got out of the car, Skylar looked away. She hated him, hated him for what he had tried to do.

After the boys put their camping gear on their backs, Nick led the way. Twigs snapped underneath their feet, and the sound of shuffling footsteps was all that could be heard as they headed down the path in silence. Though it was summer, the weather was perfect.

"Where are we going?" Kayla asked, looking down at her feet.

"Camping. Don't worry, babe. You'll have fun," Nick answered.

"This isn't my idea of fun. Whose idea was it, anyway?"

"Amanda's," Mason and Nick blurted in accord.

Amanda shrugged her shoulders. "Don't be wimps, guys. Embrace Mother Nature."

After what seemed like a couple of miles, they finally stopped to take a rest.

"Is it time for lunch yet?" Kayla whined. "I'm starving."

"Me too," Amanda agreed, seeing Everett roll his eyes. "What, tough guy? Don't tell me you're not hungry?"

Everett dropped his huge backpack and so did the others. "Here." He handed out sandwiches. Instead of handing one to Skylar directly, he gave two to Mason. Nick passed out water bottles, and Mason passed out bags of chips. They had it all planned, as if they had done this many times before. After lunch, they were on the move again.

Skylar jumped from her phone vibrating in the back pocket of her jeans. The text was from Kayla.

I want to go home. I don't like this.

Skylar felt horrible. She didn't mean to drag her cousin with her. Skylar regretted not saying anything on Kayla's behalf, but they couldn't leave her behind at the cabin all by herself. Being with the children of gods was safer, she guessed.

Sorry! Did you call your mom?

Yes. I felt bad lying to her again.

I called my mom, too, just before we left. Everything will be okay.

I know. I just hate camping.

But, you've never been.

I'm here. I don't like it.

What are you doing?" Nick asked Kayla.

Kayla giggled. "Texting Skylar."

"Wow, she can do two things at once," Everett commented.

"Shut up," Nick snapped.

"You gonna make me?" Everett challenged.

"Come on," Nick challenged, jumping from side to side with his fists up like a boxer.

"Are you serious?" Amanda stood between them. "Guys, we need to get going to safer ground before it gets dark. Stop acting like kids, and keep your testosterone in check. Grow up." Amanda scolded, rolled her eyes, and took the lead.

After about another mile, they stopped. It was dusk, and as the sun was setting, the air became cooler. While the guys pitched the tents, the girls got dinner ready. Amanda set the fire and placed a flat, small pan on top of several overlapping thick twigs. The way she arranged the wood and got everything ready, Skylar knew she was an expert camper.

"Do you guys camp often?" Skylar asked, sitting on the ground next to Amanda, watching her poke the twigs with a long thin branch, trying to get the fire bigger.

"We used to go more often, especially when we needed to get away," Amanda replied.

Skylar understood the meaning behind needing to get away. Mason had mentioned they would move from town to town to get away from the vultures. They must have gone to the woods to hide as well.

Amanda reached inside her bags and pulled out several cans.

"Beans," Kayla frowned.

"Beans and bread." Amanda shuffled her hand inside her bag again.

"The joy of camping." Nick was now standing behind Kayla. "Don't judge me if I fart all night."

"Gross," Kayla teased, and pushed Nick away.

Then Mason and Everett showed up, holding flashlights. "It'll get dark soon," Mason muttered, handing one to Amanda.

When the beans were ready, Amanda passed out the paper plates. With a wooden spoon she had used to stir the beans, she placed a lump on everyone's plate. Nick broke bread and handed a piece to everyone. Dinner was tasty since hunger pained Skylar. She had never walked this much before, and had worked up an appetite.

While she ate, she looked up to the sky, mesmerized by the glistening lights. It was a moonless night and a multitude of stars captured her eyes. Complete darkness engulfed them, and the only light was from the campfire burning, providing warmth. Under normal circumstances, camping wouldn't be such a bad experience, but they weren't there for pleasure. Their lives were at stake, or so Skylar kept hearing, but why and how? Conversation was minimal, especially since Kayla was around.

"Are we going to tell scary stories and roast marshmallows?" Kayla giggled. "Isn't that what people do when they go camping?"

"We're not people," Amanda said flatly.

That would've been a funny statement, but knowing what Skylar knew, she realized Amanda meant her words. It was awkward for a second, until Nick spoke, glaring at Amanda. "What she meant was that we're not doing the scary story thing, but you and I can roast our own marshmallows privately." He winked.

Everett rolled his eyes, most likely grossed out by them flirting. He stood up and dusted his pants. "We need to wake up before the sun rises, so I suggest we all go to bed. See you early in the morning." He headed for his tent.

"Who's going into whose tent?" Mason asked, twirling a stick in his hand.

"Don't even think about it. I'm not sleeping with you," Nick joked. He got up and tugged Kayla to him. "Come on...let's go fire up those marshmallows."

"Good night," Kayla said, walking backward, smiling at Skylar.

"I'm going to Everett's tent. See you in the morning. Don't forget to set your watch." Amanda disappeared into the darkness, but light shone from the direction she'd walked, growing dimmer by every step.

Mason raked his hair. "I guess it's you and me." He got up and led the way, beaming the flashlight on the ground.

"This? This is our tent?" Skylar stammered. The tent was small, smaller then she'd imagined. She didn't pay much attention when they were assembling it. Mason unzipped it and crawled inside.

"We only have one sleeping bag, but it's big enough for us both." Mason unrolled the sleeping bag that was tightly bundled, laying it out.

"We only have one sleeping bag?" Skylar repeated.

"Echo, that is exactly what I said."

Skylar heaved a heavy sigh. "Don't call me that."

Mason ignored her request. Unzipping it, he tucked himself in first and lay sideways. He patted the empty space next to him. "Come. I won't bite. Or if you prefer, you can sleep out there with the bugs." Then he turned off his flashlight.

Jerk! Having no choice, she slid in. Without the heat from the fire, it was cold. Shivering, Skylar snuggled and graciously took the warmth from Mason's body, or was it the heat brewing inside her from his touch? Though her back was to him, his chest rising and falling made her stomach flutter, and she was weak all over.

"Why do we have to wake up so early?" Skylar asked.

"We need to pass the swamp. We'll be crossing over to another dimension, and when we get there, time is reversed. Though the sun will be rising here, the sun will be setting there."

"Oh." Skylar tried to grasp that such things could happen.

"I forgot to change your bandages. The medical kit is in my bag." Mason turned on his flashlight. Skylar moved at the same time

Mason did. In the tight space, her body tangled around him and she ended up on top of him. The light shone between them, allowing her to see Mason's piercing eyes. She lay there, lost, as his lips were inches away. The deep breath from Mason traveled to her. She could see his lips leaning toward hers. Hot sensations coursed through her body like an untamed flame, wondering if he was feeling the same.

With a heavy, deep sigh, he looked away. "My bag is there. You think you could get off me so I can get it?"

What was wrong with her? She was falling for this jerk. Snapping out of his lure, she unzipped and grabbed the bag. "Here," Skylar huffed, practically throwing it at him.

With limited space, they sat face to face with their legs crossed. Skylar was glad it was dark so she wouldn't show her blushing and irritated face.

"Hold out your hands," Mason commanded.

Placing them out in front of her, Skylar rooted her eyes on the ground. She didn't want to look at him, afraid that if she did, she wouldn't be able to turn away, and he would know she had feelings for him.

Mason held her forearm and carefully unwrapped one of the swathes. "Impossible. Have you always healed like this?"

When Skylar looked up, Mason's eyes were wide, looking astounded. Then she gazed at the palm of her hand. She recalled the pain disappearing quickly, but she would never have imagined it to be like this. Recalling the last time she was wounded, her lips healed faster than she had ever seen any cut in her body heal before. "What did you do?" Her tone was soft, but accusing.

"What do you mean, 'what did I do?' I didn't do anything."

"This is impossible. I had a long gash. It's like I never had the cut."

"Remus healed like this." Mason traced where the wound should have been with the tip of his finger. Shuddering from his sensual touch, Skylar gasped lightly. Then he unwrapped the bandage from the other hand and traced every inch of it. The smooth glide of his touch tickled her, tingling every inch of her body. Then his hand slid up her arm, examining it. Blood rushed to her face, making her hot. She wanted more of this, more of him. Afraid of what he would do next and afraid of what she wanted to do at this very moment, she yanked her arm away.

"I don't understand," she stammered.

"I'm just as amazed as you. I don't want my family to know. I'm going to place new swathes on your hands."

After Mason wrapped them, Skylar settled back into the sleeping bag. This time she realized how hard the ground was. *Why on Earth do people like camping?* So far, there was nothing pleasant about it. Well, except maybe sharing the same tent with Mr. Rude. Though she was exhausted beyond words, it was nearly impossible to think of sleep, especially when inhabiting the same space with Mason and being very much aware of his body touching hers.

TWENTY

SKYLAR STRETCHED HER arms up to yawn and lazily opened her eyes. She jerked back when Mason appeared in her line of vision, staring at her. "Were you...like...watching me sleep?" she spluttered.

"Don't flatter yourself. I was just about to wake you up."

Why did she use such a poor choice of words? She should've known Mason would say something insensitive like that. She was almost sure he was lying, but then again, she didn't care.

Embarrassed, she crawled out of the tent first. The sun was rising, lighting the world with golden hues, revealing a splendid view. She had never seen a sunrise before. She'd never woken up early enough to see one. Just the sight of it warmed her. Though there wasn't much of the land to look at, besides the trees and the mountains, somehow the glowing sun gave beauty to it.

Skylar looked away from the campsite and saw Kayla was ready to go, and waved her hand. Kayla shook her head to reply, but Skylar was more interested in looking at Kayla's mangled hair. Since she couldn't tell from this distance, she wondered how Kayla looked after not washing her makeup off. Without changing clothes or refreshing her makeup, she wondered how she looked, too. As these thoughts surged through her mind, she turned to see Mason packing.

Skylar was staring, but she couldn't help it. The sunlight kissed the tip of his hair, radiating his body as he stood, and creating the illusion he was heaven sent. His muscles flexed when he stretched and yawned, showing a glimpse of his sexy abs.

Afterward, he folded the tent to a precise size to fit into his backpack, and the way he tossed it around his shoulders, sliding his arms through it, made her lose herself into him.

"I know Mason is attractive, but don't make it so obvious," Amanda whispered, as she continued to follow Everett's steps.

Skylar blushed. *Was it that obvious?* After thinking, she knew it was. *Darn! Why does he have that effect on me?*

After a short distance, they came upon a long bridge. Swaying slightly from side to side, it looked steady enough. Made from wood, each narrow plank was tied to the next with rope-like material. There was even a safety grip on each side, looking like a fisherman's net. It didn't look too bad from where Skylar stood, but when she approached, her courage faltered.

"Leave your bags here," Amanda ordered. "You won't need them where we're headed, but don't forget to take your flashlight."

After the backpacks were dropped, they stood closer to the bridge.

"I'm not crossing that bridge," Kayla said, shaking her head.

"It'll be fine, Kayla. I've crossed it before." Nick's tone was not convincing.

"Uh...is there another way, Everett?" Amanda looked terrified.

"Does it look like there's another way across to the other side? You'll be fine. We've crossed it before. I didn't want to come here in the first place."

"Who told you to come?" Amanda fired back.

Everett eyed Skylar. "We need answers." Then he nudged Amanda out of the way. "Might as well get this over with." He took a step onto the bridge.

"Hold onto me and close your eyes." Nick draped his arms around Kayla.

"Don't let go," Kayla said, dragging her feet.

Mason extended his hand, gesturing for Skylar to go first. "I'd rather go last. I'm going to take my time." Terrified and not wanting to show it, she wanted to stall as long as she could.

Crossing the bridge didn't seem all that bad when Skylar stood on stable ground, but as soon as she took her first step, the bridge rocked. It was already swaying, but it was a whole different story when she felt it. With her hands on the rope to steady herself, she looked straight ahead.

Curiosity got the best of her and she made the mistake of looking down. She couldn't see the bottom since she only looked down for a second, but that was enough to scare the living day lights out of her. Mountains started closing in, and so did the clouds. Winded, she took a moment to compose herself.

After telling herself to calm down, she proceeded ahead. Though her heart pounded out of her chest and her stomach felt like it would drop, she had to be brave. The gang was almost to the other side, but she was only half way there. Occasionally, Mason would turn toward her without a word. Either he was telling her to hurry or he cared enough to look back. She hoped it was the latter.

Suddenly, the bridge rocked harder. The wind wasn't blowing a second ago, but now it seemed to come out of nowhere.

"It started!" Nick yelled. "Run!"

"Run, Skylar!" Mason yelled over his shoulder.

What started and why did she have to run? She knew now. The wind blew stronger. It howled with rage. Shaking violently, the bridge had a life of its own. She ran as fast as she could, but she fell flat on her face. Her feet slipped into a gap and she started sliding off the bridge. She would have fallen off if Mason hadn't grabbed her wrist, pulling her up in the nick of time.

Skylar heard Kayla calling out for her, but she couldn't hear the words. Adrenaline zapped through her as the will to survive kicked in. Unable to breathe from the force of the gust, she took short breaths, trudging through the wind. They were almost there.

Suddenly, the bridge started collapsing, starting where they had taken their first step. Plank by plank, with a rippling effect, it plunged. It happened so fast, the section of the bridge underneath her feet plummeted. "Hold on tight to the rope!" Mason bellowed, forced to let go of his hold on her.

Skylar screamed. Holding tightly onto the rope, she was soaring straight ahead. Her body thumped hard against the face of the mountain, sending piercing pain through every nerve, bone, and muscle. Bouncing from the impact, her body slammed against the ridged rocks again. Looking up, she could see that Mason held on to the same rope she did.

"Hold on, Skylar," Mason yelled. "Whatever you do, don't let go. Do you hear me?"

"Okay, Mason," Skylar mumbled, but her voice wouldn't carry, too afraid to move even her lips. Tears streamed down her face. She had never been so scared in her life. Sure, running away from the vultures and almost drowning was pretty scary, but falling to her death was even worse.

"Hold on, Mason!" Nick said out loud. "Everett and I are pulling you guys up. This would've been a piece of cake if our powers weren't limited here."

"Hurry up. Get Skylar up. She won't be able to hold on much longer." Mason looked down at her.

Skylar was more than elated that the wind had died down, and the rope sliding upward gave her hope, knowing they were being pulled up. Not having much upper body strength, her arms burned as they trembled. Her palms were moist, making them slippery, and sweat trickled along her forehead.

Luckily, Mason had made Skylar keep the swathes on her hands. They helped her keep her grip somewhat, but it wasn't going to stop her from slipping. With shooting pains all over her body, she held as tightly as she could. Though she knew she shouldn't, she had a strong urge to look down again.

"No, no, no. Don't look down." Mason had reached the top, but they had to stop pulling. The rope was unthreading itself from the weight. "Skylar, look at me. Give me your hand."

Skylar hesitated, knowing the length of her arm wasn't long enough. To make matters worse, the loose rope dropped her lower with a jerk. Skylar screamed as the rope unraveled even more, thread by thread; there was no hope. At this point, she knew she had to accept that death was imminent. When she looked up to say her good-byes, she saw Mason drop to her and clutch her wrist just as the single thread of rope snapped.

"I got you," Mason heaved. Everett and Nick pulled Mason up by his feet, bringing Skylar up to safety. Releasing a relieved breath of air, Mason held her tightly. Her body trembled as she panted from being out of breath, and tears streamed down her face. Continuing to embrace her, the tension in his shoulders relaxed. As his hand laced through her hair, he caressed his cheek to hers.

Mason pulled back, gazed into her eyes, and ran his hands over her face, arms, and hands, looking for wounds. "You're safe." He wiped her tears. "Are you hurt anywhere?"

Skylar shook her head, unable to speak. From her peripheral vision, she could see Kayla sobbing, waiting for her turn. When Skylar was stable enough to stand, Mason gestured for Kayla to come.

Skylar clung to her cousin tightly. Their bodies shook from crying. There was no need for words. She had just escaped death, and holding onto Kayla comforted her beyond words.

"Thanks," Mason said to his brothers, taking in deep breaths. "That was a close call."

"You know we've got your back, bro," Nick smiled, patting his back.

"What happened back there? This didn't happen the last time we were here," Mason commented.

"I'm telling you and I keep telling you, it's because of Skylar, but you won't believe me," Everett whispered. "Whatever that was, it wanted her dead. If she wasn't here with us, we would've been fine. The bridge would still exist."

"I kind of agree with Everett," Nick said. "Something is different about her, but I don't think she's dangerous."

"That's why we're going to see the Oracle," Mason murmured.

"We should get going. Like now," Everett snipped. "We've lost time. It's getting dark on the other side."

"Chill," Amanda said calmly. "She almost dropped to her death. Think like a human for a bit, will ya?"

After Skylar and Kayla composed themselves, they headed out again behind the boys. After a few yards, they stopped.

"Are you ready?" Mason looked sternly at his brothers and Amanda. "This is it. There's no turning back."

"Ready for what?" Kayla asked, but they just ignored her. "What's going on Nick?"

"Hold my hand." Nick grabbed Kayla's hand while her other arm was still linked to Skylar. As they took a step forward, like magic, another world materialized in front of them.

TWENTY ONE

"**W**HAT THE...WHERE are we?" Kayla asked, looking around. She looked over her shoulder as if she could see the world she'd left behind a second ago, but she couldn't. "How is this possible?"

It was like a world within a world. At the campsite, Skylar had stood in reality, and now she was somewhere else. Though she should be just as stunned as Kayla, she wasn't. In some ways, she had expected it. It was not quite the picture she had imagined when Mason told her about the swamp. Regardless, she was mesmerized, and wondered how it could possibly exist just by taking that step— surreal.

The sun was setting, and it was getting darker and colder, just as Mason had said it would. From a distance, a blanket of thick fog stirred, gliding toward them. Just the sight of it gave Skylar a chill. Though they were standing on solid ground, it was mushy and wet. The air was humid, and mist trickled on Skylar's arms and face. Surprisingly, she was calm, but Kayla was still questioning.

"Am I dreaming? How in the world? How?" Kayla pinched herself. "Ouch."

"I'll explain later, but right now, you need to keep your voice down." Nick pulled Kayla closer and to Skylar's surprise, Mason held her hand.

Stunned to have her hand in his, she looked at him, wondering about his sudden change to niceness. Nevertheless, she welcomed it. Almost losing her life today, she didn't want to have angry thoughts toward him. After all, he did save her life, and she was grateful.

"We can take that boat," Everett pointed to the left side of a dock. A massive body of murky water blocked them from heading forward. "Hurry, but don't use the flashlights, not just yet." He led the way.

One by one, they got in. The wooden rowboat was just big enough for the six of them. Everett and Nick each grabbed an oar and pushed through the water. The eerie fog had completely surrounded them, and their vision was limited to nothing but white.

"Do you camp like this all the time, and is this your idea of fun?" Kayla whispered.

Everyone snapped their heads, narrowing their eyes at her, except for Skylar. Kayla shrugged her shoulders sheepishly, looking like a child who had been scolded.

"Don't talk. I'll explain later," Nick murmured, flexing his muscles, synchronizing the pulling and pushing with Everett.

The ride was calm, somewhat soothing. The soft, cool breeze brushed against Skylar's face. Nothing but the swooshing sounds of the oars moving in and out of the water was audible as they paddled cautiously, trying not to make too much noise. Swoosh-silence-swoosh-silence. Moving further, the fog finally lifted, giving them a better view of the path ahead, but it was dark. Flashlights were turned on, providing some light.

Though Skylar would rather be anywhere else but there, it wasn't as bad as she thought it would be, except when she looked at the trees along the bank; they looked peculiar. Oddly, the trees were black. What was even creepier were the bare branches—thin and long, like spider legs. With multiple hollow dents on the trunks looking like eyes, they gave her a chilling sting down her spine. She could've sworn the "eyes" popped open when viewed with her peripheral vision, but when she turned to look, they were just creepy trees.

Suddenly, anxiety crawled through her and her pulse raced the way it did when she watched a scary movie, anticipating something dreadful. Though she had no explanation for what she was feeling, she sensed that something was following them below the water's surface. At first, she thought she was imagining things, but then Amanda's erratic movements confirmed her fears.

Amanda suddenly turned to the left, then to the right, focusing her eyes on the water. "Can you feel them?" Amanda whispered, shuddering. "They're all around us." She huddled closer to Everett.

"Don't worry. They won't touch the boat as long as a human is with us," Everett said, looking at Kayla. "They can try to manipulate around it, but they won't appear in their true form."

"Human?" Kayla asked, but she didn't pursue her question any further. She looked upset and worried.

Abruptly, Skylar heard a low hum. She zoomed her eyes in front, behind, to the left, and to the right, to see if some kind of bug or anything else was buzzing around her—nothing. When the low hum turned into whispers, she knew it was in her mind. At first, it didn't bother her, but when it got louder, she started freaking out.

She placed her hands over her ears, hoping it would go away, but it rambled faster, overwhelming her and becoming more irritating by the second. In pain from the intensity of the voices, she curled herself in.

"What's wrong Skylar?" Mason asked worriedly when she broke out of his protective hold. His hand gripped her shoulders to calm her, but it wasn't working.

"They're...everywhere. The sounds. In my head. Make them go away."

"Hurry up!" Mason shouted to his brothers, reaching for her again.

Skylar didn't answer Kayla. In fact, she couldn't hear anyone else. It seemed as though the sounds were projecting from the water, as if the water creatures were communicating with her, but she didn't know what they were trying to tell her. Perhaps it was a warning. Soon it didn't matter. The sounds disappeared as quickly as they had started. What had just happened? Stiffly, she waited for the whispers to come back, but when they didn't, she felt more at ease.

Sitting upright, shoulders relaxed, she turned to Mason to let him know she was fine. Wondering why everyone else was focused on the water, she looked too. Waves rocked the water surrounding them, as bubbles formed around the boat. Their intensity and size grew larger by the second, like boiling water in a pot. Then the bubbles shot out, shaped in the form of human hands, reaching for the boat's occupants, but unable to touch them.

"I thought they wouldn't come near us when a human is around," Amanda sputtered.

"This is nothing," Nick bellowed. "You want to see their true form?"

"Everyone hold onto something," Everett warned. "They're trying to tip the boat."

Kayla screamed, holding onto Nick.

"Will you shut her up?" Everett said with a harsh tone.

Nick didn't say anything. Everyone was holding on for dear life. Just when Skylar thought the boat would tip, she was jerked hard. Mason's hold on her kept her rooted to the boat or she would have been flung out, like Amanda.

"Are you okay?" Nick asked, standing up to see his cousin on dry land.

"Why am I the only one off the boat?" Amanda got up and brushed the dirt off her clothes. The boat had collided with a huge boulder that was oddly set, preventing the boat from advancing. Thankfully, it was also what had prevented them from being tipped over.

Extending his long legs, Everett took a step to Amanda. He examined her body from head to toe with his eyes and the flashlight. "You'll live. Let's go."

"Whatever, Mr. Insensitive." Amanda rolled her eyes.

Mason got off the boat second to last and extended his hand to Skylar. "Jump. I'll catch you."

Skylar wanted to, but her legs wouldn't listen. Still weak, they were shaky and unstable. It was difficult to see, but she knew water separated her from Mason. Managing to stand on the edge of the boat, she could see Mason and his flashlight, so she jumped, and flew into Mason's arms.

Without a glance from him, he held her hand in silence, lagging behind the others. After several steps, he stopped. "What happened back there in the boat?"

"There were loud whispers in my ears, like they were trying to tell me something, but it was overwhelming. Why is this happening to me?"

"I'm not sure. That's why we are going through all this trouble to find the Oracle. Supposedly, they have answers to everything."

"Have you seen them before?"

"No. We tried, but they didn't show themselves to us. I guess our question wasn't worth their time."

"What was your question?"

"Before Nick's mother died, she said that our father told her there was a prophecy foretold by the Oracle that something evil would enter the human world that could possibly end the lives of all the gods' children and Hades' evil creations. Being curious idiots, we decided to risk our lives to find the answer.

"We came here before, though our journey wasn't as rough. We saw the swamp monsters the last time we were here. They looked ugly as hell, like the vultures, but they left us alone. Anyway, the prophecy states that the keeper of death will destroy us all. Hades' monsters were bad enough. We needed to know what this something evil was. We still don't know to this day."

Hearing Mason's words gave Skylar goose bumps, making her suddenly cold. She recalled Remus and Everett asking her if she was the keeper of death.

"Do you think that's what I am?" Skylar asked hesitantly, afraid of what he might say.

"No. Why would you think such thoughts?" Surprisingly, Mason tucked strands of Skylar's hair behind her ear so he could see her eyes after a sudden breeze ruffled them.

Skylar's heart fluttered. Timidly, she answered. "Remus asked me if I was."

"Remus was weird, and malicious. I wouldn't be surprised if he was one. Don't think of him. Besides, I'm sure the keeper of death would look hideous, and you don't. I mean, you're more pleasant to look...I mean...you're not."

Shyly, she shot her eyes down. She knew what he was trying to say. In a way, she wanted to think that it was a compliment. Then she remembered she never thanked him for saving her life again. Though she was humbled that he would go out of his way to help her, she knew he was doing it for himself too, especially since she'd killed Remus, or at least he thought she did. He needed answers.

"Thanks for saving my life back there. I thought...well...I thought that was it."

Mason's eyes were fixated on hers, as his lips parted to speak. He looked as though he had so much to say. Apparently changing his mind, he closed his mouth and nodded with a grin. Skylar smiled back.

"You should smile more often. I like your smile, Echo." He grabbed her hand and started walking.

They finally caught up to the rest of the gang, but they all stopped when they couldn't go any further. Strangely, dark had turned to light. It was as if they had stepped into another dimension without knowing it. In front of them was an old structure, looking almost like a castle. Vines and branches with dead leaves cascaded downward, covering a dark, narrow entrance and other parts of what was once a marvelous edifice.

"You want to go in there?" Kayla murmured, grimacing, looking terrified and annoyed at the same time. "Why? For the love of God, why?"

"If only humans continued to believe in the gods, we wouldn't be in this mess," Amanda commented.

"Why do you all keep saying 'humans'?" Kayla scoffed. "Of course we believe in God. And what mess are you talking about?"

Disregarding her, everyone looked deep in thought.

"Let's go," Everett snapped, heading in first, followed by Amanda.

"Don't worry. I got ya." Nick winked at Kayla, wrapping his arms around her waist. "It might be fun in there." He gave her a playful look.

Taken in by his charisma, she giggled like a schoolgirl, and snuggled closer to him as they strode forward. Skylar stopped abruptly when Nick and Kayla seemed to bounce back upon attempting to enter. Kayla stumbled backward and almost fell, but Nick caught her just in time.

"What just happened?" Nick huffed. Looking confused, he entered by himself without a hitch. Crooking his finger, he gestured for Kayla to come to him. As directed, she tried again, shuffling her feet cautiously. As if there was an invisible wall in front of her, she couldn't take another step.

"Nick," she called, patting nothing but air. "What's going on? Why can't I go in?"

Frustrated, Nick stepped next to Kayla, and then turned to Mason. As if they could read each other's thoughts, Nick nodded. "I'm going to have to stay here with her, aren't I?"

"I'm afraid so."

Hearing footsteps, they looked up as Everett and Amanda appeared. "What's the hold up?" Amanda asked, crossing her arms.

"It's Kayla. She can't enter," Mason replied, sounding frustrated.

"I told you not to bring her," Everett sneered.

"We knew this would happen. Somewhere along the journey, there would be a fine line where humans couldn't enter, and this is it," Nick murmured. "I just didn't think it would be here."

"We've never brought a human along, so now we know," Mason muttered.

"Hello...I'm standing right here." Kayla waved her hand. "What's going on?"

Narrowing her eyes at Kayla, Amanda spoke. "The Oracles are in there. Nick, you're gonna have to stay here with her."

Nick heaved a long sigh, looking disappointed. "Damn. I wanted to see what they look like."

"We have no idea what we are doing. You should be glad you're not going," Amanda commented.

"We're wasting time." Everett pointed to his watch. "Hurry up. Figure it out and meet me inside." He went back in.

"Let's go," Mason said to Skylar.

"Wait, wait, wait. What are you all saying? Why are we here? Who or what are these Oracles?" Kayla started rolling with her questions.

"It's okay. Everything is fine," Nick explained, placing his hands on her shoulders, trying to calm her down.

Kayla swatted his hands away. "You need to explain now, and Skylar isn't going anywhere." Kayla looked at Skylar to confirm. When she didn't respond, Kayla spoke again. "Skylar, tell them you're not going."

"I...I...," Skylar started to speak, feeling confused as to how to handle this situation.

Kayla didn't wait for her response. "No, you don't have to go. You don't even know what's going on. We're going back home." Kayla reached for Skylar's arm.

Amanda raised her hands with annoyance. "Would you just put her to sleep? We don't have time for this."

Nick swung Kayla around. "Listen. Everything is going to be okay. You need to trust me."

"I want to go home," Kayla cried. "Nick, please take me home."

Nick softened from her plea. "Look at me Kayla." She did as told. He rested all of his fingertips on her head and dim light seeped from them. "Sleep. You won't have memories of today." Nick's dark eyes turned the color of silver and then turned back to their original color.

At that moment, Skylar remembered Mason's eyes turning the same color the night she was pulled over by him. Kayla closed her eyes and Nick caught her as she fell. "She's asleep. I'll meet you back at the cabin. I'll find a way back. I have a human with me, so we'll be okay."

"Be careful," Mason nodded. Holding Skylar's hand, he guided her toward the entrance, then dropped his hand to enter first and waited for her. "Just in case."

Skylar looked over her shoulder, seeing Kayla in Nick's arms. She knew Kayla was safe. Nick had compelled her to sleep. Obviously, it worked on Kayla, but it had no effect on Skylar. Wondering if she would bounce back like Kayla, she swatted the vines blocking her way and dragged her feet. Taking baby steps, she entered without any problems. She knew for sure now that Mason was right about her.

TWENTY TWO

CAREFULLY, SKYLAR WALKED forward with Mason. A fast, cool breeze brushed her face, causing her to suck in air. This place stunk with the smell of soil and something rotting, stinging her nostrils with a repulsive stench. Ducking the spider webs, she couldn't wait to get through what appeared to be a long hallway. The flashlights gave just enough light as they headed further in.

As they continued on the path, there were more withered vines and spider webs every way Skylar turned her head. The ivory pillars were knocked down, broken and scattered on top of furniture that was hardly recognizable. Though it looked like this place would have been a splendid castle, once fit for a royal court right out of fairy tale, it was wretchedly ruined now. It clearly showed it had been long abandoned and turmoil had taken up residence there.

Out of the dim light, they entered another tunnel of darkness. Skylar thought that if she could feel death, this was what it would be like, crawling on her skin. Being the only ones there and not knowing what was ahead, her trepidation rose to the surface, ready to turn into a full-blown anxiety attack.

A short time later, the flashlights were no longer needed as another world materialized in front of them. Never would Skylar have imagined seeing such beauty. The fluffy clouds looked heaven sent, and the ground under her feet was plush and green and seemed to go on for miles and miles. To the right was a small waterfall, trickling softly, flowing into a narrow stream.

Upon approaching the waterfall, Skylar saw another entrance she hadn't seen before now. "We have to go in there?" Skylar asked, looking into the darkness, grimacing. They had just come out from a dank, dark place into this beautiful one. She didn't want to go back into darkness again.

"Come on. Let's get this over with." Everett entered first.

The dry air was comfortable and the flashlights were not needed after a short distance. They followed the bright light and stepped into the warmth of daylight. The first thing Skylar saw was a ray of light, spotlighting the center of the garden. With a radiant golden hue, it looked like they were at the end of the rainbow with a promise of treasures of diamonds and gold. Filled with wild flowers, the garden produced a pleasurable scent, and each tree sprouted its own special fruit. Following the path, she took in the beauty of the surrounding nature, but what she saw next was unfathomable.

An ivory statue was in her line of vision. As she continued, she saw many more of them, lined up side-by-side to the left and right of her in a horizontal formation. Mesmerized, she gaped at the detail in each one. Looking at her friends, she saw they were doing the same.

"Oh my god! Is this...? It can't be." Amanda gasped, looking at a statue in front of her with admiration. "This is Athena. She was goddess of wisdom and war. Nick is going to be so pissed he missed this." Athena held her head up high, holding a sword in one hand and a shield in the other.

Skylar recognized the statue next to Athena. It was Ares, Athena's half-brother. Curious, she let her fingertip glide down its cold, smooth arm. Ares was a god of war just like his sister, but unlike Athena, he was bloodthirsty and vengeful. Though it was just a statue, just knowing of his evil gave her chills.

"This must be Aphrodite." Mason examined her from head to toe. "She is breathtaking." Aphrodite's garment had a high slit, revealing her right leg. The front was low cut, showing her cleavage, and her hair was adorned with flowers. It was a perfect image of the goddess of love, who was the fairest of all.

Skylar knew she shouldn't be jealous of a statue, but she couldn't help feeling a sting from Mason's statement, assuming he would never say such words to her.

"These are all statues of gods. Are they real?" Everett looked up, placed his index finger on the lines of Zeus's robe, and ran it down with wonderment.

Zeus was huge compared to Everett. Skylar wondered if that was his actual size. She also wondered how Everett felt at this moment, to be face to face with Zeus, knowing he was one of Zeus descendants, even though it was just a statue.

"They are real to me," a small voice said.

Startled to hear such a voice, Skylar turned to see a short, rounded old woman with a cane standing in front of a colossal tree. Her hair was salt and pepper colored and long, down to her waist. Oddly, though her eyes were shut, she looked straight at Skylar as if she could see her.

"Are you the Oracle?" Mason asked. His eyes lit up with hope.

"It depends on who's asking. Since you've crossed over, I know for a fact that you are half-bloods. It's a pleasure to meet you. You are one of the last generations of the gods' children." She wobbled forward, using her cane for stability, stepping out of the shadows. "Yes, I'm the Oracle. There were three of us, but now I'm the only one left."

"There are more of us out there, correct?" Amanda asked.

"There were many, but unfortunately some have been killed by Hades' creatures. You know of the prophecy. It states that an unknown factor could possibly wipe out all of our kind, the good and the evil. I wonder if it has already begun. We called them the keepers of death."

"Unknown factor?" Amanda repeated.

"Like Remus," Everett said, narrowing his eyes to Mason.

"Yes, unknown factor. This one has me troubled. My sisters and I, god bless their souls, had been trying to determine when or how or who this keeper of death could be. Will it be in a human form? Will the keeper possess a unique ability? Unfortunately, we were unable to figure that one out before they passed away. Even Oracles don't live forever."

Amanda looked at the statues again with amazement. "Are they real? I mean...are they the real gods and now they've turned to statues? I know this is a silly question, especially since we've been told that they crumbled into nothing but ashes."

"No, they're not the actual gods. You are standing on the grounds of what is left of Olympus, the home of the gods. These statues were made and situated in the very same spot ages ago by Zeus."

This profound revelation struck Skylar to her very core. Reading about them during her school years was fascinating, but to be standing on Olympus and being a half-blood was too much to bear all at once.

Knowing everyone was busy staring at the statues, the Oracle tapped her cane once on the ground, producing a thunder-like sound. Assuming the Oracle's action was to get their attention, it worked. "Why have you come?"

"To get answers," Everett said, turning his head to her.

"I have no answers to give you. I've told you as much as I could."

"No, this is different. We don't know what she is."

It was the oddest sight to witness the Oracle turning to Everett when he spoke, especially since her eyes were shut. "Who are you talking about?"

Everett pointed to Skylar. "Her. She is the reason why we've come. She is different."

"How different?"

"If I knew would I be here?" Everett snapped.

Surprisingly, the Oracle was calm. "What I know for sure is that you have a temper. It will get you into trouble. It's the part of Zeus I never liked. He had a bad temper, causing his judgment to be obscured. As for her, I feel her heart beating in the same pattern as yours, indicating she is not a vulture of some sort. I can also feel her warm heart. Hmmm...I see she has a soft spot for someone."

Blushing, Skylar flashed her eyes on Mason, wondering if he clued in on her comment. When her eyes met his, she dropped them to her feet.

"Please," Amanda stepped in. Amanda looked at Skylar for a brief second and turned her eyes to Mason. "I feel the same as Everett."

The Oracle heaved a heavy sigh. "I don't normally get into people's business. It is one of the reasons why I refused to play your silly game the last time you tried to enter, the reason why you couldn't enter Olympus. I don't have time for ridiculous questions, but I figured you coming again must be vital. You wouldn't have crossed the bridge and passed the water beasts unless it was that important."

"We almost died on the bridge," Amanda huffed. "We went through hell. You have to see us."

"What do you mean you almost died on the bridge, my child? The bridge is sturdy."

"We didn't have trouble crossing it the first time, but this time, the bridge fell apart. There is no bridge anymore."

"Impossible. Why didn't you tell me in the first place?"

Amanda rolled her eyes. "Duh...if only we knew it was important information," she mumbled under her breath. Mason nudged her to shut her mouth.

The Oracle appeared deep in thought, unaware that Amanda made a rude comment. Mumbling to herself, she looked like she was casting some kind of spell. Suddenly, a door appeared on the tree she was standing in front of. "Come, quickly."

Everyone followed, but just before the Oracle passed through, she stopped. "No, only you." She pointed to Skylar.

"No," Mason snapped. "I go in with her."

"No, only her."

"Either I go too or she doesn't go at all. How do I know you won't hurt her?"

Skylar was extremely touched by his protectiveness.

"Child, I'm the Oracle."

"I've only heard stories about you. I've never seen you until today. My answer is no." Mason gently tugged Skylar behind him.

The Oracle stood still for a brief second. Just when they were about to walk away, she grabbed Mason by his shirt. "Very well. Just you two."

Everett looked irritated and Amanda held up her hands, giving Mason an annoyed expression. Mason gave them an apologetic look, protectively wrapping his arms around Skylar as they followed the Oracle.

TWENTY THREE

SKYLAR WAS SURPRISED to see an undersized sofa, a bed, and table set for two. In the fireplace was a huge pot. It seemed she was cooking soup. A delicious aroma filled the air and tickled her nostrils. Having not eaten lunch, her stomach gurgled with hunger pangs. She had thought they were walking into a dark tunnel, but that was obviously not the case. It wasn't cold, but the fire crackling and the coziness of the dome shaped room, gave the warm feeling of home.

"Sit down." The Oracle patted the rug next to the fireplace. Then she picked up a long wooden stick and stirred the pot. "Would you like some soup?"

Skylar was about to say yes, but Mason spoke up first. "No, thanks. We're not here to socialize. Let's get this over with, so we can get back home."

Skylar could sense Mason's uneasiness from his tone. She also noted the lack of trust he had for the Oracle. Must be his personality, recalling when he told her he didn't know if he could trust her.

"Very well." She hobbled to her cabinet and pulled out a silver bowl. Inside the bowl, she pinched clear droplets of liquid from the bottles she pulled off the shelves below. After she stirred, she placed the bowl by the side of the fire, watching it carefully, making sure it was warm but not too hot to touch.

"There. This part is ready. Now, let me look into your soul," she muttered, standing in front of Skylar.

"Look into my soul?" Skylar couldn't fathom how she would do such a thing. The Oracle couldn't even see. Well at least, she thought she couldn't, but she seemed to get around just fine.

"Come closer, my dear." She gripped Skylar's shirt, tugging her closer to her, meeting face to face.

Mason moved cautiously closer, looking like he was ready to pull Skylar away.

"Look into my eyes."

Look at what eyes? Is she for real?

Without warning, the old woman's eyes shot open. Had the Oracle not gripped Skylar's shirt tightly in her fist, Skylar would have fallen backward. Mason jerked back as well, almost stumbling. Her eyes were turquoise blue, but glassy and marble like. They looked fake, and they pulsated like a thumping heart, yet they were real. Staring back at her, Skylar was pulled into a trance and couldn't look away.

Suddenly, the Oracle gasped a deep breath, like she had come up for air from being under the water too long. With a frightened expression on her face, she pulled back. "It's you." The Oracle raised her tone at Skylar, pointing at her. "You are the unknown factor the prophecy spoke of. You are the keeper of death."

Skylar looked bewildered, wanting to run. Her mouth dropped in shock from this astounding news and her eyes were wide as she shifted them from Mason, then to the Oracle. She couldn't be the unknown factor. She didn't even know what that was. "I'm nothing. I didn't do anything," she cried, wondering what Mason was thinking.

Mason didn't move a muscle. He stood there staring at Skylar, most likely stunned, too. Breaking out of his state, he gripped Skylar's wrist and led her toward the door. "We're leaving."

"She has evil in her. You must kill her," the Oracle urged.

When Mason turned, the Oracle was already standing in front of Skylar. It happened so fast, he didn't have time to react. The Oracle snatched Skylar's hand and sliced her palm diagonally, wounding her. The swathe had prevented the knife from penetrating deeper. Drops of scarlet liquid dripped into the silver bowl the Oracle was holding before Skylar could snatch her hand away.

To their surprise, the liquid inside the bowl sizzled. The bowl dropped from the Oracle's hand, seemingly too hot to touch. It rattled while spinning endlessly. Finally, it stopped and turned into stone. Then with a puff of black smoke, it turned into ashes. All eyes were glued to what was once a silver bowl.

"Now you see. I have proof," she exclaimed with certainty, backing away, looking horrified. "Her blood is evil," she shrieked. "Did Hades create you? What are you not telling us?"

With this newfound discovery, Skylar had no words. All she could think about at that moment was how similar Remus's death was. Did she truly kill Remus? She regressed back to Mason's room. Remus slapped her so hard the impact cut her lip. In order to escape from Remus's hold, she bit down on his lip, causing him to bleed, too. He swallowed her blood. This was the only explanation.

The room started to spin as she focused on the small pool of blood on her palm. Being told she was evil tore at her heart, and her chest tightened, feeling like the air was being sucked out of her.

Turning pale, she fought frantically for breath. As if the Earth had tilted at that very moment, her knees buckled under her weight. She was about to fall flat on her face, but instead she felt two strong arms, the arms she had felt many times before, protectively surrounding her.

"Stop it," Mason snapped. "She isn't evil."

The Oracle finally calmed down. "She may not be evil, but she will bring evil wherever she goes. There are more like her out there. You must kill every one of them before they destroy us all," the Oracle warned. "Get out. Don't come back. You will bring evil to Olympus. Olympus is all we have left to remind us of what we once were."

Still in his hold, Mason lightly shook Skylar to get her attention. "Listen. Don't tell anyone what just happened. Do you understand? Everett will kill you, and I don't know what Amanda will do. You must keep a straight face when we get out."

When Skylar nodded to confirm, he turned to the Oracle. "The bridge is gone. How do we get out of here?"

The Oracle didn't respond. She kept on staring at Skylar with piercing hatred in her eyes.

Mason gripped Skylar's wounded hand and extended her arm toward the Oracle. "Tell me now before I splash her blood on you."

"Don't touch me," she jerked back. "Go back to the waterfall and follow the stream, or you can go back to where the bridge was and find the path that leads to the same stream. It will lead you back to where you were before the bridge."

"Back to the camp site," Mason mumbled. "Hurry, open the door."

The door flew open. Holding onto Skylar, he led them out. The door shut behind them, as the Oracle remained behind. Mason released Skylar from his hold and waited for her to stand steady. He ripped a strip of his shirt and wrapped it tightly around her wounded hand, trying not to touch the blood. "There. That should stop the bleeding for now. You owe me a T-shirt."

"Okay," she replied, losing her train of thought as she looked at his torn T-shirt, revealing his muscular stomach. "Mason, I'm sorry. I'm not..." Skylar started, but there was nothing she could say. She wanted to cry. She wanted to apologize for killing Remus, even though it was an accident, but she couldn't. There were no words. The fact remained—she was poison. Knowing she could kill Mason, she had to let him go. Whatever hope she had that they would be together, disappeared when they walked out that door.

Somehow managing to hold back her tears, she opened her mouth to speak, but stopped when she spotted Amanda and Everett. Her muscles tensed, and she couldn't control the rate of her rapidly beating heart.

"What happened to you?" Amanda asked Skylar.

Before Skylar could speak, Mason broke in. "She's fine. I accidentally slit her with a knife she was holding."

"Why was she holding a knife?" Amanda's gaze went to Mason's ripped T-shirt.

"Never mind. It's too long to explain. Everything is fine."

Amanda furrowed her brows, most likely not accepting his lack of an explanation, but she didn't ask any more questions. Skylar was more than happy Mason took over their conversation. She didn't know what she was going to say anyway.

"What happened in there? What did the Oracle say?" Everett jumped in.

"Not much. I knew this was a waste of time," Mason huffed. "She looked into Skylar's eyes and—"

"She what? She can't see, can she?" Amanda looked confused.

"She's strange. I don't know if we can trust her."

"So what did she say after she looked into Skylar's eyes?" Everett seemed very impatient, spitting out his words the first chance he got.

"First of all, her eyes were spooky when she opened them. Then she mumbled a few words. She said she didn't see any reasons why Skylar would be a threat. She does have god's blood, from which family line remains unclear. The Oracle also told me how we can get out without retracing our steps. Follow me."

Mason was cool and collected. Not an ounce of fear was displayed through his gestures. His words were smooth and convincing, but one question continued to replay in Skylar's mind. What were Mason's real thoughts?

TWENTY FOUR

STANDING ON THE boulders at the waterfall, they waited for Mason's instructions. Watching the soft stream of water falling from above, Skylar wanted to submerge herself under it to wash away her poison blood. Thinking she was a half-blood was bad enough, but to find out her blood could kill them was even worse—a nightmare from which she couldn't wake up.

As they continued to follow the path, the stream became narrower until there was no water.

"Now what?" Amanda asked, looking annoyed.

Mason didn't say a word. He gripped Skylar's arm and stepped over to disappear from their sight. Soon after, Amanda and Everett materialized in front of them. They were near the bridge.

"That was easy. Why couldn't we have done this instead of going through what we've been through?" Amanda said through her gritted teeth.

"What would be the fun in that?" Mason twitched his brows.

After they retrieved their camping backpacks, they headed to the cars. Since Nick's car was gone, they assumed he'd found the path by the bridge to the stream. Skylar was elated Kayla was safe at home, hopefully. Though the ride back home was silent, it was soothing for Skylar. She gazed out the window: holding on to the clear blue summer sky, holding on to the warmth from the sun, holding on to the bumpy, sometimes unpaved roads, holding on to her reality. Having slept restlessly and drained from all that she had been through, she fell deeply asleep.

When she blinked her eyes, it took her a second to realize where she was—inside Mason's car, parked in front of Kayla's house. She twisted her neck to the left and saw his small smile and that the shirt he wore wasn't torn.

Sitting up straight, she took note of the date and time. It was Sunday, 6 p.m. Though it felt like a second ago since she had closed her eyes, more than two hours had passed. Looking to the empty back seat, Skylar assumed Mason had dropped off Amanda and Everett.

Since Mason hadn't said a word, she figured it was time for her to get out of the car. "Thank you." She reached for the handle.

Mason rested his hand on her shoulder, preventing her from going out the door, and then moved his hand down to his side when she turned. "We're not safe. The Oracle is right. They will come after you."

For some unknown reason, whether it was his tone or his lack of reassurance, Skylar was disappointed. "Then I better get myself a revolver."

He chuckled lightly. "Like you'd know how to use one."

I didn't mean to be funny. "Then what do you propose?"

"I don't know. I don't understand you...who you are. I don't know—"

If words could slap her in the face, they just did. "I don't need your help," she snapped before he could finish his sentence. "And you should stay away from me because evidently, I can kill you." Skylar had had enough. Feeling dirty and ashamed, she rushed out of the car.

On her way to the front door, she tripped and stumbled to the grass. Embarrassed, she didn't look to see if Mason was watching, hoping he didn't see what she had just done.

It was too late. In the blink of an eye, he reached for her, and effortlessly pulled her up by her shoulders. In his hold, locked to his eyes, she was speechless.

"You didn't let me finish. You're always too busy assuming the worst of me. I will be there for you and do whatever I have to do to protect you. The Oracle was wrong about one thing. You are not evil. I can feel only good from you. Your blood may be damned, but you are not. There is a difference."

Skylar's already watery eyes flooded even more, and she couldn't keep the tears from falling. "Why? Why would you want to help me when your life would be in danger? You heard the Oracle. The danger and evil will follow me wherever I go. Why would you risk your own life knowing death may be imminent when you're with me?"

Mason pulled Skylar closer, tighter, and then let go to run his fingers through her hair. "I don't know. I just want to."

Tingling sensations fluttered through her body. She wanted to hear him say that he cared for her as much as his eyes revealed. How badly she wanted to pull him in and taste his lips. Snapping out of the allure of his eyes, she spoke wearily. "It's okay, Mason. You don't need to protect me out of obligation, or because you feel sorry for me. You're safer without me."

"You don't understand," he said quickly.

"You're right. I don't understand why you would risk your life for me." Skylar raised her voice, feeling frustrated. What was it that she didn't understand? If only he would speak his mind instead of dancing around whatever he wanted to say.

To Skylar's surprise, he bent lower to rest his head on hers, and tenderly cupped her face in his hands. At that moment, she was in a bubble of bliss, and nobody else existed in the world except for the two of them. Consumed by his tender embrace, she was utterly lost in Mason's world.

"I...because...," he started to say.

"Why?" she whispered.

"You're trouble, you know that?" He gripped her tighter. "Because. Just because."

Skylar would take "because," but not so much the "being trouble" part. With Mason, "because" had a deeper meaning. She understood. He was beginning to care for her in ways she wanted, but it was not how she imagined things would have turned out.

"Are you sure?"

He pulled away, looking bashful, shuffling his feet. "I'm sure." His actions were adorable. "I'm sorry about Remus. I didn't mean to—"

"We've already talked about this. The past is the past. You need to let it go."

"What does Everett know about Remus?"

"He thinks what he thinks. Eventually, he'll find out the truth. He'll get over him soon enough. Remus deserved his punishment. Gods were not as perfect as the humans think they were. Being half-bloods, we are even further from being perfect. He was cruel. As far as I'm concerned, he was the one with evil blood. I don't want to discuss him anymore. He's not worth our time."

After that, there was nothing to say. His tone said it all. It was a done deal. "So Sky," he started to say, and paused when he saw the disconcerted look on her face. Skylar's face was pale and long, as if life had been drained out of her. "What is it?"

"You just called me...." She paused and blinked her eyes. "Sky."

"Isn't Sky short for Skylar? I'm sorry. Should I not call you by that name?"

"It's just that my dad was the only one that ever called me by that name. He said that I was his heaven. That's why he named me Skylar."

Mason inhaled a deep breath. "I'm so sorry. I won't call you that anymore."

"It's okay. I always loved when he called me Sky. After he left, well, I hated him for leaving us, but now I don't know what really happened. I don't even know who I am. I'm so confused."

Mason embraced Skylar with everything he had. In his hold, she let go of the pain. Maybe someday soon, she would find out the truth about why her dad left, or if he was still alive. She wanted to stay in Mason's arms as long as she could, and she knew he would hold her until she was ready to let go.

"I'm fine now." She pulled away.

Worriedly, he cupped her wounded hand and untied the knot. "Your wound has healed quickly like the last time." He caressed the area in a slow circular motion.

Seeing dried blood on the fabric Mason was holding, Skylar pulled her hand away from him, afraid he would accidentally touch it. Not knowing if dried blood had any effect, she had to be extra careful. "I'll hold onto it." She shoved it into her back pocket.

Mason smiled warmly. "Are you hungry?"

"Little bit," she fibbed. She was beyond starving, though her hunger pains had subsided.

"So, where would you like to go?"

Skylar giggled.

"What's so funny?"

"Do you always start your sentences with the word 'so'?"

Mason chuckled lightly. "Yes, I do."

Suddenly, he started poking and tickling her. Mason opening up to her, and seeing his humorous side brightened Skylar's spirits. She wanted to squeeze him and get lost in his embrace again, where she felt safe. Her laughter got louder when the sprinklers turned on.

"Let's go before you get all wet and I have to take off my shirt again."

I wouldn't mind seeing you shirtless.

He interweaved his fingers through hers, guiding her to his car, and for the third time, he held her hand as if it had always belonged there.

TWENTY FIVE

DURING THE WHOLE ride to dinner, Skylar's lips curved into a smile. The sun was descending, streaking between the clouds with hues of violet. With the breathtaking view and Mason by her side, she was as giddy as a schoolgirl. Taking in the moment that she was actually on a date with him, she wanted to freeze time.

They drove up to the valet parking at an Italian bistro called Bella Amore. Situated on the other side of town, it was a decent sized restaurant, but clearly cozy and elegant. Looking at Mason and herself, Skylar wondered if they were underdressed. When they entered, the aroma jolted her hunger pangs again, making her think of nothing but food. As if he owned the place, he held Skylar's hand and passed by the hostess.

"May I help you, sir?" the hostess asked, dressed all in black, looking stunning.

Mason stopped in his tracks and looked up.

"Oh, Mr. Grand," the hostess said, and froze with an "oops" look on her face.

The hostess continued. "I didn't recognize you. You're not dressed. I mean you aren't in your usual attire." Her words were cautious, obviously not wanting to offend him.

Mason looked at his clothing. "Sorry. We just got back from camping and we're very hungry," he smiled, shrugging his shoulders.

"Oh, no need to apologize, Mr. Grand. Your table is ready." She gestured her hand for them to proceed.

Skylar assumed they would be sitting at a regular table, but they walked into a private room instead—a table for two nestled in the center. On top of the table, plain white, classy plates and utensils were already arranged. To give it a romantic feel, light from a small candle danced to the instrumental background music.

Leading Skylar to her seat, Mason pulled out her chair. Smiling, she sat and he placed the cream-colored fabric napkin on her lap.

"Thank you," Skylar said, gazing at the oil painting of a vineyard hanging on the wall.

With a nod and a smile, he sat across from her.

"Mr. Grand, are you ready to order?" the waitress asked sweetly.

"Yes. Please give me a second please." He turned to Skylar. "Is there anything particular you would like to eat?"

She was starving beyond words, and so she didn't care. "Anything is fine. I like everything." "We'll start with the house salad and a cup of minestrone soup. For our meal, we'll do family style: seafood linguine, mushroom ravioli, and roasted chicken. And don't forget, two glasses of water."

With a smile, the waitress left. Skylar looked at Mason with wide eyes.

"I'm hungry and I know you are, too. I like girls that eat. And I know you can eat."

Skylar giggled. "Do you own this restaurant?"

"Yes, it's one of many Nick, Everett, Amanda, and I own. We have managers to handle the business so we can kick back and enjoy."

"That's great." Skylar wanted to kick herself for giving him a stupid response. "So your cousin Amanda, too?"

"Amanda is not really our cousin. We rescued her from the vultures a couple of years ago, around the time our moms were taken from us, but we were unable to save her mom. We settled her in a home nearby. We just tell everyone she's our cousin because she suddenly appeared in our lives, not that we have so many friends. She also stays overnight when she feels unsafe by herself. We don't want people talking and spreading rumors, but don't tell her I told you that. She doesn't like people knowing her story."

"I won't say anything. I don't think she likes me anyway."

"That's not true. She sounds and seems tough, but deep inside, underneath that wall of hers, she's really sweet and caring. She has a big heart, but only when she wants to show it."

Ironically, that was how Skylar would have described Mason. "I'm sure she does. So, do you come here often?"

"Not when I want to see you. And only when I want to hear you say the word 'so' before each of your questions."

"Umm...okay." She blushed and shot her eyes to the empty plate in front of her, wondering how many dates he'd brought there.

Soon after, the waitress entered. She placed the salads, the cups of soup, and glasses of water onto the table and left. As carefully and ladylike as possible, Skylar slurped her soup with the spoon.

"How's the soup?"

"It's delicious, thank you." She took another sip. After the starters, the main dishes were served. While they ate, Mason asked her about her parents, about school, and about how she liked working at the diner. The conversation was mostly focused around Skylar, but when she asked questions about him, his answers were short and to the point. He would quickly redirect the questions back to her. Then the conversation became serious.

Mason leaned closer. "I know it's difficult to accept who you are, but you have to face reality. We don't know when these vultures will attack. We don't even know who, or what is after you, or why they want you dead. Until we figure out the reasons, you must never go anywhere alone. It's imperative that you listen to what I'm asking you to do, no matter how much you may disagree. I will be there for you as much as I can, but I need you to help me help you."

"Okay," Skylar nodded, returning to reality. But it was difficult to grasp a reality that was meant to be written in a book, or to be seen on a television show, or in a movie. "I don't go out much. I'm usually with Kayla. We're at home or at work, or out shopping or hanging out with you and Nick."

"Good. Just stay low. Watch your back. Mind who is around you, and never go anywhere by yourself, especially the movie theater restroom."

Though the incident at the theater was anything but funny, they busted out laughing. After a good round of hysteria, it got quiet.

"Eat. Your food will get cold," Mason directed.

After taking several more bites, she realized her plate was just about empty. Dinner being almost over, she felt the need to ask as many questions as possible while he was willing to speak. "Do you miss your mom? Do you think of her often?" After she asked, she realized she'd hit a sore subject. Being around him made her so nervous, asking questions was the only way she could feel at ease.

"Yes, I do. She was the best mom anyone could ask for, but I'm sure you'd say the same thing about your mom," he grinned. Then he grew serious. "I wish I'd known who I was and the capabilities I had sooner. Then, maybe I could have saved her." He looked tormented, and guilt was written all over his face.

"I'm sorry," Skylar said sympathetically. "I don't know what I would do if I ever lost my mom."

"Losing a loved one is torture, especially for those left behind. They say time heals all wounds. It doesn't. It just patches a broken heart. It doesn't get any easier over time. You just learn to live with the pain."

Skylar breathed in a deep sigh. It was exactly how she felt about her dad leaving her. She understood Mason's pain and felt as if his pain were hers. Wanting to reach out and hold him in her arms to comfort him, she stood up.

Alarmed, looking perplexed, Mason stood up, too. "Why are you standing? Are you okay?"

"I...it's just...I mean...," she started to explain, but words failed to escape her mouth.

Guiding her back to her seat, Mason placed his hands on her shoulders until her bottom touched the cushion. "I see how this is affecting you. Let's change the subject." He jiggled, tugged, and pulled a rib from his piece of chicken on the plate. "Here. It's a wishbone. The winner gets to make a wish."

"Really? I've never heard of that before."

"Where have you been? Did you live under a rock?" He chuckled.

"Maybe. Pretty much."

"Here," Mason said and placed it in front of her. "Pull."

Skylar took hold of the other side and did as instructed. Upon pulling, she broke it, but not in her favor. She frowned. "What are you going to wish for?"

"Wait. You didn't give me time." Mason closed his eyes. "Don't stare at me," he muttered with his eyes still closed.

Skylar laughed, thinking how adorable he was. "I wasn't staring."

Mason opened them. "Done. Oh, yes you were."

"Fine." She surrendered. "What did you wish for?"

"I can't tell you. Then it won't come true."

"Alright, but when it comes true, you'll have to let me know."

"Deal," he winked, placing the wishbone back on the plate.

The waitress came back several times asking if they needed anything. Skylar couldn't believe how attentive she was, but then again, she would be too if she were serving her boss. After dinner, they agreed to skip dessert and headed home. The drive home was a different view. The stars were out, dotting the sky with twinkling lights while the moon cast a golden hue. Skylar stared out, thinking how wonderful dinner was, how memorable tonight's date was, and how perfect Mason was.

TWENTY SIX

SKYLAR WOKE UP feeling as if she could float off the ground. Forgetting about what she had been through and forgetting about what danger could be ahead, her mind settled into a world of perfect bliss. Suddenly, she realized she only had one week left until she had to go back home. What would happen to their relationship? She recalled telling Kayla not to fall too deeply for Nick. Perhaps she needed to remind herself too. Her thoughts were broken by a soft knock on the door.

"Come in."

The door swung wide open. "Hey, stranger. Where did you go last night?"

Skylar had forgotten that Nick had compelled her to forget. When Kayla didn't ask questions regarding the paranormal activities that happened after camping, she relaxed her shoulders and continued their conversation. "Mason took me out to dinner."

"And?"

"Nothing happened. He didn't kiss me, if you're wondering."

Kayla plopped herself on the bed. "I didn't ask," she smirked. "Don't want to kiss and tell? That's fine."

"No," Skylar shook her head. "I wanted to. Trust me, I would tell you." Wondering how much of the last couple of days Nick made her forget, she asked about camping. "Would you go camping again?"

"Hell, no. I didn't like it at all. Why do people go camping? It's awful. The ground is hard. There's no bathroom. The only good part was spending the night with Nick. And nothing happened, if you're wondering."

Skylar arched her brow to show she wasn't buying Kayla's story.

"I would tell you. He was actually a perfect gentleman. I was quite surprised. Maybe he isn't such a bad boy type after all. You know, some boys are all talk, but they're actually sweet and sensitive."

"Just be careful," Skylar mumbled, thinking she needed to take her own advice.

Suddenly, Kayla looked serious. "You know what? I just realized we only have one more week together. It means summer is almost over. What do you want to do before you leave?"

"Not much. Let's just hang out."

"Maybe we can double date." Kayla's eyes lifted up with a sly grin. "Anyway, we better get ready for work. Looks like my mom is still sleeping. I'll fix breakfast." Then she was out the door.

"HEY, GIRLS," JACK greeted, standing in the back of the kitchen in his usual spot.

"Hey, Jack," the girls returned.

"Mona has the day off today, so it's just you girls. Oh, and the new girl starts today. She'll be here after lunch for the dinner rush."

"Okay. No problem. Mom already told me about it. I'm supposed to train her," Kayla muttered, heading to the storage room, and then she paused and locked eyes with Skylar. "I'll get your apron and your hair tie."

"Thanks."

The sound of Skylar's text message jingle rang. Thinking it was Kayla fooling around, she clicked to check. Surprisingly, it was Mason.

Hello Echo.

Skylar let out a short chuckle.

Hi.

Are you at work?

Yes.

I won't be there today. We have business to attend to.

Okay.

Remember to stay safe.

I will.

Till then.

The text from him made her stomach flutter with warmth, but she was disappointed that he could not come to see her. That was one less day to spend time together. He knew her visit was almost over. Didn't he care?

"Pretty slow for a Monday, don't you think?" Kayla said.

Skylar jumped from the sound of Kayla's voice. "Uhhh, yeah...slow."

"Okay, what happened?" She tossed the hair tie and the apron at her.

"Nothing. It's Mason. He won't be coming to the restaurant today."

"I just got a text from Nick. He says he won't be coming today either. Business, he said. I wonder what they're up to." Kayla's eyes gleamed with curiosity. "Why don't we do something tonight? Let's go out to dinner."

"Sure," Skylar agreed, tying her hair up and the apron behind her. Then she went behind the cash register and became absolutely still when she turned. Trying not to make it obvious she was staring, she peered from her peripheral vision. Kayla took the dirty blond guy and his friend to the table and came back to stand beside her.

"What's wrong?" Kayla asked, noticing Skylar's tense body.

"Nothing," she said quickly. Skylar had never mentioned them to Kayla. This was a small town. They were likely to bump into each other, she guessed, but there were other times she thought she had seen them, like at Starla, but she wasn't sure. One thing for sure, she didn't like the way they looked at her, or how they seemed to be around unexpectedly.

Her thoughts of them were disrupted when the door chimed and Amanda walked in. Without a smile, she greeted them politely. "Hi. We need to talk."

Not knowing which one she meant, Skylar assumed it was her and followed Amanda out the door. Scooting to the side of the diner, she scanned the perimeter with Amanda.

"What's going on?" Amanda's tone was not friendly.

"What do you mean?"

"Mason texted me and asked me to keep an eye on you. He even gave me your cell number. He said if something happens to you, I'm to blame. He's not this demanding, well not usually."

Skylar fluttered her eyelashes, wondering what she was talking about. She had just spoken to Mason via text.

"Okay, I take that back. He is demanding."

"I think he's afraid the vultures will come back," Skylar spoke with hesitation. How much to say, she didn't know.

"The question is why? Why are the vultures after you? I know you're half-blood, but what is it that you and Mason are not telling me?"

Skylar wasn't good at lying, but for her sake, she had to. Mason had told her not to tell anyone she had evil blood. "We're not hiding anything," she said with conviction. "I need to go back inside."

"Fine, but know that I'm here for business and not pleasure. You're stuck with me until the boss tells me to unleash you."

Skylar rolled her eyes. "Nice words, Amanda."

Amanda turned Skylar around when she headed for the door, gripping tightly around her arm. "Look, I don't know what kind of game you're playing, but I care about Mason. He doesn't care for people easily. Ever since his mom passed away, he's built a wall around himself. He hasn't been the same. He's been afraid to...care." Amanda paused with an "oops" look on her face, as if she had shared a bit too much information about Mason. "I don't understand his sudden interest in you. Whatever it is you're hiding, you should tell me right now."

Skylar had had enough. She wanted to be nice, but she could only take so much. It suddenly dawned on her that Amanda might have a crush on Mason. Wanting so much to say something to sting Amanda back, she bit down on her lip, but anger was rising inside her. She had promised Mason she wouldn't tell Amanda that she knew they weren't cousins, so she stood there, taking the heat, and letting Amanda speak her mind.

When enough was enough, she yanked her arm back and focused her eyes on Amanda's. "Don't touch me. Even if I was hiding something, which I'm not, I wouldn't tell you. Like you said to Everett, be a little human, will ya?" Skylar turned and walked into the diner.

TWENTY SEVEN

AMANDA HAD COME to the diner for four days, making sure Skylar was safe. Their conversation was minimal and so was their eye contact. Amanda came, ate, hung around, went out for a bit, came back, and left when Skylar went home.

There were no visits or texts from Mason, or even from Nick. Thinking Nick had broken up with her, Kayla moped around at the diner and at home. Skylar wanted to tell her that it wasn't the case, but she had no way to explain how she knew. Besides, she couldn't help sulking too. Between the restless nights and worrying about Nick and Mason, she hardly slept at all. It was the first time Skylar and Kayla had stayed home.

Everett and Amanda went back to the Oracle, searching for Nick and Mason since there was no word from either of them. Though they weren't sure, they guessed the guys went there to ask more questions. Amanda promised to keep Skylar informed, but now there was no word from her either.

Skylar had already said her goodbyes to Mona, Jack, and Auntie Kelly on her last day of work. She promised to visit when she had the chance. Thrilled by her first real job, Skylar wanted to come back and work again during her summers. It was definitely more than enough to pay for gas.

Saying goodbye to Kayla was difficult this time around. Leaving her cousin was bad enough, but leaving her broken hearted was tormenting. She had no choice, since she would start the local university soon and needed to attend orientation.

She was frightfully worried for Mason and Nick, but she couldn't wait to see her mom. Calling and texting to let her know she was fine was one thing, but being apart from her mom for the past three weeks was long enough, though she had been gone this long every summer. Knowing her mom was home alone, the guilt always consumed her, but now it wasn't quite as bad, knowing she had her fiancé to keep her company.

The drive back home was lonely and long, since Skylar's mind was occupied with thoughts of Nick and Mason. If they did go back to the Oracle, wouldn't they have been back by now? What if the Oracle had harmed them?

Being that it was Saturday, Skylar's mom was home waiting for her arrival. After the hugs and kisses, they chatted about what Skylar did at Kayla's house. Of course, Skylar left out a lot of the details. She told her mom that it was just as much fun as the other times. Skylar also asked tons of questions regarding her mom and dad's family tree and their ancestors. Disappointed, she didn't find the answer she was looking for. Either all was hopeless, or her mom was not telling her the truth.

The next day, Skylar went to orientation. A week later, she was living at the dorm. Missing her cousin and worried about how she was doing without a word from Nick, she texted her as soon as she got the chance.

How's college?

Fine. How about yours?

Good. You doin' ok?

Trying to get over Nick. Where could he be?

Maybe on a business trip.

Sure. I'll keep thinking that.

Some guys are not good at calling or texting when they're away.

Don't be nice. He dumped me just like you said he would.

He didn't dump you. Just give him a chance.

Skylar couldn't believe what she was saying. She didn't even know what was really going on. This conversation got her thinking. Maybe Mason had left her too. He knew her blood was evil. What if he stopped caring and just took off?

Have you heard from Mason? You can tell me the truth.

No.

I guess we were just a summer fling for them. Heavy sigh. He told me he was bad. I should have heeded his warning.

Me, too.

Talk to you soon. Gotta go.

Okay. Miss you.

Miss you, too! Hugs!

Hugs back!

The university housing looked more like apartments. Skylar shared a two-bedroom residence with a roommate. It had the necessary amenities—a kitchen, dining area, and a living room. It was small, but just enough for two people. Since almost everything was paid for through her scholarship, there was no reason to complain. She was grateful.

Skylar's roommate Emily was a biology major. She was tall, blonde, and had the fairest complexion. It had already been a week, but Emily was hardly around, and when she was, her boyfriend was always with her.

Seeing them together, all cozy, reminded her of Mason, and her heart stung. Though she tried to move on and forget about him, it was difficult. Skylar couldn't believe how much he affected her emotionally. They hadn't even kissed, and yet he'd stolen her heart in ways she'd never thought possible. They weren't really seeing each other. They'd only had one date.

On her way to literature class, the hairs on her arm pricked up. Sensing someone following her, she looked around carefully, but there were many students on campus. Who would she be looking for? Surely, no vultures would appear in the daylight, smack in the middle of a crowd. If they did appear in human form, she guessed they wouldn't attack in front of all these people, at least she hoped not.

Opening the glass double doors, she entered the classroom with hesitation. Besides her roommate, she didn't know anyone else on campus, and she wasn't even in any classes with her. Since almost all the seats were taken, she headed toward the back.

After settling in, she took out her pen and a notebook. As the professor spoke, she was heavily engrossed in the lecture, taking notes as fast as her fingers allowed. Busy looking at the whiteboard, she was unaware the guy sitting next to her had placed an envelope with her name on it on her desk. Looking down to write again, she was surprised to see it.

Skylar questioned the guy sitting next to her about it. He answered by pointing to the person next to him, who in turn pointed to the person next to her. Since there was no end to who had originally passed the note, she quickly looked around, hoping someone would wave to let her know who it was from, but nothing.

Debating whether to open it now or after class, she couldn't hold back her curiosity any longer, so she opened it.

I know what you are. Meet me at the mountains. The directions are on the back of this note. Be there at 10 p.m. If you don't come, you'll never see Mason again.

At first, she was shaken beyond words, trying to process what she'd read. Was someone playing a prank on her? With Mason being gone so long and not a phone call or text from him, it didn't seem like a joke. Who would present such a threat? A vulture? They couldn't speak, at least not the ones that had attacked her. Surprisingly, she was calm, except she felt like she'd swallowed acid, and her blood pressure shot up so fast, she felt hot all over. Whether this was a trick or not, she had to go. There was no choice.

TWENTY EIGHT

A S MUCH AS Skylar didn't want to go, she needed to be sure Mason was safe. She didn't want him to be in any danger, yet a small part of her hoped that the reason he hadn't contacted her was because he couldn't. When the lecture was over, she didn't bother to attend her other classes. Giving herself a head start, not wanting to be late—especially since she didn't know how to get there besides the directions that she'd been given—she left early.

Skylar couldn't drive fast enough. Driving on the highway wasn't so bad when there were other cars around, but the road got utterly dark when she got closer to the mountains. She hated driving when she couldn't see where she was going, and the winding roads weren't helping the situation. Feeling carsick, she rolled the window down just enough to allow the cool breeze to soothe her.

The directions she was given were confusing. She had to read them several times, and even then, she wasn't sure she was going the right way. The closer she got to her destination, the faster her pulse raced, and the anticipation of what waited for her was driving her insane.

Normally, looking at the stars and the moon brought her comfort, but tonight they had an eerie glow. As darkness engulfed her entirely, hers was the only car on the road. That alone frightened the living daylights out of her, making her feel like she was the only living soul in the world. Creeping along, the only thing she saw in front of her was the dirt road, and the only light was the high beams from her car.

Her mind was reeling with horrible imaginings. Any minute now, something ghastly would pop out and scare her. Someone that looked like a zombie would bang on the car window. That was what would happen in scary movies, and that was what this situation felt like. Skylar's muscles were so tense, she didn't realize she was gripping tightly to the steering wheel and her knuckles were white as her hands cramped up.

Desperately wanting to turn back and go home, she thought about Mason. How did she know the person who wrote the note wasn't a serial killer, luring her to the mountains where no one could rescue her? Even knowing the danger, she had no choice if it meant getting answers to where Mason and Nick had been all this time. Perhaps Everett and Amanda were with them, since she hadn't heard a peep from them either. But then again, would Amanda contact her just to tell her Mason was safe? She didn't know.

What if they were really in danger and they needed her? What could she do? They were the ones with powers. Now this pathetic rescue mission seemed hopeless. Hoping she'd followed the directions correctly, she slowed the car and turned left, and found that she was still driving on an unpaved road. Soon after, she saw a dim light, but that was all. Unable to tell if it was a house or a cabin due to extreme darkness, she parked as close to the light as possible.

The light came from a cave entrance, but not the same place she had gone before with Mason. After scanning the perimeter, knowing there wasn't much to see, she got out quickly and ran to the light. Surprisingly, there was a lantern hung on a branch of the tree adjacent to the entrance. Skylar took it down and hesitantly walked forward. The cool draft that suddenly greeted her gave her the shivers. Even wearing long sleeves didn't protect her from the sharp coldness that brushed against the fabric of her clothes. Mist floated in the air and spotted her with damp droplets.

The further she walked, the brighter the cave became, and the stench of rotten soil disappeared. Moving from one world to the next, she saw she was standing on Olympus, where she had been before. Thinking the Oracle had her hand in this, Skylar raced to the tree. Just before she reached it, a body flashed before her, forcing her to jump back and causing her to drop the lantern, which shattered. Thank goodness, she had already turned the lamp off, or it would have caused a fire.

"You've come as instructed, but I didn't tell you to come here," she hissed. "Oh, dear, sorry about the lantern."

Shocked to see someone new, Skylar stood there unable to look away, mesmerized by the woman's beauty. Her red, wavy hair flowed to her waist, accentuating her porcelain skin. She wore all black clothes with black boots. On her belt was a small dagger. With legs spread apart, hands on her hips, she was guarding the tree with her life. Why?

"Who are you and what do you want?" Skylar huffed. While her fist tightly pressed into a ball, anger and fear boiled inside her.

"You really don't know, do you?" The stranger circled Skylar, examining her from head to toe. "You can call me Alena. You don't look like how I've imagined you would look at all. Do you know how difficult it was to track you down?"

"I don't know what you're talking about and I don't care. Where are Mason and Nick? What have you done with them?" Skylar's tone was sassy and demanding. Hiding her trepidation, she spoke loudly and forcibly.

Alena laughed, sinisterly. "You thought it was going to be that easy? Just show up and take them home with you? It's been several weeks since you've heard from Mason, right? That's how long it took me to find you, especially since they wouldn't cooperate. After I found his cell phone, which he tried to break without me knowing, well the rest is history. And now you're here. It's a good thing you care about him, or else this plan wouldn't have worked."

"You've held them prisoner that long?" Skylar glared at Alena.

"Relax. I gave them some food...enough."

"What do you want from me? I have nothing to give you."

"Oh, but that is where you are wrong. Don't you want to see your friends, or shall we talk all day?" she asked with an evil smirk, turning her back on Skylar.

Alena waved her hand in a circular motion and mumbled a few words. Mason, Nick, Everett, and Amanda suddenly appeared in front of her, as if a layer of clouds evaporated, allowing a clear view. She had held them prisoner behind some kind of shield, and whatever it was, it was still there. They were all sitting closely together on one huge boulder. When they saw Skylar, their eyes lit up with hope, except for Mason's.

"Mason," Skylar called hesitantly and headed toward them cautiously. She kept one eye on Alena and the other eye on her friends, wondering why Mason didn't look happy to see her. Surprisingly, the Oracle stepped in front of her, making her halt. She had been hiding behind the tree so Skylar hadn't noticed her until now. Now she knew the reason why Alena was protecting the tree when she first got there.

"I told you to kill her," the Oracle said with anger in her tone, pointing her cane at Skylar. "Now she will doom us all."

Clenching his jaw, Mason's fists were tightly gripped as he shuddered in anger. He pounded the shield with his fist. "Don't touch her or I'll kill you myself." The palm of his hand fizzled with electrical silver light, sparkling like lightning, but it was dim. It crackled for a few seconds before the sparks went dead.

Recalling Mason's words, Skylar remembered that their powers were limited there. It was no wonder he couldn't use them to escape. Stuck there, feeling helpless, he never gave Alena the information she wanted, just so he could keep Skylar safe. She was grateful and touched that he thought of her over his family's safety.

The Oracle set her eyes on Mason, then to Skylar, and wobbled backward in a cowardly manner.

"Now, now," Alena mocked. "You already know your powers are limited here. It's one of the reasons why I tricked you to come. At Olympus, we are on equal ground. You can thank Zeus. He was always afraid someone would try to overthrow him. How smart he was. But too bad for his descendants."

"What do you mean 'she will doom us all'?" Everett demanded to know, now standing beside Mason.

"So it really wasn't that you were protecting her out of some sick obligation," Alena said. "You really didn't know. Mason kept this secret from all of you. He has chosen her over his own kind. Pity, pity, pity. Doesn't matter, you're all dead after I'm done with you."

Everett gripped Mason by his shirt. "I knew it. What are you hiding? We've been locked up here because of her? You've chosen a stranger over your own family?"

Mason didn't even fight back. He just let Everett vent his feelings.

"Stop it!" Amanda yelled. "Can't you see what she's doing? She's making us go against each other. Let Mason go."

Nick looked like he was ready to take action if Everett's anger grew, but he backed down when Everett released Mason with a shove.

"What do you want?" Mason asked Alena. "Why go all this trouble to bring Skylar here? We at least deserve an answer if you're going to kill us."

"Oh, I'm not going to kill you. I'm going to enjoy watching Skylar kill you."

Skylar flashed her eyes on Alena, then to her friends. She backed away, shaking her head. Never would she ever hurt them. She had to run, but where?

"Face your destiny, my cousin. We've been waiting for you to take revenge upon the gods' children." Alena smiled cunningly.

"I don't know who you are, and I'm not your cousin. I'll never do it." Skylar ran. From the corner of her eyes, she saw Mason slam into the invisible shield, trying to break through. When that didn't work, he was cursing, trying to shoot lighting from his hands, but to no avail. His beautiful eyes sparked silver, but that too, quickly faded. Hopelessly, he leaned against the shield along with the rest of his family, watching Skylar run for her life.

Breathing heavily, Skylar hid behind the statue of Poseidon, contemplating her next move.

"Skylar, I just need a little bit of your blood, and then you'll be free to go."

"Why do you need my blood?" Skylar yelled, running next to the statue of Hera, trying to keep track of Alena by the sound of her voice.

"Oh, don't play dumb."

Skylar turned to her right, but before she could go to the next statue, Alena was right in front of her.

"I know how to play dumb, too."

Stunned by her presence, Skylar screamed and ran. She was almost positive she knew where Alena was positioned when she heard her voice, but she guessed she'd underestimated her speed.

"I'm tired of playing games." Alena yanked Skylar's hair and dragged her in front of her friends. "Let me tell you a story about how this war began. Hades had predicted his brothers would massively reproduce to preserve their kind, while he remained in Hell to rot. Intelligent and cunning as he was, he jumped at the game. He knew that one day they would die as religion progressed, so Medusa and Hades created their own blood line, just before, you know, she got her head chopped off. I'm one of their descendants, and so is Skylar."

Glancing at their shocked expressions, she continued with a smirk. "That's right. Medusa and Hades produced offspring, creating evil blood, long before Zeus and Poseidon started theirs, and you know what's special about Skylar? Why she should be feared? When she kills a being, its special power transfers to her. Can you imagine if she was vengeful and decided to kill just to suck up your powers? There are others like her out there...somewhere. They may not even know what they are, just like Skylar. She just happened to be the first one I found."

Blood drained out of Skylar. Her pale face expressed no emotions. Having some kind of evil blood was bad enough, but knowing she was one of the descendants of Hades and Medusa was unbearable. Those two were the most hated of their kind. Now she understood how she was able to heal so fast. Mason had told her Remus was a fast healer. When she killed him, unknowingly, she swallowed his blood and took his power of healing. Remus even told her that when he attacked her.

"That's right," she continued. "Skylar has their blood. You know what that means, don't ya? One droplet of her blood on your skin, or the skin of any of the gods' children, will turn them into stone."

"I told you to kill her," the Oracle shouted again. "Just kill her."

"Shut up, you old hag," Everett yelled. "I'm getting really tired of you. You're supposed to be all knowing. Why didn't you know any of this?"

"It doesn't work that way. There is only one of me. My other two sisters are dead. We were all knowing and strong once, when we worked together as a team." The Oracle sheepishly, sadly backed away.

"Why don't you kill them yourself? Don't you have the same blood?" Skylar asked, testing her.

"I can't." She looked embarrassed at first, but then changed her expression to anger. "We do have the same blood, except mine is different. Over time, depending on the family line, our abilities and the potency of the blood changes. However, your family bloodline is strong. That means that in every generation in your family line, one of the parents had the HM blood—Hades-Medusa blood."

"Why do you want to kill them? They haven't done anything to you."

"It was my mother's wish. She was the same as me, but one of the gods' children killed her."

"We didn't do anything. We didn't kill anyone," Amanda shouted. "We keep to ourselves. We don't want any trouble. Let us go. We won't hurt you."

"I know you can't hurt me, Amanda, just like Everett. But Nick and Mason, on the other hand, can. Their blood is stronger."

"Tell her, Nick. Tell her, Mason. Tell her you won't hurt her," Amanda pleaded desperately.

"I won't hurt you," Nick started to say. "I'll just annihilate your face and crush your body beyond anything you can imagine. Zap you with my volts, fry you from head to toe, and feed you to your ugly pets."

Alena hissed like an untamed wild animal and jerked back, projecting eyes of evil. "After I kill all of you, I'm going to kill the others. There are more of you out there, hiding. We're sending the vultures after them until every one of you is dead."

"So you are the one who sent the vultures?" Amanda blared with fury in her eyes.

Alena laughed aloud. "You think I sent them? You have no idea. You hide yourselves in a little town, oblivious to the war around you. Now I've enlightened you. I take my orders from someone else. You really need to open your eyes."

Alena was distracted by the conversation. Too busy being proud to have the upper hand, she didn't realize Skylar was eyeing her dagger. Swiftly, Skylar twisted her body as pain jolted from the roots of her hair. She positioned herself in front of Alena and snatched the dagger. Skylar nicked Alena across the arm just before Alena gripped her wrist, causing Skylar to drop the dagger. Blood trickled down Alena's wounded arm as she reached to retrieve it.

"Too bad I can't kill you with my blood," Alena sneered.

Skylar didn't know where her courage came from, but she could feel the adrenaline pumping through her veins. All that was on her mind was that she needed to help her friends, and at this point, she was their only hope. Her strength and speed were not comparable to Alena's, but it didn't matter because she knew if there was a will, there was a way.

Tangoing back and forth, Alena banged Skylar into the tree. Pain rang in her head, vibrating to the rest of her body, making her see double. She could see Mason's worried face, and somehow that gave her strength. Remembering a move from a self-defense class, she kneed Alena in the stomach. Alena curled inward as she cursed and lost her grip. Without anything to defend herself with, Skylar ran, but Alena was faster.

"Where do you think you're going?" Alena placed herself in front of Skylar, making her gasp sharply. "You think you can outrun me?"

"You know what your problem is?" Skylar retorted. "You talk too much." Just the way she had been taught, Skylar swiped her right leg across the ground to knock Alena down, but it didn't happen. Alena jumped and let Skylar have it with her boot, contacting her face. Skylar flew back and whacked her body against the tree. Blood trickled down her nose and the left side of her temple, dotting some of it on her shirt.

"How convenient. All I wanted was a few drops of your blood. We didn't have to go through all this trouble." Alena leaned down to Skylar, who looked unconscious. With her dagger, Alena cautiously swiped blood from her temple. "There. That is all I need to eliminate your friends. I said you would be the one to kill them."

Pain shot through Skylar's nose, her head, and down to her feet. Her skull felt like it was split into two. Drained and out of it, she sat still and closed her eyes. It was all she could do at that moment. Her thoughts were reeling, trying to figure out what to do and how to save her friends.

With her eyes barely open, Skylar watched, anticipating Alena's next move. While Alena's back was to her, Skylar attacked her from behind, clasping her arm round Alena's neck.

"Release the barrier. You do know what happens when you touch my blood, don't you? Would you like to find out?" Though she had stopped bleeding and had wiped the blood away as much as she could, Alena didn't know that. As far as she knew, Skylar was still bleeding, and a drop of her blood would kill Alena.

"Okay, I'll do it," Alena said through gritted teeth. "But you'll have to ask the Oracle. This was her idea."

All eyes flashed to the Oracle, who was now close to the tree, her home. The Oracle extended her cane in defense, mumbled a few words, releasing the shield, and vanished with a flash.

Skylar was unaware her grip on Alena had loosened. Alena took that moment of weakness, jabbed Skylar in the gut with her elbow, and flipped her over. "Your strength is no match for me. You're so lucky I was told to keep you alive." Then she fled.

TWENTY NINE

THE BARRIER HAD been broken. Mason rushed to Skylar, helping her up, careful not to touch a drop of her blood. As expected, her wounds had already started to heal.

Standing before Mason's family, Skylar confessed the events of the dreadful night when Remus had died. After she told her side of the story, Everett and Amanda seemed forgiving, but they weren't any more welcoming than before. They kept their distance from her as if she had the plague. She didn't blame them though. One touch of her blood could kill them. The only reason they even tolerated her was for Mason's sake. Thankfully, Nick was the same as always—carefree and friendly.

From what Skylar could recall, there was never a real brotherly bond or affection toward Remus. Regardless, living with Remus and knowing he was their half-brother must have meant something. Though she knew it wasn't her fault, she couldn't help the feeling of guilt consuming her soul, and she was unable to look them in the eye when she spoke. She had taken a life—their brother's life. Though it was an accident and Remus did wrong by her, she could never forgive herself.

From what they gathered from Skylar's story, Remus died from swallowing Skylar's blood, not by contacting it, but Alena thought otherwise. From Skylar's account of the events and from the information relayed by Alena—if she was telling the truth—they concluded that swallowing Remus's blood had caused her to absorb his power of healing. It triggered her body to be more god-like so she was able to heal faster, unlike before; however, that was all. She didn't move like them or have their strength and speed. The biggest question remaining was how the Oracle was involved. Unable to find her, they decided to head back home.

Finding their way back to the campsite was not a problem, but they were faced with how to get back down from the mountain, until Skylar reminded them, she had a car. She just had to remember where she had parked it. Though there was light on Olympus, making it look like it was daytime, it was still the middle of the night in the real world.

Without a flashlight, it was difficult to see. Suddenly light appeared. Nick and Mason's bodies glowed, making them appear as if they were the center of the sun, but not as bright. Awestruck, Skylar dropped her jaw. It was the first time she had witnessed such a phenomenon. Mesmerized by this wonder, she tried hard not to stare, and looked elsewhere.

"Oh, God. Must you shine so brightly, Rudolph?" Everett mocked, covering his eyes with his hands from the intensity of the light.

"Are you color blind? Do you see red on my nose?" Nick snorted.

"I'll give you a red nose." Everett wrapped his arm around Nick's neck and ruffled his hair. Everett jumped a few feet when sparkling lights zapped out of Nick's fingers, shocking him on purpose.

"Show off," Everett murmured under his breath, rubbing his arm.

"Only when we don't have a flashlight," Mason said to Skylar, ignoring Everett and Nick.

"I see why," she said, smiling. "Are you as hot as you look?" She rethought her question, blushing. "I meant...."

Mason chuckled. "Awesomely hot." He winked. "I know what you meant."

Nick jumped in the conversation. "I'm the hot one. Hotter than Mace."

"Walking flashlights don't talk," Amanda teased. "You should get one, Skylar. You'll never get lost. It follows you wherever you go."

"Shut up," Nick laughed. "You're just jealous."

"What? That I'm not a torch like you?"

"No, that you can't light up someone's life like I can."

"Ouch." Mason nudged Nick. "Little harsh there."

Amanda scoffed. "Shut up, both of you, and find Skylar's car."

Skylar remembered she had placed Alena's instructions in the back pocket of her jeans. "Here." She handed a piece of paper to Mason, and backtracking, they soon found her car. Mason offered to drive, and two hours later, they were at Nick's house.

Instead of driving back to her college dorm in the middle of the night, Mason convinced Skylar to spend the night and head back to school in the morning. Exhausted, she agreed, knowing she couldn't make the trip in her condition, and her body ached from fist fighting with Alena. She was glad the self-defense courses had come in handy. It was too bad she couldn't tell her mom about it.

Mason excused himself from his room so Skylar could take a shower. He placed a pair of sweat pants and a T-shirt on his bed for her to change into, while he took her clothes to the laundry room to be washed.

Standing under the hot running water, she wished she could wash away her poisoned blood too. Now that she could breathe easy again, the relief of everyone making it out of there alive poured through her. She cried so hard, she gasped to take in air. Her tears fell, blending with the water droplets. Through her sobbing, she let out all her worries, frustrations, and the one question she knew had no answer...why? Why did it have to be her?

After she finished, she dried herself off, put on Mason's clothes, and headed for the king size bed.

Looking around the room, bad memories of Remus crashed through, and when she heard the door creak open, she gasped. Seeing Mason, her nerves quickly calmed.

"Your clothes are drying. I'll get them for you in the morning," Mason said.

"Thank you."

"You should go to bed. Do you have early morning classes?"

"No. I have one in the late afternoon."

"Okay, that's good. You can sleep on the right side. I'll sleep on the left. It's a king size bed, so I'm sure we can both fit."

"Of course. Thank you."

Mason moved closer, making Skylar's heart flutter euphorically. The way he came toward her, with such an alluring look, overpowered her desire and emotions. While stroking her hair, Mason spoke softly. "We should be thanking you. You came for us. You came for me. Why?"

"Because...because I know you would do the same for me," Skylar expressed, closing her eyes, enjoying Mason's caresses. What she wanted to say was that she cared for him, and she needed to know he was safe. "You were gone so long. At first, I thought you...I mean I couldn't just wait around. I had to make sure you were...I mean, everybody was safe."

"Let me see your wounds."

Skylar peered up and turned her head slightly so he could examine her. Unsure if it was purposely done, his touch was pleasant, making her feel excited and sleepy at the same time. She didn't know how long she could control herself. Any minute now her knees would buckle.

"They've healed nicely. You can't tell."

Under normal circumstances, she would probably still be bleeding or have a big gash. Instead, her cut had healed as if she'd never had one. "The pain was already gone when we were almost out of Olympus." The pain was gone when you touched me, she wanted to say, but couldn't.

"You were pretty awesome back there. Where did you learn to fight like that?"

"My mom made me take a self-defense class. You know, just in case."

"I better remember not to piss you off."

Skylar giggled shyly, but then became serious. "This isn't over, is it?"

"I think it is for now, but she'll be back. We'll have to keep our guard up. At least we know who the vultures get their orders from. When we see them, we'll know she's around. No more talking. You should go to bed."

After tucking in, Skylar scooted to the edge of her side of the bed. Lying next to Mason was not her idea of comforting sleep. Being next to him made her stomach flutter with nervousness and happiness. Feeling restless, she curled her legs in, then out, and then back in. Her arms did the same. She wanted to turn her body to him to see if he was asleep, but she couldn't.

"Sky. Stop moving and go to sleep," Mason said. He sounded groggy.

Skylar froze. She was trying not to disturb him, but the questions she had were eating at her.

"You can ask me one question," he said, as if he knew she was itching to ask.

"I can ask you one question?"

"Yes, Echo."

Skylar giggled to herself. Though she claimed she didn't liked being called that, it had become their inside joke. It was a special nickname, and she didn't mind it so much. Recalling his tattoo, she was dying to ask him the significance of it. "Why do you have the lightning tattoo on your arm?" She heard him sigh softly, seeming to hesitate before he answered.

"It's very personal, but I'll tell you," he mumbled softly. "I got that tattoo shortly after my mom passed away. In a way, it helped me to accept who I am, and the powers I possessed, though I didn't have a choice. It is a reminder for me to use it wisely, responsibly, and to protect others who can't defend themselves against evil. You know, something corny like 'with great power comes great responsibility', like how they said it in the *Spiderman* movie."

Wow! She did not expect that at all. How beautiful his words were. How beautiful he was. Knowing it was personal and knowing he had shared it with her, she was simply stunned, but she could only think of one lame word to say, "Oh." Then she remembered how it radiated when he used his powers. "Your tattoo glowed when you used your powers. I saw it light up."

"I always glow," he said matter-of-factly with a note of arrogance in his tone, not wanting to answer the question.

She would have agreed, though she wasn't quite sure what he meant, but she didn't want to fatten his ego even more, so she said nothing. Then she changed the subject, hoping he would answer more of her questions before he decided not to. "Are you afraid of me?"

"If I was, do you think you would be in my bed right now?"

Skylar thought about what Mason said and realized she'd asked a stupid question. "Do you like me? I mean...could you like me as a friend, with the dark side and all?"

"I said only one question. That was three, but I'll answer. Yes."

"Do you think I'm evil?"

"No. Now you've asked four. No more." He exhaled an irritated sigh. "Sky, turn around."

When Skylar turned, Mason was inches away. With his elbow on the pillow, his fist under his chin holding up his head, he looked down at her. Trying not to look into his eyes, she focused on his lips instead—not a good idea.

"What do I have to do or say to convince you that I don't think you're evil?"

"I...." Skylar couldn't speak, let alone concentrate on her thoughts. He was so close that if she raised her head just an inch, his lips would be on hers. She couldn't stop the heat tingling throughout her body. She wanted to be mad at him so she wouldn't have these feelings, and it didn't take long. He started acting rude again.

"Next time, don't come to my rescue. It could've all gone wrong. You could've gotten yourself killed."

The 'I want you' tingles shot away as he spoke. "What do you mean? You would rather I had ignored the note I got and just let bad things happen to you?"

"Yes. You should care about your own life and not mine. If anything happened to you...."

With both of her hands on his chest pressing lightly, Skylar was just about to push him away when she realized he'd said something sweet—'If anything happened to you'—but he never finished. "You would what?"

"Why did you come?" he continued.

"Because...because...." Smoothly, as if her hands had a mind of their own, they ran up his muscular chest, over his shoulders, and down to the curve of his biceps. She couldn't believe what she was doing.

Lost in Skylar's touch, he blinked when she stopped and snapped out of his daze. "Because you care? Well, you shouldn't." Suddenly, his soft tone sharpened. His eyes fluttered with pain, sorrow, and anger under his eyelashes. "You shouldn't care. I'm no good for you. I won't return the feeling." He snatched her hands, pinned them against the pillow with both hands on either side, and fixed his eyes on hers sternly. "No matter what you do, I won't care. My walls are too thick, sealed up tight. No one can break them. Not Nick, not Everett, not Amanda, and certainly not you. So don't waste your time. I'm broken, and you can't fix broken people."

Skylar was extremely hurt by his words, but his actions and his eyes told her otherwise. She knew at that moment that there was hope. Amanda had accidentally told her Mason felt guilty for his mother's death. Afterwards, he wasn't the same. Now she understood why he was always so protective. Now she understood when he got mad at her for coming to his rescue. Perhaps he does care, but he won't admit it. Maybe with time and patience, she could help him heal. He could be free of his guilt and hurt.

"To answer your question, you're not evil," he continued. "I knew that the moment I saw you." Then his eyes became soft. "There is something sweet and innocent about you. Perhaps that can be part of evil, who knows? But you can't be." Mason's tone trailed off when he brushed his face into her hair. "You're not evil, Sky. You smell sweet and your cheeks are soft. Evil doesn't feel good like you."

Skylar thought she was having a heart attack. No guy had ever made her heart beat so fast. No other guy had ever made her feel that way before, not even her ex-boyfriend. Then she realized what she felt for her ex was nothing in comparison to how she felt about Mason.

Slowly, Mason inched his way closer and closer to her lips. She couldn't believe Mason was finally going to kiss her. Her whole body ignited with heat and want. When his lips touched hers, instinctively, she pressed both hands on his chest. "Stop." Remembering Remus, she got really scared and became protective. "What if something bad happens to you?" She'd ruined the moment, but she didn't care. His life was more important than a kiss. Though she knew it was swallowing her blood that had killed Remus, she couldn't take the risk.

"How many times must I tell you? I guess I'm going to have to show you." Without warning, he dove in and planted his lips on hers. His kiss was soft and perfect, and much more than she imagined it would be. Though it wasn't very long, it left Skylar wanting more, sinking deeper into the mattress, swallowed up in his succulent kiss.

When he pulled away, he fell on his side of the bed. With both of his hands on his neck, he made gagging sounds as if he was choking.

Skylar was horrified. "Mason? Mason!" she called, sitting up, placing her hands on his arms.

Suddenly he stopped and pulled her in. Her legs swung over his hips and her body pressed to his chest as he embraced her tightly. "Just kidding. I was joking. See? I'm fine." It was his way of apologizing for being a prick.

"Ugh...jerk!" Skylar tried to pull away, but she couldn't budge from his hold. She was mad, but she couldn't stop giggling from his sense of humor. For a second, she remained still, enjoying her position, enjoying this tender moment as they exchanged an undeniably passionate gaze. In his arms, she felt comfort. In his arms, she was just a normal girl being held by a normal guy.

"You got me," Skylar said when Mason released her.

"Now, go to sleep. It's almost time to get up." Mason became distant again, turning his back on her.

With her eyes on his back, she wanted to reach out and touch him, wanting to help him forget his pain.

"Don't stare at me," he mumbled.

"I'm not staring," Skylar said, recalling when he said these words the last time, making her laugh.

"Oh, yes you are," he chuckled lightly. "I can feel your stare."

Skylar giggled and shook her head. "Fine, you got me again." She'd made a small dent in *his* wall tonight, and slowly she would try her best to chip it away. Holding onto their first kiss, not knowing if it meant something to him or not, she fell asleep peacefully.

THIRTY

WHEN SKYLAR OPENED her eyes, she knew it was late. She turned to Mason, but he was already out of bed, out of sight. There was a note on his pillow:

Sky,
Lunch on the table. Taking care of business. Manager out sick at Bella Amore.
Till then,
Mason

It was already lunchtime? Skylar got out of bed and saw the clothes Mason had washed and dried for her. He was so thoughtful that way. She changed, ate, called home to her mom, got into her car and headed back to her dorm.

On her way, she got a text from Kayla. She and Nick had made up and things were back to normal. Kayla had decided to attend the local state college. She commuted from home and continued to help her mom at the diner. Though they texted often, with school schedules and Kayla working, it was difficult at times.

A WEEK HAD passed. Disappointingly, Skylar had not heard from Mason, not even a text or a phone call. Wanting to take a break from studying, she texted Kayla.

Hey, what you doing?

Trying to study.

Miss you.

Miss you, too. Hope you can visit soon.

I will. Things are crazy. I have an exam tomorrow.

Have you seen Mason lately?

No. It's been a week. I'm not counting on it.

I'm sorry.

No worries. Till then.

Skylar couldn't believe she'd used Mason's words, "till then." Maybe his wall *was* too thick. Maybe it was hopeless. Not wanting to think of him, she poured herself into her studies. After an hour, she picked up her phone, hoping she'd missed a text or had a missed called from him—nothing. She thought about calling, but lost her nerve. Placing the phone back down on the table, she dove right back into her studies. Then a few minutes later, she was startled by the vibrating phone and picked it up. She was so excited to see it was a text from Mason she could hardly contain herself.

Hi, Echo

With a beaming smile, Skylar texted back.

Hi

What are you doing?

Studying

Good. You're home. Are you alone?

No. Roommate.

Remember, stay around humans. Don't go anywhere by yourself, and always bring your

phone. *If you don't return my text then I'll know something is wrong.*

Okay. Stay near humans and not aliens.

Haha. You made me laugh.

Is it even possible to get a laugh from you? Just kidding.

Haha. I miss that.

Miss what?

Thinking of you. Till then.

Miss what?

He didn't answer and Skylar knew he'd done that on purpose. After the text, it was difficult to study again, especially when he texted he was thinking of her. A part of her felt guilty. She'd lied to Mason about her roommate being home. Since there had been no signs of vultures or other strange occurrences, she figured things were back to normal.

Not wanting to worry him, she didn't want to tell him the truth. Though she thought about texting him back and letting him know she was alone, hoping he would spend time with her, she knew better. He was busy with work and she didn't want to bother him.

Her phone vibrated again. Surprisingly, it was her roommate. Emily had never texted her before, but she had given Emily her cell number.

I need help. I'm at the bio lab. Can you come now?

Room #

Biology building, first floor, room 110

I'm coming.

No questions asked, Skylar grabbed a sweater, placed her cell phone in her pocket with her keys, and walked out onto campus grounds. It was just after eight. The night sky was merciless and the cold breeze stung her face. She walked quickly, passing the dimly lit parking lot. Seeing a couple making out in a car, she looked away, but somehow it gave her comfort that humans were around.

Farther along, the campus got darker since there weren't many late night classes. Hardly ever going out this late, she hadn't realized how fast fall had crept in. Crossing her arms, she hugged herself closer for warmth. When she passed by the small café, she knew she was almost there.

The campus was huge, but during the day, it didn't seem so big. Perhaps it was the anxiety building in her. The darkness made the beautiful campus look gloomy, and she was almost positive she saw two pairs of small yellow lights following her as if they were watching her every move.

Finally, the biology building was in her sight. She just needed to cross a path and she was home free, but the path was so dreadfully dark, she didn't know if she could do it.

Out of the blue, Skylar jolted straight up. With a huff, she took out her cell phone, and turned off the vibration mode, but kept it on silent. It was another text from Emily.

Where are you?

I'm almost there.

Hurry!

What's so urgent?

There was no response.

Having a sudden idea, Skylar used her phone to shine a light along the path. It wasn't as dark anymore. In no time, she was through the double glass doors. Being inside, the cold breeze disappeared, and with plenty of light, she was able to put her cell phone in her back pocket.

The floor squeaked under her feet from her sneakers, making contact with the shining laminate floor, and for several feet, that was all she heard. Looking at the door numbers, she knew she was almost there. Room 107, 108, 109. Finally, room 110.

Skylar pulled the door open, expecting to see a room full of students wearing white lab coats and experimenting with test tubes, or hovering over microscopes, but that wasn't the case. In fact, Emily was the only student there. She stood all the way in the back, behind a lab counter, looking terrified. Trembling, she continued to stand there staring at Skylar, shaking her head as if to tell her something. Then tears flowed down her checks.

"Emily, are you okay?" Skylar started toward her, suddenly realizing someone else might have texted her from Emily's phone. She looked too distraught to be texting. Whatever the reason, Skylar was glad she had come to her rescue.

Just before she reached her, the door she had just entered made a loud, slamming noise, and then a "click." Skylar instantly realized who was behind this, and terror crept up her back. Though she had known Alena would come for her, she didn't think it would be this soon. She was glad Mason wasn't around. She wouldn't want to put him or his family's lives in danger too.

"Hello, Skylar," Alena said, looking pleased. "It's so nice to see you." Her lips slowly curved up wickedly. "You probably didn't expect to see me so soon, but you see, I have an agenda to follow."

Without hesitation, Skylar took several steps toward Emily, holding her hand to calm her down. Emily was trembling so much, she didn't know if she could get her do what she wanted her to do when the time came—namely, run. "I knew you were coming. Let her go. She is nothing to you."

"I know she is your roommate and that her name is Emily. You see, my dear cousin, I've been following you for quite some time. I know when you sleep. I know your class schedule, and I know where you like to eat lunch."

"That's enough." Skylar clenched her fists. Though she was afraid, she wouldn't show it. "You're sick, stalking me like that. Get a life. Just let her go and I'll give you what you want."

Looking offended by Skylar's words, Alena inhaled a deep, agitated breath and let air out to calm herself. "Oh, but I do need her. I can't touch your blood. Besides, she's human. So actually, I need you both."

"What are you planning to do?"

"If I tell you, then I'll have to kill her because humans can't know of us. Oops! She knows now, so I'll have to kill her anyway. Now I can tell you." Alena stood on the other side of Emily. "Cooperate, or I won't hesitate to kill her. I can always manipulate another biology smarty pants student."

"Hurry up and get it over with."

"Emily, draw her blood with this needle."

Emily looked at Skylar.

"It's okay. Everything will be okay. Just do what she says."

"But I don't know how," Emily mumbled, trying to stay composed. Her eyes were watery again. "Just because I'm a biology major doesn't mean I know how to draw blood."

"I don't care!" Alena shouted. "Just do it."

While Emily's hands shook, she picked up the syringe, and carefully inserted the needle in Skylar's arm. Skylar cringed when she missed her vein. Emily tried again...and again. Finally, she punctured her vein and drew blood.

With a loud bang on the table, Alena produced a cell phone, a revolver, and empty bullets. Skylar jumped, steadily backing away as she protectively placed her body in front of Emily.

"Nice phone, Emily. It was sure fun texting with you, Skylar. Now, Emily, unscrew the bullets, squirt a drop of her blood inside each, and screw them back up. Hurry!"

Emily flinched from Alena's sharp tone. While her hands trembled, she did as told. One by one, Emily put the bullets in the chamber while Alena held the revolver with both hands. Alena snatched the last one and slid it in herself, then cocked the gun. "There, now I'm loaded with a deadly weapon."

"You have what you want. Erase her memory of what just happened here and let her go," Skylar demanded. "You have me."

"I wish I could, but I don't have the power to erase memories like the Grand brothers. So I'm going to have to kill her. It's a shame. We were biology lab partners. You didn't know I went to the same college, did ya?" Alena aimed for Skylar's head. "I was told to keep you alive, but now that I have what I want, accidents do happen. How ironic...killed by your own blood bullet."

Unexpectedly, an intense bright light radiated, outlining the door. Then, the door flew across the room, slamming against the wall. The three Grand brothers and Amanda stood where the door should have been. Without hesitation, Alena started shooting. The loud banging noises jolted Skylar, putting her in an alert and protective mode. She pushed Emily to safety and made a courageous effort to knock Alena down, but to no avail. Instead, thankfully, it made Alena miss her targets.

The Grand brothers and Amanda hid behind the tables, dodging the bullets. Knowing Alena would try to escape, Skylar gripped her shirt. Pointing the revolver at Skylar's heart, Alena pulled the trigger, but just before the gun discharged, Mason yanked Alena's body. The bullet penetrate Skylar's arm instead.

With the hit, Skylar's body whipped back, causing her to bump her head hard on the corner of the lab table and fall to the floor. Blood streamed down her arm, soaking into her sweater. As several drops of blood painted the white floor, she cradled her wounded arm. Pain burned through her whole body as she watched Alena escape Mason's hold and dash out through the other exit door.

"Don't go after her," Mason said to his family. "She may lead us into a trap. Remember what she said before. She takes orders from someone else. It's too dangerous. We'll get her next time. I think I know where she lives. I found her loitering around the diner a week ago and I've been following her."

The others did as Mason had said, and the four of them huddled around Skylar.

Seeing Mason's face and watching him bend low to help, made her feel a sense of relief. Unable to move from the tremendous pain, she slumped over, supported by the table behind her. "Don't touch me," Skylar said softly, afraid she would kill him. "How did you know?"

"You didn't answer my text. I told you if you didn't answer it, I would know something was wrong and that I would come for you."

"I'm sorry." She looked up to see Amanda, Everett, and Nick. "I forgot I had it on silent. I guess it was a good thing?" Skylar shrugged her shoulders sheepishly, feeling bad for not answering her text. The movement caused her to yelp softly, biting her lip from the sharp pain. She was waiting for it to heal on its own, but it wasn't. After the pain subsided, she asked another question. "How did you know I was here, at the bio lab?"

"When I lost her tracks, I had a bad feeling. We were already on our way to pay you a visit. I...um had put a tracer on your phone. It's connected to mine, so I know exactly where you are." He sounded nervous, most likely thinking he should've asked for her permission.

"Oh," Skylar said, thinking she liked his protective side, but at the same time she didn't know if she liked the fact that he would know where she was at all times—just in case.

Too busy dodging Alena's bullets, they hadn't noticed Emily, but now they heard whimpering sounds underneath the lab table behind Skylar. "It's Emily, my roommate. Can you please help her?" In too much pain and unable to move, Skylar didn't have the strength to look over at her.

As Mason continued to squat next to Skylar, Amanda and Nick pulled Emily from under the table.

"Here she is," Nick said sweetly, as if he'd just rescued a cute little puppy.

Emily was still shivering. Her eyes grew wide and more terrified when she saw Skylar's blood.

"I'll be fine. Don't worry," Skylar assured her, having a difficult time getting her words out. "Don't forget your cell phone."

Emily nodded her head.

"Why don't we take her home and help her forget all about today?" Nick winked.

"Sounds like a good plan. Why don't you take Everett and Amanda with you?" Mason suggested.

"Sure, see you back at the house."

"Don't be too long," Amanda urged.

"Be careful," Everett spoke for the first time since he'd arrived.

After they left, Mason examined Skylar's arm. "I'll have to take the bullet out. Thankfully, it's not lodged in too deep."

"Okay." Skylar inhaled and exhaled uneven breaths. The combination of the pain and the blood loss made her feel like the room was spinning, and the feeling of nausea was rising to the surface.

His eyes looking mad as hell underneath those thick eyelashes, he spoke with a scolding tone. "I told you not to be brave. Look what happened to you. What if...what if," he faltered.

"I wasn't trying to be brave. I thought you didn't care," she said wearily.

"I don't." His tone was sharp and cold, but Skylar knew why. He was upset with her for making him worry and for putting her life in danger. "And you definitely need time out in a naughty corner for not listening to me."

Skylar furrowed her brows, but despite her arguments, she knew he was right. She deserved to be in a "naughty corner," or worse. This all could have been avoided if she had accepted the reality she'd been ignoring, but her reality was like a bad dream. Though she knew she was in constant danger, it was difficult to grasp. Everything had happened so fast that it was all a blur. There was no time to breathe, no time to understand what was happening around her and to her.

Perhaps thinking danger couldn't touch her was her way of coping with it all, pretending that it wasn't real, even though fear had overcome her. She had reacted the same way when her dad left. Pretending to feel nothing was better than feeling the agonizing pain. Pretending that these new terrors couldn't happen was a way to cope, to shut out the world around her. Perhaps Mason was doing the same thing, but tonight she had woken up from the dream into her reality. Not only was her life in danger, but now Emily's was as well. This couldn't happen, ever again. Who knew? The next time it could be her mom, or her aunt, or even Kayla. She had to be careful, be more aware, and completely trust that Mason knew what he was doing. Most of all, she had to accept who she really was.

Mason released a relieved sigh and his eyes became soft. "I'll be right back." He stood up and looked around while opening cabinets, and came back with some tools—rubber gloves, tweezers, scissors, cotton balls, and a bottle of alcohol. "It's going to hurt, but afterward, when you start to heal, you'll feel better. Squeeze any part of me if you need to."

With a nod from Skylar, Mason put on the rubber gloves, squatted down, and cut Skylar's blood-soaked sweater and shirt with the scissors, just enough to be able to see the wound clearly. Then he soaked the cotton ball with rubbing alcohol and dabbed it on the open cut. Skylar yelped in pain.

"Sorry," Mason said, looking distraught.

Skylar wanted to faint, and the room became dim and blurry. Her whole body burned as if she had been tossed in a fire. The intensity of the pain grew, and the rubbing alcohol didn't help, but she knew why it was needed. She turned her head, trying to think of anything but what Mason needed to do. When he reached in with the tweezers, her breathing became heavy and jagged, and the pain that had started to ease up, erupted again, pinching every nerve and muscle. At last, he pulled the bullet out.

"It's done." Mason took the towel and cleaned the surrounding area. Then he tore a section of his shirt and wrapped it around the wound. With the gloves still on, he cleaned the mess on the floor and tossed everything in the trash can.

"Thank you," Skylar whispered, looking half-asleep. Her eyes felt heavy, fluttering desperately as she tried to keep them open. She gazed at Mason, looking at him with admiration, thinking what an incredible being he was. She silently thanked him for being there, for caring enough, though he denied it. The pain had already started to subside, which was a good sign. It meant she was healing.

"Sky?" Mason kneeled in front of her. "Is the pain any better?"

"Yes, mmm, tired." Uncontrollably her eyes shut, and she could hardly get any words out.

"Now you owe me two shirts."

"Okay."

"I'm going to take you home with me. I'll feel better if you're with me while you heal."

"Mmm...don't stare." She let out a small, faint giggle.

"You took my words. And I'm not staring," he snorted.

"You're. Still. Staring."

Her body had just been through so much stress, and she lost the fight to stay awake. Just before she fell asleep, though she wasn't absolutely sure, she heard what sounded like a whisper that tugged her heart. "I'll always stare at you, Sky."

THIRTY ONE

BY THE TIME they reached Mason's house, Skylar was feeling much better. Though the pain still lingered, and the wound had not quite healed all the way, it was bearable. The nap she took in the car gave her a second wind, so she was wide-awake when Mason drove up the driveway.

"I'm feeling much better. I guess I should have asked you to take me back to my dorm," Skylar said.

Mason turned off the ignition. "It's close to midnight. I think it's safer for you to stay here for tonight. Your roommate is fine. She won't remember a thing when she wakes up in the morning. You've been through so much lately. I don't know how you've managed to stay calm."

"I'm really not calm. I'm actually terrified. I have something those evil beings want." Then it dawned on her. She hadn't thought about the night the vultures ransacked Kayla's house for a while, but now the answer was clear. "Mason...the vultures were looking for me the night they broke into Kayla's house. They weren't looking for something tangible. They were looking for me. After they knew I lived there, the robberies stopped."

"I know. I didn't know it at the time, but I realized it later when Alena explained about who you were."

"Oh." It was all she could say, and she started to shiver. Having the heater turned off, it got cold in the car.

"Let's get inside the house. Plus, we're fogging up the windows. If they see us out here, they'll think we're making out."

Skylar felt her cheeks heat up by his words.

"Nick texted me several times to make sure we were on our way. He must be worried. I didn't respond."

"Why didn't you text him back?"

"I was driving. Remember what I said to you about texting and driving?"

Skylar rolled her eyes. How could she ever forget the hot cop that pulled her over and told her texting while driving was illegal? "Yes."

"Well, Ms. Rome. Shall we go in?"

With a nod, they got out of the car and walked into the house. Seeing a dim light coming from the kitchen, Mason led Skylar in that direction. Amanda, Nick, and Everett were sitting at the rectangular oak dining table with mugs in front of them. Seeing steam rising from their mugs, Skylar assumed they were drinking something warm. She wanted to do the same.

"Where the hell were you?" Nick asked, looking annoyed.

"Obviously, I was in the car and on my way here" Mason responded calmly.

"Man, you are a demigod. You can still text me back and not crash your stupid car. Next time you don't answer my text, especially since Alena is something to worry about; I'm going to obliterate you myself. Got that?"

Mason stuck his hands inside his front jean's pockets, stood there listening, and let Nick have his say. "Are you done now?"

"No," Nick snapped, and then turned to Skylar. "I'm glad you're doing better. You look great for someone who got shot. I'm not used to thinking you're somewhat like us, kind of...I guess." He shook his head, thinking he should just keep his mouth shut.

Mason pulled out a chair for Skylar, gesturing for her to sit. He sauntered out of the kitchen and came back after a few minutes with a light blanket. After tossing the blanket around her shoulders, he went to the stove and came back with two mugs of hot tea, placing one in front of Skylar.

"Thank you." Skylar cupped the mug with both of her hands, taking in the heat, and then took a sip. It was green tea, just what she needed at that moment. Warmth traveled from her head to her toes, soothing and calming her. Gazing upon her friends, she noticed that they were fidgeting, shifting their bodies from side to side. Sometimes their lips parted to speak, but instead, they kept their mouths shut.

"What are we going to do about Alena?" Everett finally spoke, breaking the silence.

"You said you followed her. Why didn't you tell us?" Amanda leaned over the table as if she could draw the answer out of him. "Mason, you've got to stop taking matters into your own hands. You're too worried about our lives. Have you thought about how we would feel if we lost you?"

Dead silence.

Mason was just about to take a sip. His mug was to his lips, but he didn't drink. Instead, he placed it back on the table. "This isn't about my mother."

"Oh, the hell it isn't, and you know it." Amanda's tone was angrier. "You can't blame her death on yourself. You didn't know who you were. We've all lost loved ones. So stop sacrificing your life to wash away that guilt."

"Amanda is right, Mason. We've all lost our parents. I had also wished that I could have done something, but I know now that I was overwhelmed with all the weird and unbelievable craziness. We've lived together for many years, but like roommates. It's time that we start acting like brothers and work as a team," Everett urged. "Maybe, if things were better between us, Remus would have been different. I don't think he was *all* bad. I know he had a temper and was crazy at times, but maybe that was his way of coping."

Guilt wrapped around Skylar's heart. Hearing about Remus, sorrow consumed her again, especially after hearing Everett's speech about how it might have been Remus's coping mechanism. She was astounded that those words even came out of Everett's mouth. Though she disliked him, she was seeing a different side of him. Perhaps she had been wrong about him. Knowing how they had lived during the past years, she became sympathetic. Truly, she had no idea what they'd had to endure.

It must have been beyond difficult for them to lose their loved ones and then find out their father was a descendant of Zeus, who'd had numerous affairs just to keep his family line going. Not only did they deal with the loss of their parents at an early age, they were forced to accept who they were, and the powers that were bestowed upon them.

While it must have been frightening, perhaps equally terrifying was having to constantly look over their shoulders for Hades' creatures. It was certainly not a vision of an ideal life, but they seemed to have adjusted and accepted who they were. Skylar gave them each a lot of credit for their inner strength, for the ability to move forward, and for their courage. Even with all she realized, she also admitted to herself that it did not forgive Remus's actions toward her.

"So, now that we've all said our peace, what do we do about Alena?" Nick brought the subject up again as he traced the rim of the mug with his fingertip. Wiggling his fingers, he pointed his index finger into the mug and a light flashed.

Startled by the sudden burst of light, everyone's eyes zoomed to Nick with alarm.

"Sorry, my tea was cold. Too lazy to get a refill." Nick shrugged his shoulders.

"Thanks a lot. You just blinded me." Amanda blinked rapidly, adjusting her vision. "I say we hunt her down and get rid of her, once and for all." A furious look shot out from her eyes as she got up to pour more tea for herself and sat back down.

"I don't think that would be a good idea. She did say she takes orders from someone else. We've got to find the leader," Mason suggested.

Everett scooted his chair back, crossing his legs to relax. "She could be anywhere, or show up anytime. How do we find her?"

Mason turned his head to Skylar. "I once followed her near our cabin, but further up. I think she lives around there. I'm not sure. I didn't actually stick around and hold a conversation with her; however, I did see a cabin."

"Then do we just show ourselves? Announce 'Hey, we know where you live, we're here' and wait to see what happens?" Amanda snorted.

Still cupping her mug for warmth, Skylar gave a nervous cough. "I can lure her out. I'm the one she wants."

Skylar felt all eyes on her all at once.

"No. Out of the question." Mason's tone was unyielding. "It's too dangerous. We don't even know what we're up against. I won't risk your life."

Skylar let out a heavy sigh. Wanting to be part of them and making herself useful was difficult, especially when it seemed as though Mason always had the last word.

"She may have a point there," Amanda stated. "At least Alena would be the one who was surprised for a change and not us."

"I know it sounds like a good idea, but it's not. We're so tired we're not thinking straight. Let's talk about it later."

Skylar suddenly froze, worried for her mom. If Alena almost killed her roommate, who was to say she wouldn't harm her mom to get to her? "Maybe I should go home. What if Alena goes after my mom?"

"Your roommate was a means to an end for Alena," Mason said. "And right now, she's not interested in your mom. You can keep it that way by keeping your distance from her. Make your phone calls short, and try not to visit her on the weekends for as long as you can. Alena never once went to your mom's house when I was tracking her."

"How about Kayla?"

"Don't worry. I've got that department handled," Nick said.

"I'm sure you do," Amanda grumbled, rolling her eyes.

Nick gave her a "be quiet" look, lighting a fast spark from his fingertips.

"Don't you dare," Amanda flared, trying to keep a straight face.

Mason stood up. "I'm taking Skylar back to her dorm tomorrow. We can think of another plan, but we're not using her as bait." With that, he stood, indicating that his words were final.

Amanda, Everett, and Nick had nonchalant expressions on their faces. Either they agreed with Mason's decision, or they had given up on expressing their opinions, knowing Mason would have his way. With the blanket still draped around Skylar, they headed for his room.

THIRTY TWO

IT WAS ALMOST afternoon, and the ominous clouds got darker and thicker. The wind howled, tossing Skylar's hair, blocking her view. Holding an umbrella, Mason walked beside her to her dorm. Upon entering, Skylar let out a huge breath, relieved to escape the awful weather. Mason stood by the doorway, looking like he didn't want to come in and make himself at home. "Nice place."

"Yup. Small and cozy. Nothing fancy like yours."

Mason looked like he was being shy, but Skylar couldn't be sure. He glanced down and then up again, meeting Skylar's eyes.

"Do you want to come in for a while?" Skylar asked hesitantly. She wasn't sure what Mason had in mind.

"Actually, I'm not staying."

"Oh." The little bit of hope that she could spend some time with him vanished.

"I mean, *we're* not staying. I've brought you here so you can pack your bags and come back with me."

"What?" Skylar didn't know whether to feel elated that he wanted her to go with him, or upset he didn't ask her first. "You didn't mention this to me before. And what if I refuse?"

"Then—" Mason started to say, but he was interrupted by a voice.

"Hey, Skylar," Emily greeted, descending the stairs. She looked well put together, wearing a thick red overcoat. Skylar had on the jeans she'd worn yesterday and Mason's sweater that was way too big on her.

"Emily." Skylar beamed a nervous smile, tucking a strand of hair behind her ear. "This is Mason. Mason, this is Emily." Though Mason had met her informally last night, he pretended that it was their first meeting.

Extending his hand, he shook hers. "Hello. Nice to meet you."

Emily stared a bit too long, producing a friendly smile. "Hi." Looking at Skylar, she asked, "You guys dating?"

Skylar's face flushed with heat. She couldn't believe Emily asked such a question right in front of him. "No, we're...he's...where's your boyfriend?" Skylar asked, directing the attention back to Emily. It was the only way to get out of the awkward moment.

"Oh, Dex. He's on his way."

As if on cue, there was a knock at the door. Emily turned the knob, but just before she pulled the door to open it, she turned to Skylar. "Oh by the way, some guy was here to see you. He was tall, cute, with dirty blond hair to his shoulders."

Looking confused, Skylar asked, "Did he leave a name?"

"Nope. I didn't know where you were, so I told him you would be back today. I'm sure he'll stop by." Then she walked out the door.

Mason's face was blank. Skylar didn't know why she was worried what Mason would think of her having a guy visitor, but the description concerned her. It was too similar to the guy that had been gawking at her at the mall. *Did he follow me here? A stalker?* It was something to be worried about.

"Making friends already?" Mason asked flatly.

Skylar heard a ring of jealousy in his tone. Smiling, she wondered if she should tell Mason about the incident at the mall, and the shadow of a male she'd seen next door to Kayla's house. Was she being paranoid? "Am I forbidden to make friends?"

"No, of course not. You can do whatever you like."

It was not what she wanted to hear. She noted they were still standing by the door. "Should I get my stuff?"

"That was the plan."

"You mean *your* plan," Skylar retorted. "Next time, I'd like to be included in your plan."

"Fine. I'd like you to hurry. You just need warm clothes, possibly for a week."

A week? Skylar went upstairs to her room without a word. She knew deep down that being with Mason would be safer, but not for her heart. The more time she spent with him, the more attached she became, and that frightened her more than facing Alena.

Opening up her duffle bag, she shoved in some jeans and sweaters from her dresser. Next, she went into the bathroom and placed her toiletries into another small bag. Needing to change out of Mason's sweater, she put on her favorite pink sweater and a clean pair of jeans. Then she slipped into a waterproof gray jacket. She was just about to put Mason's sweater into her bag, but she decided otherwise, leaving it in her closet before heading downstairs.

Holding onto Skylar's bags, Mason opened the door, and then opened the umbrella that was big enough for two. Pulling Skylar closer to him, they headed out, as the pitter-patter sound of the rain continued to get louder and heavier with each step. Skylar was glad she'd put on her boots. The raindrops were now pounding on the ground furiously, splashing against her legs. Surely if she had worn her tennis shoes, they would have been soaked by now.

Mason opened the car door for Skylar and put her bags in the trunk, then closed the umbrella and put it in the back seat. Just before he got in, he scanned the perimeter, as he always did. From the few seconds he was exposed, his hair was drenched, dripping pearl-like droplets down the side of his cheeks, and water spotted on his gray sweater. He looked so alluring that she had to turn away. She focused on the window splattered with water, since it was difficult to see anything else but that.

"Sky, I know you're not happy with this arrangement, but it's just until things die down. Then you can go back."

Disappointed by his words, she didn't turn when she responded. "Sure. I can get my notes online. It's a good thing school just started, I guess."

After a mile, Mason turned onto the freeway. The heavy rain made it difficult to see, and the windshield wipers cleared a path only temporarily. Mother Nature was unforgiving today, adding a hurricane-like wind, along with the roaring thunder. Shortly after, lightning cracked across the puffy black clouds, flashing in and out, striking the world with beauty and danger. Silence filled the air in the car until Mason started driving faster, swerving in and out of lanes.

Skylar sat up straight. She flashed a worried look at him. "Mason, don't you think you're driving a bit too fast?"

He didn't answer. He looked at the side view mirror, then the rearview mirror, and switched lanes again. "We're being followed."

"Are you sure?"

"I didn't want to worry you. They followed us from your dorm. I think your boyfriend is unhappy with who you hang out with."

Boyfriend? They? "I don't have a boyfriend," Skylar huffed, narrowing her eyes on him, though he couldn't see what she was doing.

"The dirty blond. He was in the parking lot, trying to hide out with his friend."

Skylar turned to look, but it was difficult to see with all the rain. All she could make out were the headlights.

Seeing what Skylar was trying to do, Mason spoke, "They're in the white truck behind us, trust me."

Skylar was too busy trying to see the driver. With no luck, she turned forward and froze in place with alarm. "Mason," she mouthed. Too stunned to speak, she could hardly get a sound out of her mouth.

Skylar wasn't sure what she was seeing, but if her vision was correct, there were three huge trucks in the distance. One in each lane, they were heading straight toward them. She rubbed her eyes, thinking she wasn't seeing clearly. Surely, the rain was affecting the view. This couldn't be possible. Nevertheless, when she confirmed what she thought she was seeing, her heart hammered faster than the raindrops.

Luckily, there weren't many cars on the highway, but the cars that were in front of them swerved to the far left or right, as they tried to avoid a collision. Other cars honked their horns while braking, but those that did were hit, dead on. The cars tumbled, flipping multiple times, only to hit other cars trying desperately to move out of the way.

"Mason, MASON, MASON!" Skylar panicked.

"I know. Skylar, hold on tight. I'm going to brake."

"But there are cars behind us."

"We have no choice. Don't worry. I got this." Mason pushed down on the brake pedal forcefully. The car hydroplaned to the right. "Hold on."

Skylar gripped the first thing she could place her hand on tightly. The water from the road jetted up into the air like in a water show, but the car kept gliding sideways, until finally it spun in a full circle and stopped. With no time to waste, Mason turned the car to the right and accelerated, hoping to dodge what was coming toward them.

Out of nowhere, a long piece of ice, taking the form of a spear, darted through the trucks' tires and punctured some of them. More ice spears came soaring out of the rain, but this time, ten or more sphere-like ice balls followed, denting the sides of the trucks. One went through a windshield. With flat tires, the trucks now glided as if skating on ice, maneuvering from side to side.

"Did you do that?" Skylar asked excitedly.

"No. Must be Poseidon's kids. Where the hell are they?" Mason spread his right arm in front of Skylar, as if to protect her. "Bend down, Sky."

One of the trucks hit another and veered off, hitting yet another one. The crash caused the trucks to flip and tumble, heading straight for Mason's car. With a look of shock, Skylar held her breath. With no time to move, think, or get out of the car, she closed her eyes and prepared for the crash.

Just seconds before impact, Mason's car flew up into the air, over the trucks. Somehow, as if by magic, the water created a liquid bridge, guiding the car safely over, and then it thumped hard on the ground on the other side. Without looking back, Mason sped away as the sound of screeching brakes and metal hitting metal, blasted behind them.

"What just happened?" Skylar yelped. "Did you do that?" Everything had happened so fast. Adrenalin had rushed through her body so rapidly, she'd had no time for fear. Now that it was over, she was simply amazed, stunned and speechless.

"No, I didn't. Poseidon's kids. It's the only explanation. They can manipulate water. I had it handled. There was no need for them to show off. Lots of civilians are hurt." Mason sounded irritated, perhaps because he wasn't the hero this time around, or perhaps he truly did care for those people he didn't know.

Amazed by their abilities, wherever they were, Skylar was grateful they were there. Though Mason claimed he'd had the situation handled, Skylar thought otherwise, but kept her opinion to herself.

Looking behind them, she could see fire and heavy smoke escalating into the sky. The trucks had mostly slammed against each other, except for one. Guilt consumed her, thinking about the innocent people who'd happened to be in the wrong place at the wrong time. She couldn't dwell on being remorseful. She saw the same white truck, now joined by a black truck, tailing behind them. "It's the white truck again, but there's another one behind it."

"I see them," Mason said with a sly tone, looking in the rearview mirror. "Let's see if they can follow."

THIRTY THREE

WITH A JERK, Skylar fell back into her seat. Mason pressed down hard on the gas pedal, making the car accelerate much faster than it had been a second earlier. With a loud screech of the tires, he exited the freeway and made a fast right. The rain continued to pour with no mercy, but it didn't seem to affect Mason's vision.

Swerving in and out of lanes, other drivers honked loudly, obviously irritated as Mason cut them off. He ignored a light that had just turned red, and punched the gas even harder. Luckily, the cars on the other side were at a complete stop.

"Mason," Skylar called softly. She wanted him to slow down.

"We're almost home," he said, concentrating on the road.

When he turned a sharp left, a gush of water caused him to veer sideways to the right, sending a massive wave onto the sidewalk and splashing the pedestrians. They cursed and flipped him off.

"Sorry," he murmured under his breath.

Mason was right. Skylar noted that they were close to his house. She recognized the streets. If they had turned right, she would be headed towards Kayla's house. Looking behind them, the trucks were nowhere to be seen. "You can slow down now. I think we've lost them."

"I don't see them either."

Mason took the long way home, changing lanes and going through several small streets instead of staying on the main roads. When they pulled up in the driveway, the rain had died down to a drizzle. Heaving a sigh of relief, Skylar sat there looking at Mason, trying to comprehend all that had happened.

"Ready to go in? We should find the others," he said calmly, getting out of the car. Vigilantly, he placed his arms around Skylar's waist and scanned the perimeter. Turning the corner toward the entryway, they paced quickly. The narrow walkway forced Skylar to tread behind Mason. With her hand on his back, she focused her eyes on the ground, not wanting the raindrops to fall on her face. Suddenly, she bumped into Mason.

Skylar looked up to see the back of Mason's head as rain trickled down her face. She felt his arms reach behind him protectively. Wondering why he was acting this way, she peered over his shoulder and gripped his biceps in absolute terror. Five vultures were guarding the front door, staring back with their revolting eyes, hissing and snarling, preparing to attack. Slowly, dragging her feet, she backed away, matching Mason's steps.

"Where are Nick, Everett, and Amanda?" Skylar whispered, concerned for their lives, hoping they weren't in the house.

"I don't know, but I need you to listen. When I say run, run to the gate, okay?"

"Okay," Skylar whimpered. Her body was so stiff from fright she was unsure if her legs would budge.

A few seconds later, Mason yelled, "Run!" He snatched her arm, tugging, running as fast as he could with her by his side. They were close to the gate, but stopped when they saw two guys heading straight toward them.

Skylar recognized the dirty blond right away. How the heck had they gotten there? There was little time to consider this as she regarded them with fear. With impassive facial expressions, their hands were moving in a circular motion near their chests. What were they doing?

Stuck in the middle, Mason grabbed Skylar's hand and turned sideways, with one eye on the vultures, and the other eye on the visitors. "When you get a chance, I want you to run toward the trees and hide."

"No. I won't leave you," she retorted, holding on to his arm, deciding the odds if she ran. But what could she do to help?

"Do what I say," he demanded.

Mason pushed Skylar out of the way when the vultures leapt toward them. Just before the impact, she saw a sharp icicle-like spear, like the one she'd seen on the freeway, headed straight for the nearest vulture. Though the spear punctured its gut, it continued to charge forth.

Strategizing, Mason purposely allowed the vulture to pick him up by his waist so he could place his hands on its shoulder. With his power, Mason zapped electricity through the vulture's entire body. It sizzled, juddered, and then dropped to the ground.

The dirty blond moved his hands around his head and pushed through empty space. A massive body of rainwater copied his hand motions and plowed into two of the other vultures, knocking them down with the pressure, away from Skylar. More icicle spears soared and penetrated the remaining two, allowing Mason to finish them off.

Without acknowledging the strangers, Mason grabbed Skylar's hand and ran to the front door that was already ajar. He kicked the door open but remained by the entrance instead of charging in.

Sitting in the center of the large foyer, with their hands bound behind them, were Amanda and Everett. Standing behind them was Alena, with a few other people Skylar didn't recognize.

"Welcome to our party," Alena said calmly. "What took you so long? Actually, I didn't think you would make it past the door, but then again, I see that you had help. No, no, no, boys. Don't even think about moving your hands," she said to the strangers, pointing out the revolver she had pointed at the back of Amanda's head.

"Don't do anything foolish," Mason said to the strangers. "She has special bullets."

"Do you even know each other?" Alena continued. "Let me speed up the introductions. The blond one is Noah, and the one with the short hair is Tim. Aren't they the cutest?"

"Just shut up and let my family go," Mason demanded. With a look of fury, he tightened his fist into a ball. Dim light glowed, seeping out between his knuckles. "I'm giving you one last warning. I've told you we just want to live in peace, to be left alone. Let them go, and you can walk out of here."

"You want me gone, then Skylar comes with me." Without waiting for a response from Mason, Alena gestured her head. Understanding her nod, the guy standing to her left placed his hand on Everett's head. Light flicked from his fingertips, sending electricity through Everett's body. Everett cried out, a loud painful sound, and shuddered as if he was having a seizure.

"Stop it!" Amanda yelled.

Alena raised her hand and the guy pulled away.

Everett slumped over, apparently unconscious.

"Poor big guy." Alena bent low to see his flaccid face. "It was just a little shock. Oh, by the way, these are my new friends. They have special abilities like you. Now we can play fair."

"Lure them out," Noah whispered to Skylar, standing behind her.

"No whispering sweet nothings in her ear, Noah. Don't make me jealous now. Maybe we can kiss and make up," Alena remarked with a sinister laugh.

Noah rolled his eyes.

"Don't tell me you dated her," Skylar grimaced.

"It was like, a year ago, and I didn't know who or what she was. Never mind. Skylar, do it."

Skylar understood. They could only manipulate water, and there was no water inside. She didn't know where this courage came from, but she knew she had to do something. Guessing that Mason, Noah, and Tim would protect her, she knew she had a shot at her plan.

"Alena, I'm the one you want. Let them go. I'm coming to you right now."

"Sky." Mason pulled her back. "What are you doing?"

She turned to him and winked, hoping he would get the message. "I have a plan," she mouthed.

"No." He pulled her back again, but as she pulled against him, he finally seemed to realize he had no choice. Mason let go, and growled when Noah placed his hand on his shoulder.

Lifting her hands in surrender, Skylar carefully paced to Alena. Triumphantly, Alena grabbed Skylar by her arm. Inching backward, Alena pointed the revolver to Skylar's back. "Don't even think about following," she sneered, as her men stood protectively by her side. They stepped outside and the door closed behind them.

Outside, the rain started to pick up again. Without another option, Skylar ran with Alena about half way to the gate, and abruptly halted when Alena turned to face the front of the house. "Stop! Don't move. I told you not to follow."

With a swift motion, Noah guided the rain droplets. They swirled in an endless circular cycle, forming into one enormous sphere of water. Alena pulled the trigger. The bullet went right through and headed for Noah. He lost control of the water ball when he ducked for cover. Just before the impact, Tim twirled his hand and created a water wall. The bullet bounced and landed on the ground.

Alena's men protectively stood in front of her, but not for long, more vultures appeared at the gate. Now, clearly, Skylar and the others were outnumbered, and terror emanated from her core.

With a mischievous grin, still holding onto Skylar, Alena stepped from behind her protection. "Go get them, boys," she gestured with a swing of her arm. Growling, the vultures charged in full force with deadly looks on their faces.

Extending his arm to the sky, flashes of lightning not only shot outward from the tips of Mason's fingers, they bolted from the sky as well, as if he had called on them. Simultaneously, the wind howled fiercely, as the rain cascaded in the direction of the wind, making it difficult to stand.

The clouds rolled in with incredible speed. Thunder echoed repeatedly, seeming to mimic Mason's anger as more lightning burst out of the clouds. He carried that energy and directed it toward the vultures. Once hit, some of the vultures blistered in flames, convulsed, and sizzled to their deaths from the single blow.

Still captive by Alena and drenched from the rain, Skylar witnessed all of this with her mouth open. She already knew what he was capable of, but never would she have imagined this. He was not the showoff type to begin with, but being able to call upon the lightning from above as if he was a God himself, she was in awe.

Noah and Tim continuously shot icicle-like spears, but Alena's men used their power and broke them into pieces before they could do any damage. It was hot against cold, as they zapped each other with their special abilities. Continuing to fight the vultures, Mason ducked a blow from one and leapt over its head, then obliterated it from behind. Quickly he turned and dodged a swing, then ducked to avoid another.

One of Alena's men broke away and shot out silvery light at Mason. It nicked him across his shoulder, cutting through. Crimson liquid stained his sweater and marked the ground where he stood. When another volt came at him, he sidestepped and twisted his hips to avoid it. While flashing his power at the vulture on his left, Mason fired back with his right. The brilliant lights from each of them met half way, crackling and fizzling. The energy and light was building, intensifying, radiating like great fireworks, and blinding everyone around. It was beautiful and deadly at the same time.

Mason looked up and called on the lightning from above again. Suddenly, the shimmering flash shot through him, causing his body to illuminate just as bright as the lightning, blinding everyone around him once more. He projected that energy out from his hand, and the immense power traveled through his light to the opponent's light, blasting him as if a cannon shot him. Then Mason slumped over, as if the power had drained out of him.

As more vultures continued toward them, Noah extended his arms and swung them around, over his head, calling upon the powers of water. The water from the fountain ascended skyward, creating a continuous waterfall behind him. It cascaded to the ground, flowing like a stream, before turning into a vast sea of ice. Unable to run on ice, the vultures slipped and landed flat on their backs.

Tim extended both of his arms into the air, causing the ice to liquefy. The body of water rose and covered the vultures like a blanket, trapping them inside with nowhere to run. Mason then shot his electricity through the water. The remaining vultures and Alena's men were promptly electrocuted.

"Let her go, Alena," Mason bellowed. "You can't win. This is your final warning."

Mason, Noah, and Tim slowly trudged forward to close the space between them. Sliding her feet on the wet ground, Alena tugged Skylar toward the open gate while keeping one eye on the boys.

"Stop. I have one bullet left, and I'm not afraid to pull the trigger on your precious Skylar."

Mason stopped, gestured Noah and Tim to do the same, and raised his hands to surrender. "Okay."

Pointing the revolver to Skylar's head, Alena spoke. "Sorry guys, I'm tired of playing around. Say goodbye to your girlfriend." Alena pulled the trigger.

"Noooo!" Mason ran as fast as he could, but even with his incredible speed, he wasn't fast enough. The bullet shot out, but just before it did, Skylar jabbed her elbow into Alena's chest and fell to the ground, trying to dodge the bullet. Mason's body continued to soar, carrying Alena with him. Slamming her body against the gate, Mason sent electricity through her. The "Danger! High Voltage" sign was an understatement. Like rockets, silver lights exploded. Convulsing, her body seared, turning the color of onyx, and she went limp. When Mason finally released his hold, Alena's scorched remains dropped to the wet, muddy ground.

THIRTY FOUR

THOUGH NOAH HAD already helped Skylar up, Mason wearily stumbled to her, looking worn out and soaked from the downpour. The rain finally stopped and the sun peeked through the puffy clouds, creating a rainbow. It was a beautiful sight in contrast to what they had just been through.

"Are you hurt?" Mason asked, still out of breath, pulling Skylar into his embrace. As he always seemed to do once she was safe from having her life threatened, he pulled her back, cupped her face, and looked at her with a sigh of relief. Then he ran his hands through her hair and down her arms, looking for wounds.

Speechless, Skylar nodded her head. Having witnessed this surreal, magical moment, she was simply stunned. Now that it was over, she wanted to cry with relief. It took every ounce of effort to hold back the tears at bay. Seeing something red, she rooted her eyes to Mason's wound. "You're hurt."

"I'll be fine. Don't worry about me. I'm going to go back in to check on Amanda and Everett," he replied tersely. Then he turned to Noah and Tim. "If you have time, I have a few questions."

Inside, Amanda and Everett were still tied up. Softly moaning, Everett shook his head, trying to get himself together. The color came back to his face and the movement from his body showed he would be fine; however, Amanda looked like she was pissed as hell.

"Did you forget about us?" Amanda huffed, narrowing her angry eyes at Mason. "You could've untied me first. It only takes one second to zap your rays at the damn rope. You had all the fun and left me out. Everett was knocked out, not me. Just because I'm a girl and just because I don't have powers like you doesn't mean I can't kick ass."

Rolling his eyes without a word, Mason jetted light out of his fingertips, cutting through the thick ropes that were tightly binding Amanda's and Everett's wrists. Strangely, even with god-like strength, neither Amanda nor Everett had been able to free themselves, which led Skylar to wonder whether the rope Alena used had been "special."

Amanda stood up briskly, setting her eyes on the bloodstain on Mason's sweater. "What happened to you? Never mind. Since you'll live, you deserved it for deserting me." Then she turned on her heel.

Everyone else followed Mason to the family room. The room had leather sofas, an oak coffee table, and a huge plasma television. With a high ceiling and a few oil paintings hung on the walls, it looked elegant, like the rest of the house. Mason walked out and returned with towels in his hands.

"Thanks," Noah and Tim said in accord, draping them around their shoulders and finding their spots on the sofa.

Instead of tossing one to Skylar, Mason wrapped it around her, never taking his eyes off her. His face held no expression, but there was profound meaning behind those striking eyes. So much emotions were bottled deep within—pain, relief, and even happiness. Skylar tried to identify what he was thinking, but he let go all too soon.

Everett plunked himself on the other sofa, looking dismayed, rubbing his temples as if he had a headache, and Mason found a spot next to him.

"That hurt like hell. I don't wish that kind of pain even on my worst enemies. Looks like you've made some friends," Everett groaned.

"This is Noah and Tim," Mason introduced. "They are Poseidon's descendants."

"We knew your kind existed, but we've never took the time to look for other half-bloods," Everett explained. "Are there more of you?"

"Yes. There is a group of us," Noah answered.

Skylar noted how Amanda was admiring Noah and Tim.

"Do you live around here?" Amanda asked. Suddenly her demeanor and tone became more ladylike.

"No, but if you don't mind, we like to keep our whereabouts to ourselves. Just in case," Tim winked at Amanda. Amanda lit a flirtatious smile.

"Well, I can certainly understand," Everett supported. "We were trying to keep to ourselves, too, but Alena found us. Do you know anything about her?"

"About a year ago, Alena took an interest in Noah during our senior year in high school. She was new to our school," Tim explained. "They dated until we found out who she really was; meaning, she tried to kill us. She escaped and we lost track of her. I guess she went into hiding. Then suddenly she appeared again."

"Apparently, she was after my body, too," Noah joked, twitching his brows.

"I can see why," Amanda murmured.

Skylar let out a small giggle, her mood lightened by his humor, and especially seeing Amanda act so flirtatiously, which she'd never seen her do before. "Both of you were at the mall," Skylar said to Noah and Tim.

Noah ran his hair back with his fingers while letting out a nervous laugh. "Yeah, about that. I was told to keep an eye on you...sort of." Noah looked uneasy.

"Keep an eye on me?" Skylar questioned with a sharp tone. Her pitch elevated. "And was that you spying on me through my bedroom window from next door?"

Mason glared at Noah. If looks could kill, Noah would have been a dead man. "You watched her?"

"Look, I'm not authorized to say much, but it isn't what you think," Noah continued. "I saw her naked, but that's all."

"What?" Mason stood up, looking like he was ready to give it to him with his fist.

Noah raised both of his hands. "Relax, dude. I was just kidding, okay?"

After Mason sat back down, Noah continued. "I was instructed to keep an eye on Skylar, making sure she was safe. We know what type of blood runs through her veins. Unlike Alena, her blood is poison, but at the same time, we know she's not evil. We were told not to harm her. We were also instructed to find information about your family. Obviously, we knew where you lived. Our boss doesn't want us saying much. We wanted to make sure you were on the right team."

"You have a leader? Who is he or she?" Skylar asked.

"Sorry. I can't disclose that information."

Skylar released a heavy irritated sigh. She had hoped for an answer

"Does your leader want anything from us?" Everett asked.

"No. Our mission was to keep Skylar safe from Alena, and only interfere if it was absolutely necessary."

"Why does your leader care if Skylar lives or dies?" Mason jumped in with his question.

"Like I said before, I'm not at liberty to say much."

Mason stood up again, his fingers sparking with anger. "What *are* you at liberty to say?"

Tim stood up, ostensibly to protect Noah. Seeing Tim get up, Everett stood up too.

"Whoa...." Noah raised his hands again. "Everyone, just calm down. We're not the enemy, we had the same goal. We were trying to keep Skylar safe from Alena."

Amanda jolted up, looking like she'd had enough. "Boys, sit."

Taken in by Amanda's words, there was an awkward stretch of silence. Finally, after what seemed like forever, they all sat back down, albeit guardedly.

"Speaking of Alena, where is she?" Amanda asked, breaking the silence.

Surprisingly, no one said a word. The room was quiet for a long few seconds until Tim spoke. "Mason zapped her. It was pretty nasty. Her hair looked like Ms. Frankenstein, and her eyes popped out and—"

"That's enough," Mason interrupted, standing up. "She's dead. Death is nothing to celebrate, even if she was evil. She was someone's daughter, someone's friend."

Amanda gave Mason an 'are you kidding' look.

"Okay, maybe she didn't have any friends. Regardless, I took a life." Mason's tone was low and soft. "It's nothing to be proud of. She was our kind. I'm almost positive she wasn't born evil. Something must have triggered it, or someone influenced her. Maybe her dead mom, like she said. We are all born with a clean slate, and what happens afterward depends on people that surround us. I'm not sticking up for her. I just wish...I...she was at least a little human, after all. A life is a life. I...." He turned to Noah and Tim without finishing his words. "Thank you for your assistance. If there is anything you need, we will return the favor. We can exchange our contact information just in case. If you'll all excuse me, I need to find Nick." Mason headed out of the room.

"Our dear Nick is with Kayla," Amanda informed. "He has no idea what's going on. I'm sure he'll be upset he missed our reunion."

Mason turned to face Skylar, looking impassive. "Amanda will take you home. You have an early class in the morning. As promised, since there is no current threat to your life, you can go home now."

"I can take her home," Noah said. "I'm on my way out anyway."

Mason paused. "Whatever she wants. I'll be in my room." With that, he sauntered toward the stairs, leaving Skylar confused.

Something in the pit of Skylar's stomach told her Mason's wall could not be broken. She only wanted to chisel a piece at a time, but now, it felt like the little piece she'd chipped away had sealed itself back up. She couldn't help but feel as if Mason had just broken up with her, even though they weren't officially going out.

Nothing was clear between them. Maybe he never cared about her the way she thought he did. Perhaps he had decided she was too dangerous for him. After all, she could kill him by accident. Feeling like there was no hope, she decided at that moment to accept the fact that Mason would never care for her in that special way.

Skylar wanted to run, fast and far away from there, but no matter how far she ran, Mason was already etched on her heart, like a tattoo that would be too painful to remove.

"Noah, would you mind taking me home?" She said it nice and loud, purposely wanting Mason to hear. She didn't know if it was her tone or that she asked Noah instead of Amanda, but it froze

Mason in his place momentarily. Then without a word, he continued into the hallway, up the stairs, and out of view.

After the exchange of phone numbers, they headed out the door. Skylar didn't know whether to go back inside and confront Mason or let him be. Afraid of rejection, she got in the car with Noah and Tim. Just before passing the gate to exit, she turned and looked toward the upper windows.

Though she was unsure which was Mason's room, she thought she saw a shadowed figure peering through the curtains in a second story window. What did it matter? As she desperately blinked her tears away, she turned toward the front and focused on Noah and Tim. Grief consumed her whole body and she felt drained, emotionally and physically. All she could do was leave with a broken heart. She had known this was a possibility, but she never imagined the pain would be this excruciating. It only proved one thing. She cared for him more than she'd realized or wanted to.

THIRTY FIVE

AFTER NOAH DROPPED her off, Skylar was absolutely exhausted, and decided to skip her classes. Later that evening, she drove home to see her mom, knowing it was safe to see her again. Staying very aware of her surroundings, she kept one eye looking over her shoulder, just as Mason had taught her. Though she couldn't tell her mom the details of what she had been through, she just needed to be together with her for comfort.

"Welcome home, honey," Skylar's mom greeted, giving her a tight hug and a kiss.

"Hi Mom," Skylar said, placing her overnight bag on the floor. Her plan was to spend one night and then go back to her dorm. She wanted to escape her roommate, who would most likely ask her tons of questions about Mason. She also didn't want to put her mom in danger, so one night would have to be enough.

"From the look on your face, I'm guessing you studied late last night?"

Skylar looked confused, unsure of the question she'd asked. Thinking it was the perfect explanation, Skylar agreed. "Yup. We have exams this week." Guilt consumed Skylar, just as it always did when she lied to her mom, but she had no choice.

"Wash your hands and come to dinner. We have things to talk about."

"Okay." Skylar wondered what her mom had in mind as she entered the bathroom. She pumped soap into her palm and then ran her hands under the water. Thoughts of Mason washing her hands at the cabin rushed through her mind: the way his soft gaze compelled her, his sweet, caring tone, the way his touch drove her crazy. Missing him, her heart pained, and that was a reminder she needed to forget him. He hadn't even called or texted her to see if she had gotten home okay.

Looking in the mirror, she could see how swollen her face looked from all the tears she had shed. She had poured all her fears, frustration, anger, and hurt, through those tears. No wonder her mom looked at her strangely and asked her that question out of the blue. "Oh God." She hadn't realized how terrible she looked until that moment. She splashed some water on her face, hoping that would help somewhat, and walked out.

"Smells great, Mom." Skylar helped her mom set the plates on the dining table and sat across from her. "My favorite," she smiled. Skylar's mom had dinner ready for her upon her arrival—pot roast, mashed potatoes, and broccoli. "Thanks, Mom."

"Anytime, honey. Whenever you feel like a home cooked meal, just come home. So, how was your exam?" Gina asked, and took a bite of the beef she had stabbed with her fork.

"Fine. Being an undeclared major has its benefits, I guess. I get to take various classes, but we have lots of quizzes," Skylar replied, emphasizing the word "quiz" as she intently gazed at the mashed potatoes and patted them with her spoon.

"I see. So...boy problems?"

"Yeah." Skylar quickly looked up at her mother. "What? No, I mean...no. What makes you think I have boy problems? I'm not even dating anyone." Skylar's face flushed with warmth.

Gina flashed a huge smile. "Been there, done that. I just recognized some signs. We don't have to talk about it if you're not ready, but keep in mind, love isn't forced. Love is beautiful when it's mutual. Love is compromising, giving and taking. Sometimes it can be a lot of work, but you shouldn't have to try so hard. It takes two to make it right. There is no secret potion or remedy. It just takes two willing people, committing to communicate, taking the good with the bad. I'm sure you've heard some version of the saying; set him free, and if it was meant to be—"

"He'll run back to me," Skylar finished. She'd always shared her problems with her mom, but this one was difficult to talk about. Where would she start, and how would she explain? She just wanted to forget about Mason and move on. She decided the adage should be more like "don't set him free, he won't come running back to me," because that was exactly how she was feeling.

"Yes," Mom agreed, smiling.

"Is that what happened with Dad?" Though the topic of Dad was off limits, she needed to know. After what she'd been through and what she'd discovered with the Grand brothers, she had to get every bit of information possible, even if it meant Mom would shoot down the subject again.

"Why would you say that? You and I are trying to move forward, not backward. And no, that is not what happened," she said calmly, but Skylar could see the anger and sadness in her eyes.

Not wanting to upset her mom, she stopped pursuing her questions and changed the subject instead. "So, what did you want to tell me?"

"I'm thinking of selling our house."

"Why?" Skylar's tone was loud. She suddenly felt like a little girl, upset with her mom for not allowing her to have her way.

"Honey, I need you to understand. When Steven and I get married, I'll be moving into his home. You kind of figured that, didn't you?"

"Yes. No. I don't know, I guess." Though she had no right to be upset, she was. She felt like everything was being taken from her. Her dad, Mason, her mom, and now the stupid house. She had to stop thinking about herself. Her mom had sacrificed a lot for her. She'd vowed never to remarry until Skylar was old enough to be on her own.

Gina placed her fork down on the table, crossed her arms, and leaned forward. "Now that you're off to college and you're hardly home, I think it's time to sell the house. It's a seller's market right now, and the return would be profitable. I would like to save a chunk of that for your grad school, or for someday when you get married."

What was there to say? Though she wished she could rebut her decision, she gave her mom the biggest approving smile she could muster. Skylar was old enough to live on her own, which she was doing already, but her home, her room, was her sanctuary. The room that held her memories, where she kept her secrets and wished upon the stars while looking out the window, the room where her dad had kissed her goodnight and tucked her into bed. It was the only home she'd known and loved.

"Oh, and something else I've wanted to mention. I would like you to be my maid of honor. Steven and I agreed we would have a small wedding. We're inviting our immediate family only. If you feel uncomfortable, I'll understand."

"I would love to, Mom," Skylar mumbled with a mouth full of broccoli. Seeing her mom's eyes sparkle when she spoke of Steven confirmed she had moved on. At that moment, she knew that in order to heal like her mom, she had to let her dad go; and perhaps Mason too, but maybe, not just yet.

Gina smiled, looking relieved. "Thank you for understanding. I told Steven it was going to be mother and daughter night, so he won't be stopping by. You know, he really cares for you like his own daughter. He just isn't good at showing it since he doesn't have children of his own. So, what would you like to do? The same as usual? Watch a movie and eat popcorn, or go have a wild night out?"

"Mom." Skylar cringed at her talking about 'having a wild night.' It was the same feeling as when they'd had the 'sex talk'. "Oh, before I forget, thank you for making me take self-defense classes."

"Did something happen to you?" Gina's eyes grew wide and a worried expression settled on her face.

"No, no, no," Skylar rapidly shook her head, trying to calm her down. "Nothing happened."

Gina exhaled softly. "Okay, good. You know that you can come to me for anything, don't you?"

"Yes. I just wanted to thank you, that's all. How about we do movie and popcorn?"

"Movie and popcorn it is. Now eat your dinner before it gets too cold."

After dinner, Skylar helped with the dishes, and then excused herself to go to her bedroom to call Kayla.

"Hey, Kayla, what have you been up to?"

"Same old thing...work and school. Have you seen Mason lately?"

The sound of his name was like a stab to her heart. "No. I'm pretty sure we're done. He hasn't called." Then she realized it had only been a day. Why did it feel like it had been a week? "How are things with Nick?"

"Good. We're now dating officially."

"That's good. I'm happy for you. He better be good to you, or else you know he'll hear it from me." Skylar tried to sound cheerful. "I've got to make this short. I'm at my house with Mom. We're supposed to watch a movie, so I'd better go. I just wanted to hear your voice and see how you were doing."

"I'm glad you called. You know you can call me anytime, right? Even if you want to talk in the middle of the night. Remember what you used to tell me? There are other fish in the sea. The sea is massive, with lots of good fish."

"Yeah...but most of them are fishy," Skylar sighed.

Kayla busted out laughing. "You've never said that before."

"That's because I know better now. They are slimy and they stink."

"Hmmm, sounds like you're describing someone I know. I mean, I don't think he's that, but sometimes those fishes just need a little bit more time in the water before they get caught. The particular fish I'm talking about seems like the type that when he swims, he swims deep. I think he is just being careful. He doesn't want to be eaten by a shark, not that you are one. Just remember that, okay?"

"Don't worry. I'll be fine. I've been through a lot worse. Anyway, Mom says we'll be at your house for Thanksgiving this year."

"Yeah," Kayla squealed. "Jack bakes the most delicious, perfect turkey. Speaking of which, Jack and Mona send their love."

"Tell them I miss them, too. They're so funny together." Skylar chuckled just at the thought of them. "Well, I'll text you when I get a chance. Miss you."

"Miss you too."

"I'll talk to you soon," Skylar said with hesitation, missing her cousin. Closing her eyes tightly, she exhaled a deep breath, as if to release the tension.

"You okay, Skylar? You want to talk more?"

"No, I'm fine. I need to go. I don't want to keep my mom waiting. I'll talk to you soon."

"Okay. I'm here if you need me."

"Okay. I'm hanging up."

"Bye."

Click.

THIRTY SIX

SKYLAR SPENT THE rest of the week attending classes and trying to drown herself in her studies. With midterm exams coming up, it wasn't hard to do, but every once in a while, thoughts of Mason would pop into her mind. She missed him, but she had to be strong. She almost wished the vultures were after her, just so she could be with him. At least his protection was better than not seeing him at all, she guessed, but that was a crazy, desperate thought. *Oh, forget it. Forget him.* But she didn't want to.

With the turn of her key, she entered her dorm apartment. Emily was sitting at the dining table with her boyfriend eating lunch. "Hey, Skylar," Emily greeted.

"Hey, what's up?" Dex grinned.

"Hi," Skylar replied, placing her key back into her backpack.

"Would you like a sandwich? I have extra," Emily asked, pointing to the kitchen.

Skylar smiled. "Thanks, but I'm not hungry. I'm going to take a nap." She headed upstairs.

"Oh, by the way, that guy came by to see you yesterday. You know that guy...what's his name?"

Skylar froze in place. Her heart stopped for a second, and then thumped faster than she could catch her breath. Heat shot up from her heart to her face. It was like reopening a wound she'd been trying to heal. "Did he leave a name?" *Wrong question.* "I mean, what color hair?"

"Oh, the dirty blond, I think. Dex was here." She turned to him. "It was the dirty blond, right?"

Dex grunted, stuffing his mouth, only half-listening to their conversation.

Emily continued. "Dex said the guy wanted to speak to you. He asked how you were doing, and looked very concerned. Were you sick or something?"

Disappointed, Skylar's heart dropped, unable to answer. It was as if her words had been caught in her throat, immobilizing her ability to speak.

"Anyway," Emily continued. "A guy doesn't just drop by to see how you're doing. I think he has a thing for you." Her tone went up a pitch. "Right, Dex?"

Dex let out a grunt again, taking another bite while nodding.

"Thanks for the message," Skylar said, and headed to her room.

For a brief second, she was almost happy. For a brief second, she'd had hope. That vanished quickly when Emily told her the color of the visitor's hair. Shutting the door behind her, she dropped her backpack on the floor, took off her shoes, and plopped onto her bed, wondering what Noah wanted. Taking out her cell, she checked her messages. After scrolling through her emails and texting her mom back, she couldn't suppress the somber feeling. What did she expect? She just had to accept the fact he didn't care for her as she'd hoped.

Exhausted from lack of sleep, she closed her eyes, trying to forget the world and think of absolutely nothing. Inhaling and exhaling deep breaths, her body began to relax, drifting peacefully to the sleep she yearned for.

Repetitive tapping sounds woke her up. When she opened her eyes, she saw it was dark. Had she been asleep that long? Not wanting to get up, she continued to lie in bed, irritated and confused as to where the sound was coming from. Feeling groggy, her body wasn't in tune with her surroundings. Suddenly, fear struck, sharply sending the frantic energy right through her gut, bringing her fully awake, and she froze.

The first thought that came to her mind was the vultures, but if they were there, most likely they would've found a way to enter already. Hearing the sound again, she realized it came from her window, but it was impossible for anyone to be knocking on it since she was on the second floor.

Tap...tap...tap! Annoyed, she opened the blind, peered down, and saw a rock hit the window. "Mason?" Anchoring the blind so it wouldn't fall on her, she slid the window open. "Mason. What are you doing?"

"Didn't you get my message?"

"What message?"

"I came by the other day."

"You did?" Skylar was confused. She was sure Emily had told her it was the dirty blond, but then again, she said Dex had told her. Did he even know what he was talking about? Only two guys had ever visited her—Mason and Noah. Possibly Dex had forgotten the color of the visitor's hair. He must have agreed to the first thing Emily said, she guessed.

"Are you going to let me in, or do I have to talk to you out here in the rain?"

Stunned and elated by his appearance, Skylar didn't know what to do. "I'll be right down." Just like that, her anger and pain vanished, and she was once again, hopelessly in love. What was she going to do when he left? She was only setting herself up for more pain. She should tell him to go home instead, but it was too late. She'd already invited him in.

Walking into darkness, Skylar turned on the downstairs lights. Emily and Dex were gone, most likely out for dinner. She tried to steady her nerves, but it was impossible. Her heart thumped erratically as she opened the door. "Hi," she welcomed him shyly. "Come in."

Mason entered, looking delicious and suave as always, but he had bags under his eyes. He looked tired, like he hadn't slept for days. With stubble along his jaw line—which was actually kind of sexy—it was hard to resist the urge to run her fingers through it. Even with bags and stubble, he looked just as hot as she remembered him—totally not fair.

His hair was wet, but not drenched, from the light rain. Pacing to the sofa, he settled himself comfortably. After crossing his legs, he placed his arms lazily behind his head for support. Skylar wanted to sit right next to him in his arms, but knowing better, she sat on the other sofa.

"I came to warn you, and also to see how you're doing," Mason said. "Alena is no longer our problem, but whoever is in charge may still come after you."

Skylar wasn't worried about who was going to come after her at this moment. All she cared about was that Mason had come to tell her some bad news, and then he would leave. It wasn't an "I miss you" type of visit. It was all serious business.

"You could've texted. It would've saved you a trip." Just like that, she built a defensive wall around her heart. Mason didn't say a word, most likely thinking he should've done exactly that. "Thanks for the warning. I can take care of myself." Her tone was soft and flat. It was all she could say without falling apart in front of him.

"You think?" he chuckled.

Did he find this amusing? Anger rushed through her, but she didn't know why. She had no right to be mad at him. So why was she so angry? Because she fell in love and it wasn't returned? This was her fault, not his. He was always there for her, risking his life. Thinking she should be thankful instead, her anger eased.

"Noah and Tim said I could call them if I needed their help," Skylar said, unable to look at him in the eyes. Focusing on her thumb instead, she twirled it over her other thumb. "So...you don't need to worry so much. I've already taken up too much of your time. I'm sure there are other things you'd rather be doing." Skylar stood up, heading toward the kitchen. "Let me get you something to drink." She wasn't sure if Mason was thirsty, but she needed to walk away. Water started to pool in her eyes. She didn't want him to see her this way. What was wrong with her? Why did she feel the need to cry?

"Sky," Mason called out.

Startled from the demand of his tone, she turned. When she did, Mason was right in front of her, toe-to-toe. He embraced her tightly, snuggling his head to the side of her neck. Then his hands cupped her face. "Sky," he whispered, tenderly.

Tears that were already threatening to fall streamed down Skylar's cheeks as her lips trembled. "Please, don't say another word. You can just leave. I'll understand. It's my fault for caring. You've already warned me that you could never care for me."

"Sky, don't you know why I've come?"

Assuming the worst, she tried to prepare herself for the twisting of the knife in her heart. Waves of hot and cold rippled across her ribs. Layer by layer, her heart was tearing apart from the sharp pain occupying every inch of her chest.

"Sky, I can't do this anymore."

"I know." Her eyes continued to focus on his sweater, too afraid to look him in the eyes. Her spirit was already breaking. She didn't need more reminders by seeing the rejection in his eyes. Instead, she inhaled the scent of his after-shave and molded into him, thinking this would be the last time she would feel his arms around her like this. "It's okay. You can leave."

"I want to, but I can't. I care. Do you hear me? I care too much. I've missed you. I can't sleep. I can't eat. Every waking moment I think of you. Every second of my sleepless nights, you're on my mind, and if somehow I sleep, I dream of you. You're all that I can think of. I tried to stay away, but I can't. I'm sorry. I had to see you. I'm sorry if I've ever hurt you or wronged you in any way. It was not my intention. I didn't want to feel again. Before you, my life was empty and cold, but you made me feel alive again, a feeling I thought was buried so deep from all the pain and loss that it could never resurface."

Skylar couldn't believe what she was hearing as her tears continued to fall. The sad tears turned into happy ones. The sweet words Mason was whispering overwhelmed her, making her weak in the knees. If not for his hold on her, she would have fallen, as he continued to make her legs feel like jelly with his words and his touch. Her arms that had been dangling at her sides, moved up to the curve of his neck.

"Mason," she whispered, peering up to meet his eyes. "I've missed you too. I've been a mess."

Still cupping her face, he pulled back and wiped her tears. "You missed me too?" He sounded completely surprised.

"More than you know."

"I'm sorry to put you through all that. I told you I was broken and that I couldn't be fixed, but somehow you've torn down the wall I built around myself, and no matter how hard I try to resist you, I can't. I didn't want to care for you, but I do. I knew you were trouble the moment I set my eyes on you...at least trouble for my heart." He produced the biggest grin Skylar had ever seen on his face. "I care about you, Skylar Rome, in more ways than I ever meant to."

"I care about you, too, Mason Grand," she giggled, taking in the delight that erupted within her.

"I don't know what it is that I'm feeling for you, but I want it. I've never felt this with anyone before. I want to know what it feels like to really love someone, and to be loved back just the same. I want to know love with you, if you'll let me."

At this point Skylar was speechless, but she managed to nod. Blinking her eyes, she soaked in all of his words, the words she had been so sure would never pour out of his mouth.

Mason continued, "Everett and Amanda were right. I've been so consumed by the pain of losing my mother and the guilt over not being able to save her life, it was controlling me. I had forgotten what it felt like to really live, to care, to love, to be happy. I lived my life just passing through. I think I was just waiting for you," he smiled again. "Everett, Amanda, Nick, and I need to start acting like a family. Perhaps they were already. I just got lost. I didn't want to be a part of something that I may lose one day. Now I know I'd rather have it and risk feeling the pain than not have it at all. You helped me realize that. This past week without you has been pure torture. I want you in my life, even if it kills me."

Skylar suddenly remembered she could literally kill him, and she took several steps back. Mason seemed to understand the meaning behind her gesture and pulled her into him again. "Don't be silly. I didn't mean that. You know you can't kill me with your kiss, thank goodness. If you could, I would've been dead by now. Not being able to kiss you? Now that would really be torture."

Happiness filled her. Mason was always reassuring her that she wasn't poison, and he'd even proven it by giving her a life-affirming kiss in his room, the kiss she'd held onto until this day.

"So, now that we've got that settled, how about I take you to dinner? It must be around dinnertime. Are you hungry?" His hands held hers and guided them to the front of his chest, kissing each of her knuckles.

"Yes," Skylar nodded, enjoying his attention.

Mason pulled her in again. "I've missed holding you. I've missed the way your scent seems to follow me wherever I go, the way you always repeat what I say, your smile, your laughter. I've missed every part of you, Sky. You made my wish come true." Mason reached into his back pocket and pulled out the wishbone. "I kept this with me, hoping. Do you remember this?"

"I made your wish come true?" Skylar repeated his words, looking flabbergasted. "Yes, I remember. What did you wish for?"

"I wished that you would care for me as much as I cared for you. That you would have the patience to wait for me. To put up with my dark side and give us a chance when the time was right, or that my feelings for you would disappear so that I wouldn't care."

"You wished for that?" Skylar couldn't believe it. Those times she thought it would be impossible, it was right there all along. She just had to be patient. For him to not want to feel anything if the feelings weren't reciprocated? Well, that simply showed how much he did care. She had set him free because she had no choice. Like her mom said, since it was meant to be, he came back to her, thankfully, but setting him free had been easier said than done.

Mason continued to hold her and gaze lovingly into her eyes. "You are the only wish I've ever had. And maybe what I'm about to do would come right after." His eyes became playful.

"What would that—"

Skylar was unable to finish her words. Mason dove in and conquered her lips, molding them perfectly together. Gently and slowly, his lips tasted hers, leisurely savoring every touch, every moment, and every thrill. At first, Skylar stood still, unable to believe what was happening. When she finally realized Mason was kissing her and it wasn't a dream, she took in the reality, looped her arms around the back of his strong neck, and pulled him in tighter.

Responding to him, she kissed him back with hunger and passion. Hot, tingling sensations poured through her soul like a wild blaze, driven by all the anger, sadness, wanting, hurt, and most of all from simply missing him. She couldn't believe he was there. They were sharing this tender moment, knowing that this time, his kiss meant so much more than the first.

Like two lost souls finally understanding each other, their bodies entangled, and their kisses intensified. His hands explored her every curve, as she moaned from his touch. Oh, he was experienced all right, from what she could tell. He knew exactly where to place his hands to make her come alive, completely unraveling her.

Suddenly he pulled back, panting, his hot breath on her. "You're going to the naughty corner."

"What?" Skylar's eyes shot open, remembering him telling her several times that she needed to go to the naughty corner for not listening to him, for risking her life. She gulped nervously, yet it sparked excitement at the same time. "What happens in the naughty corner?"

Mason's brows arched playfully. "You'll see. I'm taking you there now." He pulled her in for another kiss. With his lips on hers, he ran his hands down the length of her back and on to her thighs. Effortlessly, he lifted her up, carried her to the dining table, and carefully lay her down.

Captivated by the sweetness of his display, his playfulness, his caresses, she didn't know how she got there when she looked up and saw the dining room lights as his lips moved downward. Every place he touched, every place he kissed, she could feel the heat rising from within, burning hotter by the second. Quivering, a feeling she didn't want to have end, erupted through her whole essence. How wonderful it was to be in his embrace, to feel his desire, to fulfill the need.

"I think I'll have my dessert first," he teased, trailing sweet kisses down her neck, then up to her ears. "You owe me two shirts, but I'll gladly take yours." With his chest pressed to her, she could feel his heart racing just as fast as hers was. Lowering his hands to caress her sides, he slid his fingers under the hem of her sweater. Flesh upon flesh, she ignited, and heat exploded from her head to her curling toes.

"I love it when you wear pink," he whispered, kissing her around the area of her bare stomach. "But we need to stop. Not here and not now." Seductively, his soft kisses traveled upward until he held her gaze, while his hands laced through her hair. "I want to do right by you. I want to know you. Spend time with you. We need to take it slow, okay?"

Skylar nodded, trying to calm her breathing that had gone into overdrive. "Ouch," Skylar yelped. Her body jerked slightly, and she looked at Mason with wide eyes.

"Sorry, did I hurt you?" With one long stroke, he ran his hand down the front of her body, making sure she was fine. "I kind of...." Raising his hand, he wiggled his fingers, and released small sparks. "...sizzle from your touch. I call this the love shock, baby." He paused, and then gave her a mischievous, crooked grin. Oh, that grin he worked so well, lassoing her with one whip, reeling her in, and roping her into Mason's world. Skylar could do nothing but smile immensely, but shyly. That was way too hot and sexy for her ears.

"I want to try something," he continued. Delicately he rubbed the flesh surrounding the area near her belly button, where her sweater was already uplifted. Light illuminated dimly from his fingertips as he moved them in a circular motion. Pleasant warmth kindled at first, then gradually flared deeper and the heat dispersed. The hot, sensual wave of desire coursed through every inch of her, completely taking her in.

"Mason," she yelped a pleasurable cry, barely a whisper caught in her throat, surprised from the sensation. It was almost the same feeling he had unknowingly caused when he was asleep, but with more intensity. Panting and breathless, erotic vibrations erupted, especially in areas she could never possibly have guessed they could, just from that simple touch. Losing control, she arched her back to him as she took all of his tantalizing energy in.

With the sound of the doorknob turning, Mason snatched Skylar off the table and took her to the kitchen with the speed that she was learning to love. Feeling light headed, grinning, and feeling the flush on her cheeks, Skylar ran her fingers through her hair, straightened her clothes to look presentable, and tried to suppress the lingering hot sensations. Just as Emily entered, they walked out of the kitchen together.

"Hey," Emily exclaimed, looking surprised. Her eyes focused on Skylar. "What happened to your hair?" she asked slowly. "Static much?"

Skylar brushed her hair back again, imaging what it looked like. Lighting up an embarrassed smile, she diverted the conversation. "Hey, you remember Mason, don't you?"

"How could I forget?" she curled her lips flirtatiously. "Dex will be coming by soon and then I'll be off. I'll catch you both later." She headed up the stairs.

With a flash, Mason pulled Skylar into his arms. "I don't like your body away from mine too long." Mason ran his fingers through her hair to settle the rest of the static down. "Let me help you. I didn't know I could do that," he chuckled.

Giggling, she replied. "I didn't know you could do that either, but I like the naughty corner." She decided that had she known what he'd meant by "naughty corner," she would've gone a long time ago.

"I know you do. Let's get out of here and get some dinner." Mason released her and waited for her response.

"Let me grab my purse." Skylar slipped on her jacket, grabbed her small black purse from the sofa, and walked out the door with Mason. The cold breeze slapped Skylar's hair on her face as she huddled into herself. The dark sky was somewhat merciful tonight compared to the nights before since the rain had stopped.

Hand in hand, they walked down the path to the parking lot. He had held her hand before, but this time it meant so much more. His fingers intertwining with hers felt so right, so at home, as if they were made for her to hold. All the pain and torment she had felt disappeared, as if it had never existed.

"Are you cold?" Mason asked, taking smaller steps to match hers.

"I was a second ago, but not anymore." Skylar gazed down toward their clasped hands. A glowing dim light shone from them. Skylar's smile was as bright as the light, knowing the warmth that flooded through her body was Mason's doing. "I'm fine now. I'm perfect." Indeed she was. She was in a state of bliss as he guided her to his car.

Mason had changed for the better, to the man she was always so sure existed behind those hopeful, soul-burning eyes. He battled the hurt, the grief, and the regrets to get to where he was, here and now. He wasn't the only one. Skylar knew that she had also changed. Being called "Sky" wasn't as heart wrenching as it used to be. Not only that, with Mason's help she'd accepted who she was, and that would help her prepare for whatever danger lay ahead.

Her gut feeling told her there would be a heavy storm coming soon. How heavy? She would not know until it hit. That was the most frightening part. Who knew what they would be up against? She had been forced into a war that started long before she was ever born. She was what the Oracle called "the unknown factor" or "the keeper of death," but knowing Mason would be there for her, that alone was enough. It had to be.

EPILOGUE

"WHERE ARE WE going?" Skylar asked.

"I have a surprise for you." His tone was cool, but his eyes beamed with excitement.

Changing lanes and turning right at the light, Skylar recognized the familiar roads. If her sense of direction was correct, they were headed to Starla. After parking in the back of the building, Mason gripped her hand and led her through a private back door. Upon entering, they went straight to the bar.

"Do you own this restaurant too?" Skylar wasn't sure, but since the employees were more attentive to him than the other customers, it was the only explanation. Without a word, he grinned humbly, so she took that as a yes.

Mason pulled her in and batted his eyes with a serene look, moving in at a snail's pace for a kiss.

"So, what's the surprise?" Skylar asked, pushing him back a bit just before his lips brushed hers. When she pulled away, she was startled by something, like a blurred image of a man. Whatever it was, it moved with inhuman speed. She didn't want to lose sight of him, but it was too late. He was gone.

"Ouch, rejected already," Mason whined, curling his lips downward, looking adorable while expressing his vulnerability.

"Sorry," Skylar shrugged, still trying to figure out what she had seen. "A girl's gotta play hard to get."

"I don't know if I like you playing hard to get." He frowned. "Keep my seat warm, I'll be right back. If someone tries to take it, tell him he's making a huge mistake. I will scorch him and fry him up extra crispy. Nick doesn't call me 'Mace the Ace' for no reason. I'm really good with my fingers." He wiggled them, twitching his eyebrows playfully.

Indeed he was, in more ways than one. With a wink and a sweet kiss on her lips, he walked away. Skylar twisted her neck to see Mason stride toward the back. The women sitting at the nearby tables followed him with their eyes as he passed by. Skylar gloated inwardly as she continued to watch until he disappeared from her sight. *Mine. Hands off, ladies.*

Waiting for Mason, she focused on the people around her, trying to figure out who or what she had seen earlier. She couldn't help feeling edgy. Though Alena was gone, she knew there were others after her and the danger was ever-present.

The bartender placed a glass of water in front of her, even though she hadn't ordered one. She recognized him from the last time she was there.

"Thank you."

He smiled and attended to another customer.

Sensing a body next to her and thinking Mason was back, she turned and smiled, but that smile disappeared shortly after. "Sorry, but this seat is taken."

"I don't see anyone here except me, sweetheart. Why don't I buy you a drink?" the stranger said.

"Thanks, but I'm here with someone. And if you don't mind, like I said before, this seat is taken."

He was young and attractive, but she suddenly felt a chill. Though she was flattered, she couldn't help the inexplicable frightening connection, as if somehow she knew him. Was it in the familiarity of his scent, or his voice? Whatever it was, it was definitely something she couldn't pinpoint. Brushing away the thought, she figured since she had been through so much, paranoia was kicking in.

He leaned in closer, too close for comfort. "Your blood smells sweet."

Skylar jerked back. She wasn't sure what she'd heard through the loud music. Surely, he said she smelled sweet and not her blood, but she didn't like his words either way. "He'll be back soon."

"Are you sure? I'm really fun to be with," he murmured, running his index finger down the back of the hand she had resting on her glass.

"Ouch." Skylar pulled her hand away and jumped from the sharp sting. Apprehension crawled through her as she wondered if he was like Mason. Instead of stirring with questions, she ignored it. She didn't want the stranger to realize she knew. That would confirm she was one of them. And she definitely didn't want to make a fool of herself in case she was wrong, so she kept her mouth shut.

"Sorry. I shocked you," he said flatly, without looking at her. "There's a whole new world out there. A world that can be placed in your hands. Why don't you come with me?"

"She's not going anywhere with you," Mason stated with hostility in his voice, appearing just in the nick of time. "Sorry, but this beautiful young lady is taken, by me. If you'd like to fight for her, I suggest we take it outside."

"Perhaps another day." The stranger stood and sized Mason up. They were the same height. With a nod, he walked away.

"Are you serious?" Skylar gripped Mason's arm. "What if he took you up on your challenge?"

He arched his brows. "You think I can't take him?"

"No, of course not. I'm afraid of what you'd do to him."

"I would fight for you, don't you know that, Ms. Rome? I'm not a cheater. It would be man to man, not man to my...." He wiggled his fingers. "And believe me, I would win."

Indeed, he had been fighting for her. Fighting all the evils they'd encountered so she could live. Even fighting his demons, trying to define what she meant to him. He had been there for her from the moment all the crazy things had happened, and for that she would be forever grateful. Melting inside, all she could do after that was say softly, "I know now." Then she gave him a long, luscious kiss.

With a grin, Mason turned to the bartender. "Hey Ben, get us the usual. We'll be in the back room. Thanks."

"There's a back room?"

Without answering Skylar's question, Mason led her through the crowd. "Come on, Echo."

Music filled the air as the customers laughed, ate, and enjoyed themselves. On the way to the back, she passed by so many bodies. The restaurant was packed, but luckily, they were headed to a private room.

When Skylar entered, the room was dim, and the surrounding candles gave it a romantic feel. With excitement overflowing, Skylar looked at Mason. "I like my surprise." The room was cozy and there were two round tables set for two. Though the room looked different, it reminded her of the private room at Bella Amore. "Are we expecting anyone else?"

The door flung wider. "Skylar," Kayla greeted.

"Kayla?" Skylar wrapped her arms tightly around her cousin, her eyes gleaming with happy tears.

Skylar released her cousin and embraced Mason with all of her might.

"Hey, I'm here too," Nick said.

"Sorry," Skylar said, giving Nick a hug too.

"This is fantastic. We finally get to do the double date I've always talked about," Kayla exclaimed.

"Are we gonna stand here all night, or shall we sit?" Nick said lightly when the waitress walked in with their drinks.

"I ordered drinks for us at the bar," Mason said, pulling out a chair for Skylar.

The two couples settled into their seats and ordered their dinner.

"This is cool. Our own private room," Kayla said, taking a sip of her water.

"Mace's idea," Nick grinned, raising his bottle of beer to him.

"Mace?" Kayla questioned. Then she nodded, looking at Mason. "Never mind."

"I knew Sky would like to have dinner with her favorite cousin." Mason winked at Skylar.

Kayla blinked multiple times. "Did you just call her Sky?"

"Yes." Mason looked baffled.

"Skylar let you call her Sky?" Her tone went up a pitch. "Nobody calls her Sky except for her...." She paused, looking at Skylar with hesitation.

Resting her hand on Kayla's shoulder, Skylar gave her a serene expression. "It's okay. I'm okay with it now."

With a hug and a heartfelt smile from Kayla, Skylar turned to Mason. "Sorry. Kayla knew that the only person to call me by that name was my dad."

Mason raised his hands toward Kayla as if to surrender. "I promise I got her permission first."

"Fine. Remember what I said when you came to my house that night," Kayla warned.

"Yes, I remember. If I mess with Sky, I'm messing with you, too," Mason said nonchalantly, as if he was saying it for the tenth time.

"What? When did this happen?" Nick's eyes were wide with curiosity.

"Never mind," Kayla and Mason said in accord.

As they laughed, the conversation was mainly about school and work. The waitress walked in with their dinners and left. After dinner, they ordered dessert. Realizing how late it was, Kayla needed to get back home. Another double date was set for the next week at another restaurant the brothers owned.

Clicking the car remote to unlock it, Mason opened the door for Skylar. Standing face to face, she couldn't believe she was there with him. Looking at him with loving, caring eyes, she spoke. "Thank you for being there for me. Thank you for risking your life for mine."

Mason brushed his hands tenderly on her cheeks. "I told you I would be there for you, and I meant it." He kissed her lips slowly, tenderly. After he pulled away, he continued to gaze at her.

"You're staring," Skylar teased, expecting him to say he wasn't, but what she heard next tugged deeply at her heart.

"I'll always stare at you, Sky," he said softly. His words flowed out like the icing on a cake—so sweet and smooth. "To some, you're the keeper of death, but to me, you're the keeper of my heart."

Peering deeply into his eyes, her heart melted and she practically floated off the ground. Speechless, she leaned forward to kiss him. Just before their lips touched, Mason reached into his pocket and pulled out a small box.

"I have something for you. I had this made especially for you. I want you to know that you're my girl and I'll always be there for you."

"Mason," Skylar exclaimed with a twinkle in her eyes. "I don't know what to say." After Skylar opened the box, she held its contents up to the light. "It's beautiful."

After taking it from Skylar's hand, Mason wrapped the silver chain bracelet around her wrist. Turning it to its correct position, he traced the shape with the tip of his finger. "It's a lightning bolt. You flashed into my life like lightning and gave me strength and hope. You radiated the darkness in me and brought life into my soul. You light my life, Sky. You're brave, mesmerizing, intoxicating, and dangerous to me in every way, but I can't help myself. You made me care."

Skylar's heart fluttered a mile a minute and she was swooning from his loving words. "I love it. Thank you. I'll never take it off," she said, embracing Mason tightly.

"Sky," a male voice said, interrupting the moment.

Skylar pulled back and fixed her eyes on Mason, waiting for him to say something. He was staring back at her with a glow in his eyes. Obviously, he hadn't called her name.

"Sky." Skylar heard again.

There was only one other person that would call her by that name. Surely it couldn't be, after all these years. Mason turned his body, apparently he'd heard it too. Following Mason's gaze, she saw a man with a long trench coat and a fedora hat standing tall by the front of the car. It was difficult to distinguish who he was in the dark, hidden behind the glare of a parking light. To get a better look, Skylar took a step forward.

"Sky," he said in a low tone again.

Skylar's heart pounded out of her chest. She felt a flood of anxiety in her stomach. Recognizing the voice she hadn't heard since childhood, she whispered one question. "Dad?"

BOOK 2 OF

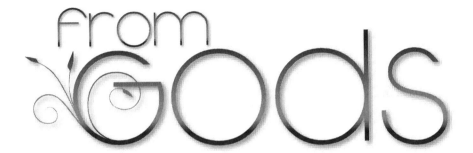

COMING SOON . . .

A SNEAK PEEK OF **SOMETHING GREAT**
by M. Clarke/Mary Ting
a New Adult novel

Startled, I twitched, and turned my body to his voice. There he was, all six feet of him, peering down on me with that smile that could make me do just about anything. Though there was nothing to laugh about, especially seeing this hottie in front of me, I couldn't help but giggle from his words.

He wore beige casual pants and a black sweater that fit perfectly to the tone of his body. His hair was brushed to the side, showing his nice forehead. Whatever kind of cologne he had on made me want to dive right into his arms...maybe it wasn't the cologne, but just him.

"Pretty cheesy, huh?" he chuckled.

I shyly giggled as I stared down at my shoes. What's wrong with me? Answer him. "Umm...kind of," I smiled as I peered up, only to have him take my breath away again.

"Sorry. I just had to say that. You looked so lost and vulnerable. Did you need some help?"

Great! To him I was just a lost puppy...lost and vulnerable. "I actually found what I was looking for." I was staring into his eyes, melting, feeling myself sinking into him. Snap out of it!

"You certainly did," he said with a playful tone.

Arching my brows in confusion, I thought about what I'd said. From his perspective, my words had been about him.

"We meet again, for the third time."

He was counting?

"You left so abruptly at Café Express, I didn't get to ask you for your name."

"Umm...my name? Oh...my name is Jeanella Mefferd, but you can call me Jenna."

Extending his hand, he waited for me. "I'm Maxwell. But you can call me Max."

Nervously, I placed my hand in his to shake. It was strong, yet gentle...just right, and heat blazed through me from his touch.

"Are you here with someone?"

"Yes." I looked away shyly.

"Are you lost? Do you need some help?"

"Actually, I was looking for the restroom. Since I didn't know where it was I thought I'd ask the bartender, but I guess there isn't one, and I'm on my way to the restroom." I rambled nervously as I slowly pulled my hand back to point in the direction I meant to go. I had just realized we were holding hands during our short conversation. "So...I'd better go."

"I'll walk you there."

What? "Oh...no need. I'm sure I won't get lost." Feeling the heat on my face again, I turned before he could say another word, but it didn't matter what I had said. His hand was gently placed on my back, guiding me to the women's room. I turned my back to the bathroom door to thank him, but he spoke first.

"I think this is my stop," he muttered, looking straight at me. "I'm not wanted in there. What do you think?" He arched his brows, and his tone held a note of challenge.

Huh? He wants to go in with me? I gasped silently, as I was still lost in his eyes. "I think the women in there will throw themselves at you." I couldn't believe I'd said those words. I couldn't take it back. What was I doing, flirting with him?

He seemed to like what he heard. His arms reached out, his muscles flexing as he placed one on each side of me on the wall. With nowhere to go, I was trapped inside the bubble of his arms. He leaned down toward the left side of my face and brushed my hair with his cheek. "You smell...delicious," he whispered. His hot breath shot tingles to places I hadn't expected them.

Out of nervousness and habit, my left index finger flew inside my mouth. Max gave a crooked, naughty grin and slowly took my hand out of my mouth. "Did you know that biting one's finger is an indication one is sexually deprived?" His words came out slowly, playfully, but hot. "I can fix that for you, if you'd like."

He did not just say that to me! I parted my lips for a good comeback, but I couldn't find one. Feeling my chest rise and fall quickly, I tried to control the heated desire. Sure, he'd helped me once, but that didn't mean we were friends, or flirting buddies, or that I would allow him to fix my sexual deprivation. Oh God...can guys tell if you haven't done it in a very long time? This had to stop or else...oh dear...I wanted to take him with me into the restroom.

Needing to put a stop to the heat, I placed my hand on his chest... big mistake. Touching him made the heat worse, and tingles that were already intensifying burst through every inch of me. I had to push him away.

As if he knew what I meant to do, he pulled back, but his eyes did the talking instead. There was no need for words; I felt his hard stare on my body, as if he was undressing me with his gorgeous eyes. His gaze was powerful, as if his eyes were hands; I felt them all over me, completely unraveling me.

Just when I thought I was going to faint, his eyes shifted to mine again. "It was really nice to meet you, Jenna. I'm sure we'll see each other again, real soon. I better let you go. Your someone must be waiting for you. By the way...." There was a pause as he charmed me with his eyes again. "You...took my breath away. If I were your someone, I wouldn't let you out of my sight for even a second, because someone like me will surely try to whisk you away." He winked and left.

A SNEAK PEEK OF **CROSSROADS**
Crossroads Saga, Book 1
by Mary Ting

Crossroads, Between, Beyond, Eternity, Halo City

Slowly I turned my back toward him and tried to wrap myself inside his wings again. I wanted to be back in the arms of an angel, back to the feeling of peace that was so desired. He fidgeted away from me, mumbling, "This is too dangerous. I won't be able to control myself." His voice was worried and low.

I didn't heed his warning. When I pulled him closer, he ultimately gave in, and held me gently with both of his arms and wings this time. All I needed was his touch, for him to hold me that way; it made all the difference in the world. I was safe again. Without thought, I turned toward him.

The look in his eyes was so tempting, telling me that he wanted me too. I knew it was impossible for him to want and need me the same way, but his eyes told me something else. The depth of my yearning and what I wanted to do at that moment were undeniable.

I leaned toward him and tenderly placed a kiss on his supple lips to thank him. It was an innocent kiss. What was the harm in just one small kiss? I was extremely surprised that he didn't push me away. I was even more surprised at myself, since I was never the type to make the first move.

"Thank you for saving me," I whispered, looking straight into his soulful eyes, as something came over me. He was right. It was dangerous, but it was me who couldn't control myself. His eyes gave me permission to continue, so I gave him another kiss, but slower and longer this time. His lips were warm and sweet like honeysuckle, just how I imagined they would be. When he kissed me back it was hesitant, but it was enough to spread heat through my body like a blazing fire.

Still holding me, he pulled me away with a sudden jerk as his eyes pierced into mine with anger. His left hand was tightly wrung around my hair and the other gripped my shirt so I could feel the tightness from it. Panting, wanting more of him, I forgot how to breathe, and so did he.

His eyes, still fierce with anger, gripped me even tighter as he slightly pushed and pulled me, fighting and uncertain of what he wanted to do. Feeling petrified, I had to prepare myself for the consequence of my actions, for I knew I had crossed the line.

I was waiting for him to release me and push me away. I also anticipated the lecture he would preach about how humans and angels couldn't have any physical contact. Recalling the last time, he suddenly stopped as we almost kissed. Then, he drew me even closer, and kissed me hungrily. Passion that I never knew could be possible claimed both of us. My toes curled, feeling immense pleasure that tingled to the very depth of my being as my fingers tugged lightly on his muscular shoulders. Then his wings were totally wrapped around us.

We were in the dark, just Michael and me inside the cocoon of his wings. I couldn't believe what was happening...our first real kiss. Pressing his whole body against mine, I could feel his heart racing just as fast as mine was. We both lost control, and every part of me quivered with intense pleasure I had never felt before.

AN EXCERPT FROM **ETERNAL ECHOES**
by Angela Corbett
Emblem of Eternity, Book 2

I took a deep breath as I came out of the memory. I was getting better at keeping my flashback reaction less noticeable, but I still steadied myself against the gate. Alex noticed. "Are you okay?" he asked.

I nodded, my breath less ragged. "I'm fine."

"Are you sure?" He came over and stood behind me, a commanding presence. His hands were a gentle weight on my arms as he turned me toward him. At first, he seemed to be looking for signs of distress, but as our eyes caught and held, I knew his thoughts were in other places, and mine were headed there, too. His hand slipped feather-light over my arms and down until they rested above my hips.

Like I was having some sort of out-of-body experience, I watched as my hand went up to his face, tracing the line of his jaw. "We shouldn't be doing this," I said in a very unconvincing way.

It wasn't that I didn't mean what I said. I did. And I still had enough blood flowing to my brain to vocalize it. But I was having a hard time convincing my rational side I shouldn't be making out with Alex. Especially when my rational side was practically screaming that I'd kissed Emil last night and to be fair, I should also make out with Alex. My rational side told me I wouldn't want a double-standard. My rational side had lost its mind.

"Why?" Alex asked, inching slowly closer, his eyes dark in a way that made my legs feel like pudding.

There were so many possible answers to that question, with reasonable arguments why we shouldn't proceed, that I wasn't sure which to choose. I started with, "What if the bracelet doesn't work?"

Alex glanced down at my bracelet, giving a very slow smile I could only describe as predatory before eying me like he was preparing for an attack. Apparently a couple of centuries of sexual frustration will do that to you.

"It will," he answered, still moving toward me.

"How can you be sure?"

Alex's mouth curved slightly in a smile part rapacious, part entertained. "I've been waiting a *long* time for a relationship with you, Evie. And for everything that comes with it. I wouldn't have given you the bracelet if I wasn't sure it would work. I gave it to you because I intend to put it to use."

Sheesh! Judging by his dark, focused gaze, I knew he wasn't kidding.

"I don't think it's a good idea." I shook my head, like that would emphasize my argument and stop his sultry advances. It didn't.

His arms went around me tight, pulling me to him. My chest crushed into his, the hard planes of his stomach obvious even through our clothes. He stared down at me, not loosening his embrace. My breath was shallow as I stared back, wondering how long it would be until we both lost all common sense. He moved his lips over my cheeks, the soft skin brushing wispy strokes over my face. When he got to my ear, he took the soft pad in his lips and nipped lightly, then whispered one word. "Why?"

Why? Why what? Had there been a question? I fumbled around in my head for what we'd been talking about. Oh. That's right. Bad idea. This is a bad idea. Why is it still a bad idea? What was my list again? I did more fumbling and found one. "What about Emil?"

I felt Alex tense, his shoulders becoming taut under his shirt. "He's not invited to this conversation."

Geez! Alex had always been overbearing, but apparently when it came to sex, he was not only overbearing, but alarmingly primitive. Again, I attributed the aggression to decades of pent up frustration.

"Don't you think he'll be pissed?"

Alex kept kissing down my neck, and I moaned. His hands moved around to my stomach, unzipping my coat. He quickly discarded it on the ground.

"We all agreed to the rules," Alex said, his hands moving lightly under my sweater, inching it up ever so slightly. I'd never been addicted to anything, but imagined this was how addiction started. A little at a time. Alex pulled my sweater over my head, then kept kissing back up my neck and along my jawline. "We're not doing anything wrong."

I looked at where our hands were, and the clothes slowly making their way to the ground. We were about to be doing things that were wrong in a very good way. "I guess it depends on your definition. Emil would think this is seriously wrong."

The muscles at Alex's jaw ticked, his eyes glittering with a combination of passion and anger. "I told you," he said, moving swiftly, one arm sliding under my thighs, the other around my back. He lifted me, cradling me in his arms, and walked down the row of stalls to an empty stall at the end of the barn. Fresh hay was scattered in large mounds, creating a soft bed on the ground—albeit a scratchy one, but better than the dirt floor. He laid me down gently in the hay then straddled me, the years of want and need, written across his face. "We're not talking about him." With that, he was on top of me, the kiss aggressive. I could feel my soulmark burning, and my bracelet seemed to be giving off heat as well. If this kept up, I wouldn't be surprised if the whole barn burst into flames.

A SNEAK PEEK OF
THE GHOSTS OF RUE DUMIANE
by Alexandra Weis

Shaking her head slightly, she moved on to the hallway that separated the bedrooms from the rest of the cottage. Just as the slender fingertips of light retreated from the hallway, Danica came to the first bedroom door. She pushed the thick cypress door open and reached into the dark, windowless room for the light switch. When she flipped the switch on the wall next to her, the small room became drenched with warm light from the lamp mounted in the ceiling fan above. The dome over the lamp had been covered with frosty glass, muting the harshness of the bright light. Soft blue paint covered the walls while a matching blue carpet had been placed on the floor. Overhead, the ceiling had been left an austere shade of white.

Danica leaned against the doorframe and reflected on the various stages of childhood and adolescence she had gone through while occupying this room. The rainbow-painted walls her mother had painstakingly decorated for her had been replaced with posters of boy bands and television heartthrobs until her mother had died. After the funeral, Danica had come home and removed all the posters in a fit of rage, wanting to be surrounded once more by her mother's rainbows. The last year she had spent in this room, she had felt comforted by those rainbows, as if her mother's love had been forever sealed beneath the paintbrush strokes on her walls.

"I missed this old place," she whispered.

A sudden rush of cold air moving down the hallway caused Danica to turn away from the bedroom door and peer into the darkness behind her. She took a few steps further down the hall until the aroma of cigar smoke mixed with a hint of brandy wafted in the air around her. Danica remembered that smell. It had always filled her bedroom whenever the dark man would appear.

"Is it you?" she softly called into the hallway. "It's me, Danica. I've come back. Just like I said I would."

Danica walked briskly past the entrance to the master bath to the final door at the end of the hall. Without hesitation, she pushed the cypress door open and walked inside the master bedroom. The light from the large picture window overlooking the courtyard shone into the room, accentuating the deep burgundy color of the carpet beneath her feet. She stepped into the center of the room and observed the ceiling fan above. Danica waited, straining with every breath to hear the slightest stirring.

"Welcome home," a man's wispy voice resonated around her.

A hopeful smile curled the edges of Danica's heart-shaped mouth. "Thank you, Gaston. It's good to be home."

ABOUT THE AUTHOR

 Author Mary Ting resides in Southern California with her husband and two children. She enjoys oil painting and making jewelry. Writing her first novel, Crossroads Saga, happened by chance. It was a way to grieve the death of her beloved grandmother, and inspired by a dream she once had as a young girl. When she started reading new adult novels, she fell in love with the genre. It was the reason she had to write one-Something Great. Why the pen name, M Clarke? She tours with Magic Johnson Foundation to promote literacy and her children's chapter book-No Bullies Allowed.

Website: www.authormaryting.com
Facebook: www.facebook.com/CrossroadsBook
www.facebook.com/AuthorMaryTing

Twitter @MaryTing
Email: authormaryting@outlook.com
Blog: www.marytingbooks.blogspot.com
Follow Mary Ting & M. Clarke on Goodreads.

Made in the USA
Charleston, SC
18 October 2014